fever

Also by Bernice L. McFadden

NONFICTION
Firstborn Girls

FICTION
Tisoy
Praise Song for the Butterflies
The Book of Harlan
Gathering of Waters
Glorious
Nowhere Is a Place
Camilla's Roses
Loving Donovan
This Bitter Earth
The Warmest December
Sugar

WRITING AS GENEVA HOLLIDAY
Groove
Heat
Seduction
Lover Man

fever

A Novel

Bernice L. McFadden

Writing as Geneva Holliday

PLUME

PLUME

An imprint of Penguin Random House LLC
1745 Broadway, New York, NY 10019
penguinrandomhouse.com

First published in trade paperback in the United States by Broadway
Books, a division of Random House, Inc.

Second American edition published in the United States by Plume,
an imprint of Penguin Random House LLC, in 2025.

PLUME and the P colophon are registered trademarks of
Penguin Random House LLC.

Book design by Diahann Sturge

LIBRARY OF CONGRESS CATALOGING-IN-PUBLICATION DATA

Names: Holliday, Geneva author
Title: Fever: a novel / Bernice L. McFadden writing as Geneva Holliday.
Description: Second American edition. | New York, NY: Plume,
an imprint of Penguin Random House LLC, 2025.
Identifiers: LCCN 2025021107 (print) | LCCN 2025021108 (ebook) |
ISBN 9780593472842 paperback | ISBN 9780593472859 ebook
Subjects: LCSH: African American women—Fiction |
Female friendship—Fiction | New York (N.Y.)—Fiction |
LCGFT: Romance fiction | Novels
Classification: LCC PS3563.C3622 F48 2025 (print) |
LCC PS3563.C3622 (ebook)
LC record available at https://lccn.loc.gov/2025021107
LC ebook record available at https://lccn.loc.gov/2025021108

Printed in the United States of America
1st Printing

The authorized representative in the EU for product safety
and compliance is Penguin Random House Ireland, Morrison
Chambers, 32 Nassau Street, Dublin D02 YH68, Ireland,
https://eu-contact.penguin.ie.

For my sistah friends,
the women with whom I laugh the most

Everybody's got the fever . . .
Fever isn't such a new thing,
Fever started long ago.

—"Fever," music and lyrics by PEGGY LEE

fever

"You see, what had happened was . . ."

Geneva

Pfizer and other pharmaceutical companies that have jumped headfirst into the sexual-stimulant market are in for some bad news. It seems that there is a new, natural sexual stimulant on the marketplace called Cupid. It's cheap, it's organic, it doesn't require a prescription, and it can be purchased from your neighborhood incense dealer. The makers of Cupid, Roscoe and Jo-Jo Barker of Cambria Heights, Queens—by way of Kingston, Jamaica—say there are no side effects associated with the stimulant, but in order for it to be 100 percent effective, large quantities of water need to be consumed when taking it.

This story and more tonight on the six o'clock news.

* * *

I gave news correspondent Sade Baderinwa one last look before I pressed the off button on the television remote. I would try to remember to watch the news that evening. Not that I had a man to use that Cupid stuff on, but I would one day—sooner than later, I hoped—and it wouldn't hurt to have a little extra ammunition in the bedroom when I finally met that special someone.

I settled myself flat on my back again.

The lights were off and the candles lit, and I even had

a little oil burning in a simmering pot on the windowsill. Clean sheets, a little Jean Naté dabbed behind each ear, and Barry White's greatest hits playing in the background.

Eric was out somewhere, and my baby girl, Charlie, was napping in the other room.

I'd been taking care of myself for some time now. I mean after I got pregnant from my ex-husband and that bastard had the nerve to demand that I get an abortion, I vowed that that would be the last time that man got any more of my good loving! And to sock it to him good—I had that baby!

Not that that lowlife son of a superbitch acknowledges her. When I announced I was keeping the baby, he told me that he wasn't going to be involved. He said, "Geneva, if you have this baby, you're having it and raising it on your own!"

I just looked at him and said, "How's that different from the first time around? I was married to your sorry ass when Eric came along, and I raised him on my own!"

Well, she's here now, and I gotta tell you, she drives me crazy, but I can't imagine life without her. She is the second best decision I ever made. Eric Jr. was the first.

Since Charlie's been born, I've been practically sexless. Oh, there's been a little stink finger here and there, a little caressing of the breast, some tongue kissing . . . but none of the toe-curling booty calls I was used to getting from my ex-husband. So I had to take matters into my own hands, literally! And plus, Crystal and I made a celibacy pact. No more of this senseless sleeping around. We would save ourselves for Mr. Right and stop giving ourselves over to Mr. Right Now!

I learned about ten different ways to pleasure myself, and that alone has kept me from stripping naked and running through the streets like an insane person!

"Right, Mandingo?" I whispered as I turned. Mandingo was waiting patiently beside me. Well oiled, he glistened beneath the candlelight.

"Okay, baby, I'm almost ready," I whispered as I stretched my body alongside Mandingo's and slowly began to caress my nipples. "Ohhh," I moaned, then glanced over at Mandingo and said, "You should be doing this for me, you know?"

I chuckled as I moved my hand up to the soft mound of flesh beneath my chin. There I allowed my fingers to feather-stroke my skin.

That really turned me on.

"Mmmmm," I groaned, already feeling moist between my legs. "I'm going to make it nice and wet for you, sweetie," I told Mandingo, even though I was thinking about the cedar-colored cutie who frequents the diner where I waitress.

He always sits at my station, always orders a decaf, two slices of whole-wheat toast, followed by a glass of orange juice. He reads *The New York Times* while he's eating, and when he's done, he leaves me a five-dollar tip, even though his meal costs only $3.50.

I like to pretend that he comes there just to see me, even though he doesn't say much more than "Good morning" and "Thank you" to me.

But, hey, it's nice to dream, right?

Now when I see him coming, I imagine that he's Mos

Def and I'm Alicia Keys, and I start humming the melody to "You Don't Know My Name" as I reach for the decaf coffeepot.

And he don't know my name because we don't wear nametags on our uniforms.

Anyway, it's just a fantasy; besides, he don't look too much older than my own son. I probably remind him of his own mother.

Slowly I moved my hand from my breast and pushed it down to my belly and the triangle of black hair below.

My clitoris was already pointed and erect, so when my pinky finger accidentally brushed against it, my body shuddered and my toes curled. "Shiiit," I squeezed out between clenched teeth. "Okay, Mandingo, I'm more than ready for you, baby."

Reaching over, I plucked the little red and white striped plastic penis from the pillow, hit the on switch, and set it to HIGH.

Mandingo pulsated into action; vibrating so hard, he almost slipped from between my sweaty fingers. "Aren't we the eager one," I laughed before I closed my eyes and guided his pointed head to my pleasure place.

Mandingo bucked as I eased him in and out, in and out, in and—

"What's going on, Manny?" I asked, my eyes flying open and my head jerking up off the pillow.

Mandingo's vibrations were becoming spastic.

"C'mon now," I urged, and rolled the tip of his head across my clitoris. The joy was minimal. Mandingo was losing power.

"No, no!" I screamed, and brought Mandingo to eye level. "What? What? It can't be your batteries, I just changed them."

I slapped Mandingo upside his narrow head a few times, but all he did was sputter weakly.

"I'm sorry, I'm sorry," I cried. "Just please don't do this to me, not now!"

Mandingo coughed, buzzed once, and then died.

"Nooooooooooooooooo!"

Crystal

I thought, My life must really be bad, because I was standing in a liquor store on a Saturday afternoon, and it wasn't even two o'clock yet. But I needed some Merlot; I had to have some Merlot.

Some Merlot, Jill Scott, and a hot bath.

"Yes, how can I help you?" The Asian storekeeper stared out at me from behind two sets of glass—the one shielding him and the bifocals that made his eyes look as large as serving platters.

"Um," I said, and pressed my finger against my lip, "what type of Merlot do you have?"

He smirked at me. "What kind you like, lady?" he yelled. "I got Australian, California—"

"Um," I cut him off, "you know, I think I'd rather have a Shiraz. You have Shiraz, right?"

He shot me a look that said: What the hell do you know about Shiraz?

His eyebrows climbed to his receding hairline.

"Or, uhm, maybe a Petite Syrah?"

Now I was just showing off. I knew my wines. He was so used to black people coming into his store and asking for a pint of Bacardi white or E&J that he became

tongue-tied when someone my color asked for something different.

"Ohhhh, you got good taste, lady." He grinned, and
two rows of blanched teeth appeared. "I got something
very, very nice for you," he said, and disappeared through
a narrow opening in the wall behind him.

When he returned, he was holding two bottles of
wine.

"This from my special collection," he said, then leaned
in close to the glass and sputtered, "Reserves."

I blinked at the pale cloud his breath left on the glass
and watched as it faded slowly away. "Really?"

"Oh, yes. You see, I'm a big—how you call it?—um,
wino!"

I burst into laughter.

"What so funny?"

"You called yourself a wino!"

"So? That's not what you call someone who likes good
wine?"

I could barely talk, I was laughing so hard. "N-no," I
managed to say.

After setting the bottle down, the shopkeeper threw
his hands up in the air. "So what you call it then, since
you are such a Miss Smarty-Pants?" he spat.

"A wine connoisseur."

"That a funny word. You just make it up?"

"No."

"Hmm."

He eyed me for a moment before he snatched up the
bottles and held them up for me to see again. "Okay,
which one you want, Miss Smarty-Pants?"

* * *

Back in my apartment I immersed myself in a tub of warm sudsy water. My head was swimming from the wine, and my hands were trying to do things they ought not to have been doing.

"Stop it!" I shrieked, snatching my hands out of the water. Looking down at them, I began to scold them. "You know what happens when you start touching places that have been neglected for too long, don't you?" I used my left one to slap the right one and then vice versa. "Don't you?" I stressed as the suds dripped guiltily away from my fingers.

I hadn't had sex in more than two years.

"Whose big idea was it for me to become celibate?" I asked out loud, my voice bouncing off the blue glass tile and back to me.

After my live-in boyfriend turned out to be a drug addict, and the old boyfriend Earl whom I'd turned to to ease my pain turned out to still be the same womanizing creep that he'd promised he no longer was, I decided that I would become celibate.

Well, that promise lasted a little over four months, and by then I was so horny, I started foaming at the mouth every time I saw a good-looking man.

And so rather than continue making a fool out of myself, I pulled out my black book and started calling up exes of mine that would not mind a roll in the hay with no attachments.

That went on for about a good three months before I got tired of giving myself up over and over again. So I just stopped having sex altogether. I changed my number, started chanting, and committed myself to celibacy.

I told myself that the next man that lay on top of me would be my husband—so help me God.

Hey, it worked for Jackée Harry!

So I began masturbating—not that I hadn't before, but two years into my celibacy, it was nearing chronic levels.

I'd found all sorts of ways to get myself off.

Lying on my stomach with my hands beneath me while I did a slow grind in my fists. On my back, my middle finger up inside of me while I rolled my clitoris between my thumb and index finger. In the tub, me up on my elbows as I scooted my behind across the porcelain until my vagina was directly under the water that rushed out from the spout. That was a hell of a climax, but it left my elbows sore.

And then there was my "toy"—the butterfly vibrator that was wrapped in a silk handkerchief and hidden beneath my Bible in the nightstand drawer.

But three months ago, I'd stopped the self-pleasuring. I mean, it seemed to me that I wasn't staying true to my promise of celibacy.

Sex was sex, whether it involved two people, my hands, the faucet, or the butterfly, right?

So I stopped getting myself off and took up yoga and started running five miles a day.

The good thing that came out of not masturbating was that my body had never looked better. The bad thing was that I was a bit nasty. Well, at least that was what my mother, Peyton Atkins, kept telling me.

"Crystal, you're always blowing your top. You're so snappish. Are you getting some on a regular basis?"

Peyton, in her early sixties, had suddenly shed her conservative views on sex and had become my own personal Dr. Ruth! It seemed as though every conversation we had, my mother found a way to bring up sex.

For instance, I would mention a particular television show, and her response would be something like, "Have you found your other erogenous zones yet?"

It was damn annoying was what it was, not to mention embarrassing. Who the hell wanted to discuss their sexual activities, or lack thereof, with their mother!

She'd even gone so far as to send me a gift certificate for my birthday to White Lotus East. I didn't know what the hell a White Lotus East was, until I went on the website, and oh, my God! I knew my mother had flipped the fuck out! The website had all this information about sacred-spot massages, female orgasms, and performance anxieties!

I was horrified and called my mother up and told her so.

"My sex life is my personal business," I kept reminding her.

"Yes, it is, dear," Peyton would calmly reply, "but it seems to me that the Out to Lunch sign hanging on the front door of your *business* has been hanging there for three years too long."

I loved my mother, but sometimes I just couldn't stand her.

"Goodbye, Mother!" I would say before slamming the phone down.

She was right, of course. I had been a bit uptight since I'd stopped fucking. But I was determined to stick to my commitment, even though I felt a meltdown coming on. I just hoped it didn't happen when I was anywhere near the male persuasion, because there was no telling what I would do.

* * *

The bathwater turned cold, and all of the bubbles were gone by the time I stepped out and wrapped myself in a powder blue oversized bath towel.

I moved from the bathroom into my bedroom and dropped the towel to the floor. In front of my full-length mirror, I took a moment to admire my slim waistline, washboard stomach, and bootylicious bottom.

After I moisturized myself with baby oil and slipped into my favorite oversized T-shirt, I headed out to the kitchen where the rest of my Merlot was waiting for me.

Alongside the glass of wine was my day planner. My eyes were drawn to April 22, a date that I'd encircled in red, scrawling beneath it: "Lunch with Karen Shaw." Around the date I'd also drawn daggers dripping with blood.

Karen Shaw, like the rest of us, had grown up in the projects. She was part of our little crew growing up; well, at least until Geneva popped up pregnant and Noah came out of the closet. After those two incidents, Sonia, Karen's mother, decided that we were a bad influence on her little girl and forbade her from being in our company at all.

The poor child spent her last two years of high school with her nose in every book the library had to offer; Sonia was determined to make her little girl a success.

And she had succeeded, to some extent anyway. Karen was accepted to Vassar, where she obtained a degree, and then she went on to marry a Frenchman who just happened to be a doctor and who just happened to be white, and in some odd exchange that we all never quite understood, Karen took her husband's surname, dropped her first name in favor of her maiden name, and now was known as Shaw DeJeuné.

To go along with her change in identity, she got a nose job, got Botoxed, lightened her already light skin, shaved off her eyebrows and got some permanently tattooed on, and dyed her hair blond.

We all thought she'd lost her mind. Well, most of us. Chevy didn't see a thing wrong with it.

Karen, I mean Shaw, lives in Los Angeles now. She's quite famous in the voice-over circles; she's the one you hear on the commercials that advertise the drugs of various pharmaceutical companies—well, it's her voice you hear toward the end of the commercial. Come on, you know the one that rattles off the 101 possible side effects that one could experience after using said drug . . .

Anyway, Shaw and her plastic surgeon husband were coming to New York to attend a medical conference, and oh, joy, she wanted to get together and have lunch.

The last time she'd come to town, I was stuck spending a whole weekend with her, and it was torture!

First, I vowed never to see that confused child again,

and then I thought that might be too harsh, so then I vowed never to do it alone again, which was how Geneva and Chevy got invited.

* * *

I took a few sips of my wine and flicked on the Bose radio. Al Green's "Let's Stay Together" floated from the white box, and I found myself immediately lost in the music.

I was feeling warm from the inside out and began to dance myself round and round on the kitchen floor, totally lost in the song until the spell was broken by the clamor of my ringing telephone.

"Hello?"

"Crystal, girl." Geneva's sad voice filtered through.

"Hey, I was going to call you to remind you about lunch tomorrow," I said, and then I realized that Geneva was panting urgently as if she were in the midst of a panic attack. "You okay?"

"Guuuuuuuurrrrrrrrrrl," Geneva hollered, "Mandingo's dead!"

And just like that, my best friend provided me with my first hearty laugh of the day.

Chevy

I stood there staring at the ATM while the line of people behind me made annoying sounds. Someone even had the nerve to shout, "Hurry up, bitch! Damn!"

I couldn't believe what I was seeing; I was down to $32.26!

How the hell was I supposed to go out to lunch tomorrow with $32.26?

"Lady, do you need some help or something?" asked the tall dark brother with a crew cut and Pinocchio-length nose, who'd stepped up alongside me.

"I don't need no goddamn help!" I spat at him, and then placed the palm of my hand inches away from his face. That's when I saw the sad shape my acrylic tips were in.

The brother shook his head and took his place back in the line.

"This can't be right," I whispered to myself as I pressed the cancel button on the panel, snatched my card from the slot, and stormed out.

I was broke. BROKE!

Again, my conscience whispered to me as I marched down Fulton Street toward home.

My unemployment was done, over, finis!

I thought I would have secured a job by the time my last check rolled around, but no such luck and now I was destitute.

* * *

I crossed Kingston Avenue, ignoring the man who was hollering, "Hey baby girl, you need a ride?" out of his two-door, baby blue, convertible Mercedes coupe. I looked around to see if the brother was worth my time, and then I saw the license plate. It read: "MRMAN2U." What kind of vanity shit was he on? And so I rolled my eyes and kept on stepping.

I was so upset that I wanted to jump in a taxi and ride the next few blocks home, but that was six dollars I couldn't afford to spend.

Schoolchildren sidestepped me as I barreled down the sidewalk muttering obscenities and flinging my hands in disgust.

A man sidled up beside me and said, "Hey, sweetie, where you in a hurry going?"

I turned my head to see that he was the dirtiest, grubbiest-looking piece of walking garbage that I'd ever seen.

"Fuck off," I said, and hastened my pace.

"Hey, hey, don't be like that. I just want to get to know you," he said as he reached out and touched my shoulder.

I spun around, weave flying, eyes wild, and screamed, "Have you lost your ever-loving mind? You don't know me like that, don't be putting your hands on me!"

Pedestrians stopped and stared.

The man—brown teeth, white lips, bloodshot eyes and all, an obvious crackhead—had the nerve to reach his hand out and touch me again. I stepped back and glared at him. "Are you crazy?"

"Crazy for you, baby," he sputtered back at me.

"You can't be serious."

"Serious as a heart attack, mama." He grinned and offered me some type of awkward swagger that reaped laughter from the onlookers.

"Please, you wouldn't know what to do with this," I said, pointing down to my crotch. "I am a woman. W-O-M-A-N! Not a crack pipe!" I shouted before walking away and leaving him wide-eyed in the middle of the sidewalk.

It's difficult being a fine woman in New York City; you got every Tom, Dick, and Crackhead after you!

* * *

Back in the house, I hurried over to the rack of wine and snatched off the large sheet of yellow paper on which Noah had written: "DO NOT DRINK."

Grabbing up a bottle of Cabernet Sauvignon from the prized collection, I took a water glass from the shelf and filled it to the brim with the dark berry-colored liquid.

By the time I was done gulping down the second glass, my head was spinning and my stomach grumbling.

Opening the door to the Sub-Zero, I peered in at a spotted banana, a half-empty bottle of champagne, and a white carton containing three-day-old chicken and broccoli.

Removing the bottle of champagne, I opened the freezer and looked blankly at the frozen chicken, pork chops, and ice cubes—all of which had been there since Noah's last visit, and that had been more than six months ago.

I knew I would stand a better chance with the Chinese food, so I pulled out the container, poured the contents onto a plate, and popped it into the microwave.

A lot of good it did me—three bites, and it was gone.

Leaving the plate on the counter, I carried my glass and the bottle of champagne into the living room and turned on the twenty-seven-inch plasma television where, on the screen, twenty or so hos were booty-shaking their way through a Snoop Dogg video.

Flopping down onto the couch, I let my eyes fall on the employment section of the Sunday *New York Times*.

It was already a week old.

I had had every intention of perusing the want ads, but time had just gotten away from me; I mean, there were those two nightclub openings, and then of course I had to catch up on my beauty sleep, and before I knew it, it was Friday.

And I wasn't about to look for a job on a Friday. That was somebody's Sabbath, wasn't it?

Saturday was no good. That was usually my nail-and-hair day, but the meager amount of money left in my bank account had ruled that out.

Well, a new edition of the *Times* will be out tomorrow, I told myself as I closed my eyes.

But can you spare the $3.50? my conscience asked.

My eyes flew open, and I reached for the paper and started with the administrative assistant listings. Most of the ads were placed through agencies, and I really didn't feel like being bothered with those shysters.

I moved on to sales. Not that I wanted to be up on my feet all day smiling into the faces of the rich and famous, but the discount on the clothing was tempting.

Travel was last on the list. There were plenty of jobs for reservations agents and even a few for corporate travel agents. I'd been one of the latter for the past ten years, but I'd been "excused," if you will, from all of the top agencies in the city, and they were the ones currently advertising. I doubted that any of them would be eager for a return engagement with me.

I was just about to throw the paper down when I spied the following:

TRAVEL/PERSONAL ASSISTANT

POPULAR RADIO PERSONALITY NEEDS PERSONAL AS-SISTANT WHO IS YOUNG, VIVACIOUS, AND WILLING TO WORK LONG HOURS AND TO TRAVEL DOMESTICALLY AND ABROAD.

SALARY IN THE HIGH FIVE FIGURES.
ONLY SERIOUS CANDIDATES NEED APPLY.

I read the ad about five times before I decided that I was a serious candidate, even though I didn't find the long hours appealing. But who in their right mind would?

I wondered which radio personality it was.

Maybe Wendy Williams or Michael Baisden, I thought, as I gathered up the paper and started upstairs toward Noah's office. I would email my résumé and cover letter immediately. Shoot, it didn't matter that the ad was practically a week old; my mother told me nothing beats a fail but a try.

Crystal

After I'd laughed until my sides hurt, Geneva and I decided to spend the rest of the warm afternoon at the park with Charlie.

We shared a bench and some conversation; two mother hens keeping a close eye on Charlie, who was darting here and there in a vigorous game of tag with three other children her age.

"So Little Eric's still not working?" I began, broaching the subject that was at the top of Geneva's list of complaints.

"Uh-huh," she said, her eyes still peeled on Charlie.

"Well, what happened to the McDonald's gig?"

Geneva momentarily let her eyes travel to mine. "What you think? The same thing that happened at Burger King, Popeyes, and Best Buy."

"He walked out?" I was astonished.

"Yep." Geneva's response was clipped as she turned her attention back to her daughter.

"Did you talk to him about going back to college?" I probed.

"I talked, his father talked, my mother talked, you talked. We all talked until we were blue in the face, but he got his heart set on this music thing, and ain't nothing gonna change his mind."

"Damn," I muttered, slumping against the hard wooden back of the bench.

"Well," Geneva started, her tone a bit hard, "not everybody can hold double degrees and be a big-shot director."

I bit back my response. Was I supposed to feel ashamed about having an education? And with regard to my position as director of the Ain't I A Woman Foundation, well, it wasn't what it seemed to be. I worked long hours and put up with a lot of corporate, old-boy, all-white, all-male, stuffed-shirt bullshit!

Sometimes I felt that Geneva was jealous of my accomplishments. She could have the same life I did, if only she'd apply herself and stop being so goddamn lazy. But I kept that thought to myself.

I just rolled my eyes and looked up at the sky.

"Charlie! Get your behind up off of that ground right now!" Geneva yelled.

Charlie shot her a wicked look and then slowly raised herself up off the ground.

"Well, how's the band thing going anyway?" I asked.

"Girl, the Lord only knows. Eric be out until all hours of the night. Say he practicing, but I don't know what he's out there doing."

"He's got a girlfriend now, right?"

"Yes, who I have yet to meet," Geneva snapped before she wriggled up her nose and the girl's name spilled sloppily out of her mouth. "Juuuuuuuuuuuulie."

"Oh, Geneva," I laughed. "Why do you always say her name like that?"

"I don't like her," Geneva snapped again.

"How can you not like her? You've never even met her."

"I don't need to meet her. She's probably just some gold-digging booty-shaker who's going to trick Eric into getting her pregnant, and then his life will be ruined."

My mouth dropped open. When did Geneva become so cynical?

"Now, Geneva, I think that Eric knows how to protect himself. And besides, that boy's got a good head on his shoulders. He's focused on his dream and—"

"Crystal, please." Geneva waved her hand at me. "Let's not fool ourselves. Eric is nineteen years old; he's focused on what other boys his age are focused on, and that's pussy!"

I just shook my head. I knew it was true. I put my hands up in surrender.

We sat quietly for a while. I was lost in my thoughts when crackling sounds pulled me out of my reverie. I looked over, and Geneva was shoving mounds of Wise potato chips into her mouth. At five foot five and two-hundred-plus pounds, Geneva is hefty, but not obese, although I could see that obesity was going to be the next stop on her food train.

Geneva had tried almost every popular weight-loss system: Calorie Counters, Jenny Craig, Weight Watchers, Slim-Fast, and both the Atkins and South Beach diets, but her commitment time was short; the longest she'd ever stayed on any one program was thirty days.

Not that I didn't think she was beautiful—she was—and could even be gorgeous if she'd wear a little mascara and lip gloss and maybe do something else with her hair other than wearing it in a snatch-back. But that has always been Geneva—Ms. Plain Jane.

"Hey, um, did you take your walk today?" I asked casually.

Geneva had promised that she would try to do at least a mile on Saturdays and Sundays.

"Humph," she said as she shoved another handful of chips into her mouth. She chewed for a while and then hastily brushed away the crumbs from around her lips before saying, "How many blocks from the projects to the park?"

Puzzled, I answered, "Well, that's four. Why?"

"Okay. How many blocks make a mile?"

"Ten, I think." I wondered where she was going with this.

"Well, I walked from my apartment to the park and I'll walk back, so that's eight blocks, which means I would have done just under a mile."

I rolled my eyes in dismay.

Geneva looked deep into the chip bag and then held it up. Tilting her head back, she opened her mouth and poured the last few salty crumbs onto her tongue.

"Oh, I'm sorry, did you want some?" she asked, turning innocent eyes on me.

I shook my head.

Charlie rushed over to us, out of breath and giddy with excitement. A small blond-haired white girl trailed close behind.

"Mama, look. Dis is Mary. She my best friend."

Both Geneva and I grinned.

"That's nice, baby," Geneva said, then looked into Mary's pink face. "How you doing, Mary?"

Mary shrugged her shoulders and whispered, "Fine."

"C'mon, Mary! C'mon!" Charlie screamed, and tore off across the park again.

"Damn, I wish I had their energy," Geneva mused aloud as she dug into her backpack and pulled out a sixteen-ounce bottle of Pepsi and her pack of Newports.

"Now you're not going to forget about lunch tomorrow, are you?"

Geneva gave me a strained look. "How can I forget when you keep reminding me every ten minutes?"

"Look, I just don't want you backing out at the last minute," I said with the most carefree attitude I could muster.

"What the hell did Karen do to you the last time she was here?" Geneva asked, giving me a wry look.

I just shivered at the memory, raised my hand, and whispered, "Don't ask."

Geneva started to press me, but I was saved by my ringing cell phone. I reached into the breast pocket of my denim jacket and pulled out the phone.

"Oh, it's my mother," I said as I looked at the number and then flipped the phone open. "Hey, Mom."

"Hey, baby. Where are you?"

"In the park with Geneva and Charlie."

"Oh, tell them I said hello."

I wave at Geneva.

"Hey, Mama," Geneva yells back.

"What's up, Mom?"

"Well, baby, I'm calling to ask you a favor."

That was something different; Peyton Atkins wasn't one to ask for much of anything, especially a favor. She said when someone did you a favor they always wanted something in return.

"O-okay," I said a little hesitantly.

"Neville is coming into town."

"Really? When?" I asked, nudging Geneva as I mouthed, "Neville is coming." Geneva couldn't seem to read my lips and just gave me a confused look.

"Um, next week."

"Oh, so what do you need me to do, meet him at the airport or something?"

"No. I . . . well . . . I kind of told his mother that he could stay with you."

My mouth dropped wide open.

Neville had been a good friend of mine when we were growing up, but we hadn't seen each other in years, and the only communication we'd had was a Christmas card here and there and maybe a postcard in between that. But really and truly time had made us strangers, and I didn't see how I would be able to have a strange man sleeping under my roof.

"You did what?"

"I know, baby. I didn't mean to. It just kind of slipped out."

"Well, I don't know, Mom. You know we haven't seen each other in years and—"

"I would let him stay here with me; I mean, he's like

the son I never had, but I'm going to Vegas with the club that week."

"Oh."

"I mean, if you really don't want to do it, I'll just call Beth Ann and tell her that Neville has to find someplace else to stay."

"Well, why can't he get a hotel?"

"Crystal, Neville isn't financially blessed like you and me. He can't afford it. He's just scraping by on that island."

The line went quiet, and I chewed my bottom lip, trying hard to make the best decision. "Well, how long would he need to stay?"

"Oh, just a few days is all. And you know Neville, quiet as a church mouse. He won't be any trouble at all."

"Well, okay, I guess a few days won't hurt me," I said, caving as usual.

"Are you sure?"

"Yeah, tell Ms. Beth Ann I said it was okay and I look forward to seeing Neville."

"Oh, thank you, baby. I'll call you later with the details."

"Bye, Mom."

The line went dead and I turned to Geneva.

"Who's coming when?" she said.

"Neville."

"Neville . . . Neville." Geneva's face lit up. "Well, I haven't seen him in years!"

I nodded my head.

"And?"

"And he's staying with me."

"Really?" Geneva's face twisted.

"Yeah, I know, but it's just for a few days."

"Are you cool with that?"

"Yeah, I guess," I said, knowing full well that I wasn't.

Geneva was opening her mouth to say something else when one of the little girls Charlie had been playing with began throwing a hissy fit after her mother had told her that it was time for them to leave.

"No, no, no, I'm not leaving!" she screamed as she jumped up and down.

The mother, a small, dark-skinned, fine-boned woman gave us an embarrassed look. The white mothers didn't seem too disturbed, but the black mothers all folded their arms and twisted up their faces in disgust.

"That child needs her ass whupped," Geneva grumbled under her breath.

The mother reached for her child, and the little girl promptly bit her hand and then hauled off and kicked her on the shin before tearing off across the park, leaving her mother standing there stunned and embarrassed.

Geneva and I exchanged looks before Geneva shook her head piteously and laughed. "Damn, I didn't know they made them in black."

Geneva

Sunday came and I found myself staring down at the only four outfits that I assumed would be appropriate for the luncheon. And by appropriate, I mean that they fit.

A turquoise sleeveless summer dress; a black linen flare skirt with matching camisole top; a pair of white capris and a floral orange and green sheer poncho; and a red and white Captain & Tennille sort of getup. All size eighteen.

I looked down at my bulging gut and slapped it in dismay. "Why won't you just go away!" I wailed, and then reached over and plucked a sugar-coated doughnut from the green and white Krispy Kreme box on my nightstand.

Turning back to my sparsely filled closet, I stared at my out-of-date wardrobe. The only clothes I owned that fit perfectly were sweatpants, T-shirts, and my work uniforms.

"Shit!" I bellowed.

"Shit!" echoed behind me, and I spun around to see Charlie standing there, mimicking my stance.

"Don't say that, baby," I said as I bent over and

tweaked her nose before walking around her and back toward the bed.

"Why?"

"Well, it's not a nice thing to say," I mumbled, examining the waistline of the black skirt to see if there was a secret dart there that I could open.

"Is it a potty word, Mommy?"

"Yes, it is."

No dart. Damn.

"Then why you saying it then?"

"Mommy made a mistake." I reached for the turquoise dress and pressed it up against my body for the fifth time.

"Why?"

"Why what, baby?"

"Why can you use potty words and I can't?"

I gave her an exasperated look. "Because I'm an adult."

Charlie considered my response, and then her face scrunched up tight. I tossed the dress down in favor of my pack of cigarettes that sat alongside the doughnut box.

Reaching for the matches, I looked down at Charlie and said, "Go on to your room, baby, so Mommy can have a cigarette."

Charlie pinched her nose and began her nasal chant, "Secondhand smoke kills, secondhand smoke kills," as she marched out of the room.

I lit my cigarette and inhaled the calming nicotine. Three puffs and my mind cleared. "I know what I'm going to do," I mused out loud to the curl of smoke. "I just won't go."

Proud of my decision, I picked up the phone and called Crystal's apartment.

The phone rang twice and then her recorded voice came on. Hanging up, I racked my brain for the number to her cell phone. Another three puffs from my cigarette and it magically comes to me.

Crystal

I looked at my watch again; just a quick glance, but Shaw caught the move. "Ooooh, Crystal, am I going to have to take that little ol' Casio right off your wrist?" She laughed and gave my wrist a light tap.

"It's not a Casio, Shaw, it's a—"

"Oh, pooh! Stop being so sensitive," she said, then took a moment to straighten the diamond-encrusted Rolex on her wrist . . . for the eighth time. "You've lost your sense of humor, Crystal."

I was fuming. Fuming! Where was Geneva? Where was Chevy? I'd been sitting there listening to Shaw go on and on about her fabulous California life, her wonderful rich doctor husband, her Range Rover, her Mercedes sedan, and her new granite kitchen countertops! Her fucking Pekinese dogs and Siamese cats and her vacation homes in Mustique and Sri Lanka!

Really, how much more could I take?

"Now, what about you Crystal? Tell me all about your little life," Shaw said as she folded her hands beneath her chin and batted her eyelids before leaning in, like she was really interested in my *little life*.

Oh, is it my turn to talk now?

"Well—" I began just as Shaw's cell phone rang.

"Oh, pooh!" she yelped, and dug into her Louis Vuitton purse for her eight-hundred-dollar cell. "Hello?" she said, and then, "Oh, Pookie Bear, how are you? . . ."

* * *

Pookie Bear is Shaw's pet name for her husband. I looked at my glass of wine and said to myself, What the hell? I picked it up, drained it, and then raised the empty glass high enough for the waiter to see. "Another," I mouthed.

If I have to be here alone with Shaw, I might as well be drunk, I thought.

The song "Boogie Nights" was suddenly chiming all around us and I bopped my head absently to the tune. A look of horror spread across Shaw's face, and she covered the receiver of her phone to ask, "Is that coming from your pocketbook, Crystal?"

I jumped a bit when I realized that, yes, it was coming from my pocketbook. "Shoot, I forgot I had Eric download that song for my new ring tone." I laughed as I hurriedly pulled my Nokia from my purse.

Shaw shook her head in dismay before returning to her conversation.

"Hello?"

"Hey, Crystal." Geneva's voice was pensive.

"Hey," I responded. "Where are you?"

"Home. Um, listen, girl, I don't think I'm going to make it—"

"What!" I screeched, and Shaw as well as a few other

diners turned disdainful eyes on me. "Hold on," I said to Geneva, and then to Shaw, "I've got to take this outside, the reception in here is terrible."

Once outside, I pressed the phone back to my ear. "What the hell do you mean, you don't think you're going to make it?"

"I can't find—"

"Oh, you're coming all right. You agreed to this two weeks ago, and you're coming!"

"But I—"

"No buts, Geneva. If it's the money, I told you not to worry about that. I got you."

"That's not it. I just can't—"

"Let me tell you something, Geneva. I refuse to sit here and suffer through hours of conversation with Ms. Perfection—"

"That's not it. I—"

"Miss Know-It-All, Kiss-Face, I've-Been-All-Around-the-World-and-Other-Places!"

"But you see—"

"I mean, really, what other places can you actually go? I mean, does she expect me to think she's been to the frigging moon too?"

"Crystal!" Geneva screamed. "I don't have anything to wear!"

I yanked the phone away from my ear and then pressed it back. "Geneva, you have plenty of things to wear."

"Sure, I would have plenty if they fit."

"Nothing fits?"

I knew she'd put on more weight, but now wasn't the time to start needling her about it.

"Nothing."

I snatched a glance over my shoulder and caught sight of myself in the large pane of glass in the restaurant window. "Look," I said in a sedate voice as I removed the smart silk scarf from around my neck and then slid the chunky gold bracelet from my wrist, "come casual. I'm casual."

"But, Crystal—"

"No, really," I continued as I undid the pearl teardrop earrings from my lobes and dropped them, along with the rest of my bounty, into my leather sack purse, "just throw something on and come on down."

"Oh, okay," Geneva breathed before she hung up.

* * *

Shaw looked up when I approached, and, after offering me a mock smile, she ended her conversation with a round of annoying kisses and the ever-sickening "I love you, honey bunny."

Flipping the phone closed, Shaw batted her Bambi eyes, smiled brightly, and asked, "So who was that?"

"Geneva," I mumbled, and daintily placed my napkin back onto my lap. "She's running a little late."

Shaw looked at her Rolex. "What about Chevanese?"

"I haven't heard from her yet." The heffa was probably going to blow me off.

"Oh, well, I get to have you all to myself for a few more minutes!"

Oh, goody.

"I still can't believe that Geneva had another baby, especially at her age," Shaw began as she lifted her glass of champagne and sipped.

"Yeah, well," I grumbled as I picked up my own glass of wine.

"I mean, um, she had it hard with the first one. A boy, right?"

Now Shaw knew good and well Geneva had a son. Had she had her memory removed right along with the cellulite in her thighs?

I nodded my head.

"I mean, living in the projects and all. She still lives in the projects, right?"

"Yes."

Shaw shuddered.

"Wow," she murmured in disbelief. "And she had what—another boy?"

"A girl."

"Ah, yes," Shaw breathed, and then ran her fingers slowly down her perfect neck. "What was her name again? Chamomile? Corona? Condoleezza? Camry—"

"Chartreuse," I barked, then played it off with a cough. "Chartreuse," I said again sweetly.

"Oh, I knew it was some ghetto—" Shaw began, then stopped short and changed gears. "I mean, I knew it was something *different*."

"We call her Charlie for short," I added before I threw my hand into the air to get the attention of a waiter again.

"Cute," Shaw said, taking another sip of her champagne. "Same father?"

I looked at Shaw and the expression she wore was one of an innocent child, but I knew her question was far from innocent. It made Shaw feel good to see other people not do well. I knew she wanted me to tell her that Geneva's baby was from a different man and that she was not only still living in the projects but on welfare too. That information would have just made her day.

"Yes, it's from the same man, Shaw."

"Hmm, that's nice. But I thought they broke up." Shaw's eyes narrowed, and I could see fangs growing out of her mouth. She wanted blood.

"Well, they got back together for a while." Why was I even answering her questions? That was Geneva's personal business.

"Now"—Shaw leaned in closer and grabbed a breadstick from the basket that sat between us—"she's working at your company, right?" Then she snapped the breadstick in two. I found myself jumping at the sound.

I drained my glass of wine. The wine wasn't going to be enough; I was going to need a gin and tonic to deal with this beast.

"Yes, she was, but not anymore." I didn't want to tell her that Geneva was waiting tables at a diner.

"So she's on the state?" Shaw said with a triumphant smile.

"No, she's in food services," I quickly retorted. "And she's in school." Albeit, it was some no-name online university—but a school just the same.

Shaw's smile faltered and then recovered. I waited for the next question, the final one that would leave Geneva's sordid life gutted and skinned on the table before us.

"Charlie. Hmm, that's a cute little nickname for a girl," Shaw chimed before she looked down at her watch again.

Thank God, the inquisition was over.

"Waiter!" I called.

"Would you like to order an appetizer?" the waiter inquired after I gave him my drink order.

"Yes, let's," Shaw chirped as she snapped open the menu.

I was on my second gin and tonic and not hearing a word Shaw was saying when I looked up and saw Geneva peering uncertainly through the glass door of the restaurant.

"Oh, there she is," I said with a heavy sigh of relief.

"Where? Where?" Shaw twisted her head this way and that.

"Right there," I said, pointing toward the door. "That's her in the flowered miniskirt."

"No, it's not," Shaw squeaked in disbelief. "She got so fat!"

Geneva lumbered toward us, the hem of the skirt inching up her thighs with each step she took.

I gulped down my drink and forced a smile.

The white blouse was nice; I remembered when she'd picked it up on sale at Macy's. But that skirt, Conway for sure.

Her Payless white slingbacks were scuffed at the toes, and I could see, by the horrific smile plastered across Shaw's face, that she'd seen that too.

"She's gained a few pounds, yes," I eked out of the corner of my mouth, "but she just had a baby."

"Yeah, three years ago," Shaw whispered as Geneva made her final approach.

"Sorry I'm late, girls," Geneva huffed as she tugged the bottom of her skirt before looking down at Shaw and smiling. "Long time, girl!"

Shaw must have temporarily misplaced her tongue because although her mouth sat wide open, not a word came out. She just sat there gawking, her eyes rolling up and down Geneva's body.

So I jumped up and said, "Hey, girl, you look fabulous!" and came around the table and embraced her. "And you smell good too."

"Jean Naté, girl, you know how I do." Geneva chuckled and then turned back to Shaw. "Show me some love, Karen, I mean Shaw," Geneva said, and spread her fat arms wide open.

"Um, um, okay." Shaw rose on stiff legs and kind of fell into Geneva.

"It's been a long time, a long time," Geneva gushed as she squeezed Shaw's size-four frame against her. "You look good, girl. California really works for you."

"Yeah, yeah it does," Shaw muttered into Geneva's bosom. "You—you . . . look good too," she stammered after Geneva released her.

"Thank you."

Geneva smiled, sat down, picked up the menu, and said, "I'm starving, let's eat!"

Noah

"She had on what?"

"You heard me."

"I'm not sure that I did," I laughed.

"A flowered skirt."

"Oh, that's some Woolworth shit right there!"

"I *said* Conway," Crystal spoke between clenched teeth.

"Same difference."

"Okay, enough, Noah. We can't spend our entire conversation talking about Geneva. And besides, she's our best friend, so it ain't right."

"You're right, Crystal. Okay, next subject. You getting any yet?"

"Next subject."

"Okay, then that is a clear no."

"I said next subject, Noah!"

"Hmm, Zhan and I are getting new neighbors."

"Really? What happened to the old man next door?"

"He died."

"Oh, sorry to hear about that."

"I ain't. He was a pain in my perfect ass!"

"Noah, that's not nice."

"Well he wasn't nice to me. I still swear I heard him call me a nigger."

"You never told me that."

"A sand nigger."

"A sand nigger?"

"Yeah, that's what they call the Arabs here."

"That's terrible. . . . He thought you were an Arab?"

"I guess so. This process in my hair, along with the sallow-looking color my skin has taken on since we don't get any friggin' sun here must have led him to believe— Oh, don't let me get started."

I didn't want to rant and rave about the London weather, the lack of sun, or the fact that I was about to go bonkers holed up in that fucking flat all day long. At first, being a kept man was fabulous, but that got old fast. So my lover, Zhan, made a few phone calls for me—he knows the entire world—and got me a design gig with Sola Fashions. Now, I hadn't been in the creative part of the business for decades. When I went to FIT umpteen years ago, my teachers could have bet their pensions that I was going to be the next Ralph Lauren—my designs were that fabulous—but I took a different track and ended up on the merchandising side of the industry.

So when Zhan told me to pull out my portfolio and take my little cute ass over to Sola, I whirled on him and asked him if he'd lost his ever-loving mind! The drawings in my portfolio were over twenty years old and I'd kept the damn thing only for nostalgia's sake!

But my baby, quick as a whip and sharp as a blade,

took my face in his hands, leaned in close, and said, "Exactly, darling. All of that stuff has come right back around again."

No truer words had ever been spoken! Fashion is so repetitive.

Sola allowed me to work from home. Which was wonderful because I didn't have to deal with office politics or attitudes.

I took my daily walks, sometimes caught a movie or a yoga class, but really and truly, what I really needed was more hours of companionship than Zhan could give me. I was so starved for company that I behaved like a happy puppy when Zhan walked through the door every evening. My tail just a-wagging as I jumped all over him. It was sick.

But that was about to change because it had come down the grapevine that a multiracial gay couple was moving into the vacant flat next door, and it was said that one of the pair worked at home, just like me!

Finally some company!

"Anyway, there's a gay couple moving into the old man's apartment."

"Really? Have you met them?"

"Yeah, I met Aldo. Aldo Randello. He's older, Italian. A very handsome, white-haired gentleman with the body of a weight lifter. I think he might be a financier. I'm not sure, though. He was pleasant enough, but not overly friendly. His mate, well, I've only seen him from the window. I haven't had a chance to introduce myself. He's a gorgeous black man. Much younger than the Italian. I think Aldo said his partner's name was Ray-Ray."

"Ray-Ray? Ray-Ray and Aldo?" Crystal blurted out in between her reeling laugh. "Now that doesn't even sound right! In fact it sounds like a bad sitcom or the name of two radio hacks that work the lonely two-to-six morning slot on some forgotten AM station!"

I looked at the phone and shook my head. Pressing the receiver back to my ear, I said, "Well, shit, I don't care if their names are Frick and Frack. I finally got me some homosexual company right next door."

"I guess that's all that matters," Crystal breathed. "So when are you coming back for a visit? I miss you."

"Oh, maybe at the end of the summer. I need to get on a plane right now and come there 'cause Miss Drama ain't paid me a dime in rent for three months."

"Noah, are you surprised?"

"Well, I guess not."

"We told you not to leave Chevy in your house. You'll have to evict her to get her out, you know."

"I know."

Beep. You have one minute left for this call.

"Well, that's about it, Noah. I'm about to get cut off."

"I'll call you next week."

"Okay. Love you."

"Love you more."

Geneva

Monday morning came, and I found Eric sprawled out on the couch, his entire body, including his head, buried beneath the green and gold striped comforter.

I could just imagine what time he'd come in that morning, so I tried my best to be as quiet as possible as I pulled two frying pans from the cupboard and set them on the stove. In one I placed four strips of bacon, and in the other, two eggs. While the food was cooking, I pulled the ironing board from the closet and set it up in my bedroom. I should have pressed my uniform the night before, but I was just too damn tired to be bothered. So now I had to multitask.

Touching my finger against my tongue, I hesitantly tapped it against the iron. "Damn," I muttered. It was still cold.

Moving back to the stove, I turned the bacon and slid the eggs out onto a plate.

"Charlie, you got your clothes on yet?" I yelled from the kitchen, forgetting about Eric.

"No."

"Charlie, please get dressed, baby!"

"I can't, Mommy, I don't know how."

I rolled my eyes and marched into Charlie's room. "I'm not in the mood for this nonsense today. You hear me, girl?"

Charlie was sitting on the edge of her bed, cradling her doll in her arms and staring at Bugs Bunny on the small color television Noah bought her when she was just five months old.

"If you turn off them cats and rats you'll be able to get dressed, little miss missy," I bellowed, and reached for the remote. Charlie let loose a glass-shattering scream.

"Stop it!" I shushed, and then warned, "You keep screaming like that and people in here will think I'm murdering you. Then BCW will come."

"Who's BCW, Mommy?"

"Bureau of Child Welfare," I said, tweaking her nose. "Just make sure you keep using your inside voice and you won't ever have to find out."

Pulling her onto my lap, I reached for the pink and blue T-shirt I'd laid out for her.

"Socks first, Mommy," Charlie instructed. Since she was able to speak, she'd always been very precise about which article of clothing should go on first.

"Then the shirt," she added.

"You know how to do this yourself, Charlie."

"Now the pants," she ordered, all the time keeping her eyes on the television.

When it was time for the shoes, she fell into a fit of giggles as she wiggled her feet this way and that until I got so frustrated with her, I screamed, "C'mon, Charlie, now! Dammit!"

"Potty word! Potty word!"

I was just about to threaten my child with a toss out our fifth-floor window when the smoke alarm began to blare. Dropping her off my lap, I rushed into the kitchen.

The bacon had burned to ashes, leaving the smoking grease behind.

Reaching over the sink, I struggled with the window until it finally flew open. The smoke began to sail out, but the alarm was still blaring. And on top of that, Charlie was mimicking the sound!

Grabbing the closest kitchen chair to me, I climbed up onto the seat and pulled myself onto my tippy-toes, trying desperately to reach the silent button on the smoke alarm. I thought, I must be shrinking, because I've had to perform this act a million times and never had this much difficulty reaching it.

"Did you burn the breakfast again, Mommy?" Charlie asked in an exasperated tone.

I ignored her, trying hard to keep my balance on the chair while I reached for the button.

"Can I have oppie meal then?"

"It's oatmeal, shorty." Eric's voice came first and then his hand was on the small of my back, while he reached effortlessly up with his other hand and pressed the button.

I was spent and it was only seven thirty in the morning. I wanted to cry, but I knew there was no time for tears, because I still had to press my uniform, fix Charlie's breakfast, get her shoes on, drop her off at the nursery, and still get to work on time so that I could smile my way through an eight-hour shift.

"Mom," Eric said through a yawn as he helped me

down from the chair, "get yourself together, and I'll fix the squirt here her oatmeal and drop her off at the nursery."

"Hey, I ain't no squirt!"

* * *

"You late again, guuurrrrl!" the overweight fry cook, Arthur, yelled at me as I dashed in.

"I know that," I snapped, and hurried past him, down between the boxes of canned vegetables and into the two-by-four-feet storage closet that doubled as a locker room.

"Abe been looking for you!" Arthur shouted back to me as he poured a mixture of egg, sausage, and red peppers into the skillet.

"Yeah, what else is new?" I said sourly as I tied my apron around my waist.

Out in the dining area I plucked a blank order pad from beneath the counter and rushed toward my station, where five annoyed patrons sat waiting.

"Hey, girl," Darlene, the short, bowlegged, blond-haired Dominican waitress, greeted me.

"Hey."

After I took the orders, I went to make sure all the coffeepots were full.

"You know, Abe was looking for you," Darlene said as she sidled up beside me.

"Yeah, I know," I responded, stooped down now behind the counter searching for a box of Equal.

"He seemed kind of pissed."

"Oh, he always pissed. That old man gotta—" I started as I brought myself erect again and came face-to-face with my boss, Abe Myerson. "Heart of gold," I finished, offering him a sweet smile.

"Eva."

"Geneva," I corrected him. "I've worked here for damn near three years, Abe. It was Geneva when you hired me, and it's still Geneva."

"Yes, yes, whatever you want to call yourself, you're late again," he said, tapping the crystal face of the pocket watch he always seemed to have pressed into the palm of his sweaty hand.

"Yes, I know that."

"I told you I need people to be on time. I told you I would have to let you go if you were late again."

I didn't even say a word; I just slowly removed my apron, folded it neatly in half, and rested it down on the counter.

"What are you doing?" Abe asked, his eyes bulging with surprise.

"Well, you're firing me, aren't you?" I said coolly.

"Eva."

"Geneva."

"I don't want to fire you. You're the best waitress I have here, but you leave me little choice. I'm running a business. When you come late you cost me money."

"I totally understand and you're right. Me being a single mother of two should have no bearing on why sometimes things happen that would prevent me from getting here on time, even if I stay late to make up the time."

Abe sighed.

"I mean, the fact that you trust me to close and to even drop your money off at the bank—the fact that you can trust and depend on me should count for something."

Abe blinked, and the color in his face began to get all blotchy.

"Don't feel bad, Abe. You gotta do what you gotta do."

Abe's hand came up and slowly pushed the apron back across the counter toward me. "Just try a little harder to make it here on time, please," he mumbled before turning and walking away.

I smiled triumphantly. I'd won again.

* * *

By the time four o'clock rolled around, Darlene and I were sitting at the counter, sipping coffee and reminiscing on the days when one could enjoy a cup of coffee and a cigarette. Those days were long gone. At least in New York State they were.

The bell rang on the entrance door, and Darlene and I exchanged looks. "Rock, paper, scissors?" I suggested.

"Okay."

"Shoot," I said, and we each threw our hands out. Mine in the shape of a scissors, and Darlene threw out a fist.

"Scissors beat rock, don't it?" I said jokingly.

"In what universe?" Darlene laughed. "But I'll take this one just because I'm cool like that," she added, hopping off her stool and walking over toward the customer.

On her way back, the bell on the door rang again, and Darlene's head turned, then did a quick double take before she let out a low, provocative whistle.

I made a face at her and turned around to see who it

was her fast ass was salivating over this time, and to my surprise there stood my son, dressed in basketball shorts and Nike T-shirt, holding a basketball and grinning like a damn fool.

I gave Darlene a hard slap on her arm. "Don't be looking at my son like that," I warned before I turned to Eric. "What you doing here, baby? You come to take your mama out to dinner?" I teased.

"Nah." Eric blushed. He was having trouble keeping his eyes off Darlene's bosom.

"Don't you have something to do?" I turned on Darlene, who gave Eric one last appraising look before reluctantly moving off to the other end of the counter.

"I'm here. Over here," I said, snapping my fingers in Eric's face. His eyes were glued to Darlene's tight behind as she swished slowly away.

"Oh, yeah, um," Eric started, then finally looked at me. "Yeah, I wanted to let you know that I'm going to Philly tonight with Deeka."

"Philadelphia?" I questioned. "What for?"

"Well, Deeka got us a gig down there."

"Who the hell is this Deeka person?"

"Mom, I told you, Deeka Jones, he's our acting manager."

"Uh-huh," I said. "Philly, I don't know about that," I said warily.

"Oh c'mon, Mama," Eric whined, and bounced the ball nervously.

"Don't bounce that ball in here, boy."

"Sorry."

"Well, how are you all going to get down there?"

Eric nodded his head toward the diner's front window. "Deeka's gonna drive us down in his whip."

My eyes followed Eric's to the glass pane, and I saw a big black SUV parked along the curb. There was a man seated in the passenger seat, talking and laughing on a cell phone. His eyes were clad in dark shades. His jawline was sharp. I screwed up my face; I already didn't like him and I hadn't even met him.

"Is that him?" I said, squinting. "He looks familiar. Have I ever met him?"

"Nah."

"I don't know, Eric. How well do you really know this guy?"

"Ma, he's cool."

"Yeah, but that ain't answering my question."

"C'mon then, let me introduce you."

I smirked at my child. I knew I needed to stop treating him like a baby, but he was still my baby and it was hard.

"No, I'll meet him some other time when I don't smell like grease," I said. "But write down his name, phone number, and license plate number," I added, handing him my order pad and ink pen.

Eric took the items from me and hastily scribbled down the information.

"I don't know the plate number, but everything else is there," he said, pushing the pad back at me. "I'm going home to change and then we're out," he said, leaning down and pecking me quickly on the cheek.

"When will you be back?"

"Late, so don't wait up." Eric double-dribbled the ball

as he started toward the door. I opened my mouth to chastise him again, but before I knew it he was out the door and climbing into the SUV.

The truck pulled off, and I ran over to the door and watched it until it disappeared.

I just shook my head. I didn't know about this Deeka fellow.

Chevy

I never did meet Crystal and the others for lunch that day. And no, I didn't call to cancel or explain.

But typical anal Crystal, she called the house about eight times. I didn't answer not one time. All I can say is thank God for caller ID.

I'd slept most of Monday away. By three p.m. I was still in my pajamas but had made some progress; I'd moved from the bedroom to the couch downstairs.

When I went into the kitchen to fix myself a bowl of cereal, I saw that the light on the answering machine was blinking. I knew the only messages I could possibly have were from Crystal and the bill collectors, but I pressed the play button anyway.

You have four new messages.

Beep.

"This message is for Chevanese Cambridge in reference to her Chase credit card. Please call 1–800–258–6658, extension 238 to discuss your delinquency."

Beep.

"Chevy, I know you're there. Pick up. Pick up! Okay, be like that. Call me—uhm, it's Crystal."

Beep.

"Chevanese Cambridge, please call Dr. Hugo at 212–689–5596 to arrange payment for the dental work we performed on you three months ago. We've sent you numerous invoices. We don't want to send this to collections. You are a valued client."

Beep.

"This message is for Chevanese Cambridge," a feminine voice said. "I am in receipt of your résumé and cover letter and would like to set up an interview as soon as possible, please call me, Dante Whitaker, at . . ."

I stood straight up. I couldn't believe my ears, so I pressed the button again and again, playing the last message over and over until finally it seemed to ring true.

After the fourth time, I found a pen and scribbled the number on the back of the envelope for the Con Ed final-notice bill.

Picking up the phone, I hurriedly dialed the number.

"Dante here."

"Uhm, yes, this is Chevanese Cambridge, I—"

"Ah, yes, Chevanese, so glad to hear back from you so soon. I received your résumé and was very impressed, very impressed indeed."

"Thank you."

"I would like to set you up for an interview as soon as possible."

"Okay," I said as I looked at the small wall calendar above the phone.

"How's today at five?"

I was dumbfounded. My weave was a mess, my nails were atrocious, and my chin was covered with black-heads.

"Chevanese?"

"Five is fine," I said.

* * *

I would be interviewing at La Fleur Industries located on the fiftieth floor of 30 Rockefeller Plaza. I'd never heard of La Fleur Industries. It sounded more like a perfume company than a radio station. But oh well, a job is a job, right?

I fixed myself up pretty damn good if you ask me.

Pulling my weave back into a tight bun, I found some nail polish remover in Noah's room and cleaned my nails of the lime green polish I'd been sporting. Plucked a few stray hairs from my eyebrows, popped in my hazel contacts, smeared some foundation over my chin, and slipped into my cream-colored Anne Klein skirt suit. I debated over the Jimmy Choo black pumps, but the pink Judith Leibers won out. Grabbing the matching handbag, I was out the door in two shakes of a dog's tail.

Once in the building, I presented my driver's license to security; they in turn gave me a white visitor's badge and instructed me to go to the fiftieth floor.

Stepping off the elevator, I found myself standing on a bloodred shag carpet that followed the length of the hallway. A small Asian woman dressed in a kimono was standing there. I assumed the sister wanted to get on the elevator, but before I could step around her she put her hands out and said in a small voice, "Please to remove your shoes?"

"What?"

"Please to remove your shoes," she repeated.

What the hell was this shit? I thought as I slipped off my shoes and hesitantly handed them over to the woman, who then promptly scurried away down the hall and disappeared around the corner.

"Welcome," a fairylike voice called to me from the other end of the hallway. I hadn't noticed the reception area. I squinted and could barely make out the woman who was seated behind a large marble desk, beckoning me over with a wave of her hand.

This was getting stranger by the moment.

I started toward her.

When I finally reached her, I was practically out of breath. That hallway must have been a mile long.

"Hello, I'm Chevanese Cambridge and I'm here to see Dante Whitaker."

"Oh, yes," she said. She was a big girl, with broad shoulders and Kewpie doll–like cheeks. Her hair was a mass of blond Shirley Temple curls, but the suit she wore was definitely Dana Buchman. I didn't know Dana dealt in plus sizes.

"Welcome, Chevanese, I'm Jheri," she said before reaching for one of eight clipboards on her desk and handing it to me. "Please fill this out, and Dante will be with you shortly."

I thanked her and moved to one of four chocolate-colored leather club chairs. And just as I was getting comfortable, the Asian shoe confiscator returned.

"Tea?" she inquired as she stood before me, head bowed.

She had a bamboo platter in her hand that held a small jade-colored teapot and teacup.

"'Scuse me?"

"Tea?" she said again.

What the fuck? My eyes traveled slowly from the tea-toting designer shoe–napper to Jheri, who smiled sweetly and said, "It's really very good."

I preferred coffee myself but didn't want to refuse the tea, especially if it was part and parcel of the interview process, so I set the clipboard aside, thanked the girl, and took the platter from her.

The girl bowed profusely and then left.

Resting the platter on my lap, I carefully poured the hot liquid into the cup. It was green. I looked again at the receptionist.

"Green tea is a powerful antioxidant," she said, smiling.

I nodded as though I understood what the hell that word meant and then cautiously lifted the cup to my lips and sipped. It didn't taste like anything, so I sipped again and again until the cup was empty.

Just when I was trying to decide where to place the platter, the girl reappeared and took it from me.

I have to admit, I was totally weirded out at that point. It felt like freaking Disney World.

Retrieving the clipboard, I was about to write my name when the receptionist declared, "Dante will see you now."

"But I—" I started to say that I hadn't even had a chance to fill out the application when Jheri cut me off and pointed toward the white paneled wall behind me.

"Through there, down the hall, and it's the first office on your left."

I turned and looked at the wall and then back at her. "Through where?" Did I look like I was from *The League of Extraordinary Gentlemen* or something? Did I look like I could walk through fucking walls?

"Right there," she said, wagging the pen for emphasis.

I turned around again, sure I'd missed something, and the wall had magically disappeared. Beyond the door-sized space was a cream hallway and what looked like a white fur carpet.

My mouth dropped open and I turned back to the receptionist in awe.

"I know, I know," she said, nodding her head with a godlike aura.

* * *

My legs were a bit shaky when I stepped from the receptionist area and onto the fur carpet.

Wooden doors with glass windows lined the right side of the hallway, offering a clear view into the offices and the view beyond. Employees were going about their business; some were on the phone, while others typed intently on their computer keyboards.

When I reached the end of the hall there was one office on the left side. The door was different from the other office doors. The window was blacked out and the wood had been painted a glossy midnight blue.

I knocked softly.

"Enter," a voice said.

Pushing the door open, I peered into an opulent office complete with silk-covered walls and a plasma-screen television.

"Hello?" I called timidly.

"Yes, yes, come in," a voice instructed. "I'll be right with you, Chevanese."

Stepping in, I pulled the door closed behind me.

In no time a small person entered the room from what I assumed was a bathroom off to the left. At first I thought I was seeing a woman, because she was dressed in a soft pink off-the-shoulder peasant blouse and white capris. She had a beautiful copper-tone complexion and wore her hair in a mass of cascading black curls that looked as if they had been drenched in olive oil, a look Prince had made famous. But upon closer inspection and after I decided that the eyeliner was permanent and not Maybelline—I realized that this person was not a she, but a he.

Drying his hands vigorously on a paper towel, Dante said, "Sorry about that, but when Mother Nature calls . . ."

I smiled.

"So," Dante began as he leaned back into a leather wing-back chair and plucked my résumé up from his desk, "you have had quite a career so far."

I nodded proudly.

"I see you've worked with some of the top travel companies in the city, as well as a few stints with the higher-end hotels."

"Uh-huh."

"Tell me, Chevanese—"

"Please, call me Chevy."

"Chevy, hmm, I like that. Tell me, where do you see yourself in five years?"

Rich and famous is what I wanted to say, but instead I said, "I hope to be the host of my own talk show."

"Really? What kind of talk show?"

"Television. Something to do with fashion and travel."

"Interesting," he mused, and then what followed was something I'd never experienced in an interview before. "So you wouldn't be interested in my position, then?"

"I'm sorry?" I said confusedly.

"I mean, you don't plan to make La Fleur Industries your life's work, right?"

I didn't know what was happening here, so I just slowly shook my head.

"Good," Dante said, and grinned. "Would you call yourself a hard worker?"

"I'd call myself a workaholic." Lie.

"I like that, because the person you'd be working for—if hired—is just that, a workaholic."

"Exactly who would that be?" I asked, leaning forward, eager to know who the celebrity radio personality was.

"Anja."

"Anja?" I repeated stupidly, and then the name finally registered.

Anja was the top female radio personality in the nation. Just a year ago her radio show had gone national, and people all over the country were tuning in to hear her interviews, pointed commentaries, and gossip about well-known actors, musicians, and politicians. "Anja the

Anaconda!" I blurted out, then slapped my hand over my mouth. "Sorry," I muttered.

Dante laughed. "It's okay. She's well aware of what her haters call her," Dante assured me, and then he asked, "Are you a fan?"

Was I a fan? I was one of her biggest fans. She was a rich, beautiful, brawly, black female! Anja was my idol! She didn't take no shit, and when I grew up I wanted to be just like her.

"Yes, I am. A big fan," I said with a wide, genuine smile.

Now this whole setup made perfect sense. Rumor had it that Anja was the child of a Japanese mother and African father. She was born in California, but when her parents divorced she and her mother moved across the country to north Philadelphia, where she had learned the hard knocks of life.

"That's good," Dante said. "I like your vibe, Chevy. I like your spirit, and you certainly have the look."

"Thank you." I beamed.

"Get up, do a little runway for me."

"What?" I said, blinking in disbelief. Was this an interview or a fashion show? Then I reminded myself that this was Anja's show and that Anja was eccentric.

I rose from the chair and walked a bit stiffly from one side of the room to the other. Turning to look at Dante, I could tell by the expression on his face that he was not impressed.

"Did I tell you that the starting salary is seventy-five thousand dollars, with a twenty percent bonus at the end of your first year?" Dante said as he picked disinterestedly at his cuticles.

Well, he didn't need to say any more. I placed one hand on my hip and strutted back across the room, head tilted toward the ceiling, swinging my ass like I was Tyra Banks up in that bitch!

"Bravo! Bravo!" Dante yelled as he clapped enthusiastically.

Geneva

Wednesday evening, and Charlie was down at my mother's house, playing with her cousins. Eric was in the bedroom, primping in front of the mirror.

I would be working the weekend and off Thursday and Friday.

One large Papa John's cheese pizza, a six-pack of Corona, and some Ben & Jerry's ice cream would be my dinner and dessert, topped off with a movie rental and a little late-night action with my handheld showerhead.

"How's this look, Ma?" Eric's voice sailed over to me. When I turned around to look at him, instead of seeing my son, I saw the ghost of what his father used to be: tall, chiseled, and gorgeous.

"Wow!" I screamed.

When did Eric's shoulders and chest get so wide? When did that mess of fuzz beneath his nose actually become a mustache?

"You look sexy, baby," I breathed.

Eric blushed. He wasn't one of those stuck-up good-looking boys. I didn't think he was really aware of what a great specimen he was.

"Oh, Mom," he said with a shy smile.

"Well, you do," I pressed, and then pulled myself up into a sitting position. "Hot date?" I inquired.

"Nah, me and the band are playing at this club."

"Really?"

"Yeah, the Spice Club, somewhere in Brooklyn. Williamsburg, I think."

"Williamsburg? Where the hell is that?"

Eric just shrugged his shoulders.

"You better call your uncle Noah and find out where it's at. Williamsburg could be some cracked-out neighborhood."

"I don't think so, Ma."

"Well, I'd feel safer if you checked with Noah anyway."

"You want me to make a long-distance call just to find that out, Ma?"

I nodded my head.

"You're trippin'," Eric laughed.

Yeah, I guess it was a little absurd. I screwed my face up and said, "Will Juuuuuulie be there?"

"Yeah, I suppose," Eric said without looking at me.

"I don't understand. Why haven't I met her yet?" I said, folding my arms across my breasts. "Are you ashamed of me?" I needled.

Eric took a long tired breath before he began. "I told you, Mom, her schedule is real tight with school and work—"

"She's going to Brooklyn to see you play, so why can't she come here to meet me?"

"Mom"—Eric spoke quietly, but his tone was stern—"I told you that you will meet her, so stop sweating me about it, damn."

My mouth opened, then closed. Who the hell did he think he was talking to? I wasn't one of his friends in the street. I opened my mouth to tell him just that, and all that came out was: "Anyway, how you all getting there?"

I know. I can be such a wimp sometimes.

"My man Deeka is going to pick me up."

"Oh, really?"

"Yeah," Eric said as he brushed a piece of lint off his black slacks.

"The same one from the other day, right?" I said, the skepticism heavy in my voice.

"Yeah, the brother who wants to manage us."

Immediately I was alarmed. I'd watched one too many VH1 *Behind the Music* episodes to know how people get caught up in crooked contracts.

"You didn't sign any papers, did you?"

"Ma, I—"

"'Cause you know you need a lawyer to look those things over. There are sharks out there looking to take advantage of every young person trying to make a way."

"I know, Mom, I know."

The intercom buzzed loudly.

"Oh, damn—I mean, dang—that must be Deeka," Eric said as he rushed to the intercom. "Who is it?"

"Deeka." The voice was deep, sexy, and familiar.

"A'ight, come on up."

I grimaced. Now I would have to get up and make myself look at least welcoming. I tightened the knot in the red and white scarf I had wrapped around my head, smoothed the ragged T-shirt over my breasts, and then decided at the last minute to go into my bedroom and throw on a gray pullover sweatshirt.

By the time the knock came on the front door, I was ready.

Eric swung the door open and said, "Hey, man," to a figure I couldn't quite make out in the hallway.

"Hey," the husky voice came back, and a dark hand was extended.

"Don't you have any manners, boy?" I shot out, eager to see this Deeka person who was trying to take advantage of my baby.

Eric shot me a dismayed look, then stepped aside. "Come in, Deeka."

I straightened my back and put on the most serious face I could muster. Then I heard a car alarm begin to wail outside my window.

"Yo, I think that's your ride, man," Eric said.

"Dammit!" I heard Deeka mumble, and then the sound of his feet hurrying down the hallway toward the stairwell followed.

Eric moved to the kitchen window and peered out. "Oh," he said as he looked down at the street. "I think that kid's ball hit Deeka's truck," Eric said more to himself than to me before yelling, "Yo! Take it easy with that ball, yo!"

Shaking his head he turned around and looked at me, then said, "A'ight, Ma, I'm out. See you when I get back."

* * *

The last thing I remembered, before sleep won out and my eyes fluttered shut, was Letterman's gap-toothed smile. When I finally rolled over and opened my eyes, it was ten minutes to three in the morning.

My gaze fell on the television screen and the awkwardly walking living dead that lumbered toward the frightened white woman standing near a gravestone. I watched for a moment before reaching for the remote and shutting the television off.

My bladder was full, and I struggled out of the bed and shuffled my way out of the bedroom and down the hall toward the bathroom. Yellow light was seeping out from beneath the closed door. That wasn't unusual; I kept the bathroom light on twenty-four hours a day for Charlie.

My eyes were half shut as I pushed the door open and began rolling my T-shirt up around my waist, and then I heard the steady sound of urine hitting the ceramic inside of the bowl.

My eyes flew open, and I found myself staring at a man's back. Of course, I was still half asleep and thought I'd walked in on my son, like I had a million times before. I was about to open my mouth and chastise him about not locking the door when the figure turned around and I was face-to-face with the man from the diner!

"Oh! Oh!" I squealed, bringing my hands up and over my eyes and then taking them down again because I was sure that I was seeing wrong. I mean, why would the Mos Def to my Alicia Keys be taking a piss in my bathroom?

When I peeked at him again, I could see recognition quickly blending with the embarrassment on his face. I threw my hands back over my eyes and cried, "I'm sorry! I'm sorry!" as I backed carefully out of the bathroom, bumping into the sink and then bouncing off the wall before losing my balance completely and falling backward onto my behind.

"Ma!" Eric shrieked from behind me as he fitted his hands beneath my armpits, trying desperately to hoist me up.

"This is your mother?" Deeka was astonished, and I could tell by the tone in his voice that he'd recognized me as quickly as I had him.

"Yeah. Now help me." Eric's voice was etched with fear.

Deeka started to lean over, but I threw one hand up and said, "No, no, I can get up by myself." I had dreamed about him touching me a million times, but in those dreams I wasn't sprawled out on the floor in a dingy T-shirt, my head wasn't wrapped in a washed-out head scarf, and I certainly didn't have dimpled thighs!

Oh, the shame!

"You sure?" Eric's voice was filled with concern.

"Yes," I whispered. I was so embarrassed, I couldn't find it in me to look at either one of them. "Just go away," I breathed.

"I-I'm sorry, Ms.—" Deeka started, but I interrupted his apology by shaking my hand at him and sputtering, "Just go!"

"C'mon, man," Eric said, and his hands eased from beneath my arms. I turned my body a bit so that Deeka could slip by.

They walked toward the door, and Eric said, "I'll see you tomorrow."

"Yo, man, I'm really sorry," Deeka murmured.

"Don't worry about it, man."

When the door closed, Eric was at my side again. "What happened?" he asked as he knelt down beside me.

"Just help me up," I choked out behind hot tears of embarrassment.

Chevy

Thursday morning, Dante called to say I had passed the first interview sequence and was on to the second round. This time I would be ready. I would be flawless because I would borrow the money from Crystal to make that happen.

"Hey, girl."

"Hey. What's going on with you? Haven't heard from you in a minute."

"I know. Look, I need to borrow some money."

"Goddamn, Chevy. No small talk, no foreplay, you just bend me over and stick it in, huh?"

"Crystal, I know I owe you, but I really need help."

"Help with what? A Dolce & Gabbana bag on layaway?"

"No, no. I'm up for a second interview with Anja."

"Anja? What is that, some new clothier?"

"Anja the radio host."

There was a long silence before she whispered, "Anja the Anaconda?"

"The very same."

"How'd you score that?"

"I applied, like everyone else," I snapped.

"You applied? You mean you applied yourself to some man's dick and he got you the interview, right?"

I was in shock. Crystal wasn't usually so gully!

"I ain't no ho!" I screamed at her and banged the phone down on Noah's black granite countertop a few times so that she knew I was not amused.

When I pressed the receiver back to my ear, she was laughing.

"I'm just kidding, Chevy. But let me ask you this: why would you want to work for a woman like that? I understand that she's a cutthroat, lowdown snake. Hence, the 'Anaconda' term."

"Seventy-five thousand dollars a year," I quietly responded.

"Oh. Well, that's different," Crystal said. "But for real, Chevy, I hear she's one tough cookie and a bitch to get along with. One of the admins here at my company used to work for her."

"Yeah, what she say?"

"She can't say a word. She signed a confidentiality agreement that's good for ninety-nine years, and if she breaks it she'll lose everything she has and be jailed for life."

"Get the fuck out of here," I laughed.

"I'm serious. I've seen it."

"Damn."

"So do you still want to work for her?"

"Did you not hear me say seventy-five thousand dollars a year?"

* * *

Crystal deposited five hundred dollars into my account a few hours after we spoke, and I went right out and got my weave touched up, my eyebrows and my legs waxed, a facial and a manicure and pedicure, and still had enough money left over to get a new pair of stockings and a blouse.

I was sharp!

I arrived at La Fleur Industries twenty minutes early and went through the same routine: shoes, tea, Dante.

After Dante and I talked, he ushered me down the white fur–carpeted hall to another office with a large red door.

Dante knocked.

"Enter," the familiar radio voice instructed.

Dante whispered, "Good luck, girl," and hurried away. I pulled my shoulders back, checked my breath, cleared my throat, and pushed the door open.

The room was done up in about twenty shades of white, giving it a beach house sort of feel. There were splashes of red here and there—framed paintings, throw pillows, and ceramic vases.

My eyes coveted everything in that office before finally falling on her.

Anja the Anaconda in the flesh!

Anja was seated behind a smoky gray glass desk that was nearly the length of the glass wall of windows behind her. Her hair was piled into a neat bun at the top of her head, giving her already Asian eyes a more severe slant. Her pouty lips were done up with an iridescent pink gloss. She wore a lime green sleeveless top that looked as if it had been painted on. I was sure she wore no bra, because her nipples reached out to greet me before her hand did.

I made a mental note to find out who her "boob man" was, 'cause those were the perkiest breasts I'd ever seen.

"Hello, Chevy," she said as she pulled her six-foot-one frame out of the leather chair. I couldn't help but marvel at her track-star body. I wondered if it was all plastic surgery, or if at least some of it came from hours at the gym.

She extended her hand, and I was temporarily mesmerized by the three diamond-clustered bangles that hung from her wrist.

"Hello."

"Please sit," Anja said. "Dante was very impressed with you," she began as she leaned back and pressed her palms together.

I nodded.

"He tells Anja that you'd like to host your own television talk show one day."

He tells Anja?

"Yes, that's right."

"Well, you know that here at La Fleur, everything and anything is possible."

"Yes, Dante expressed that."

"Anja is not a pussycat to work for."

"Yes, I've heard that," I said confidentially.

"Anja is fair, but hard."

Okay, this was weird; she was referring to herself in the third person? I nodded again.

"This is no place for wimps or slackers. Do you understand?"

"Yes."

"The workdays here are rarely less than twelve hours."

Twelve hours! "No problem," I lied.

"Most days you'll start at seven and end at seven, except for the nights when I have my Divalicious parties, those days can go on until four a.m."

"Yes."

"And then of course, Anja will still expect you back in the office by seven."

I blinked. This bitch was crazy!

"That's not a problem, I require very little sleep," I lied.

"Anja does special broadcasts a few days out of the year in different parts of the country and sometimes out of the country. Anja assumes your passport is up to date."

"Yes, it is."

"Good. So how does all of that sound so far?"

Insane! "Exciting."

"Now, you would be Anja's personal assistant, and a good part of your day would be to fetch Anja things. But there will be days when Anja will need you to assist her during Anja's interviews. There will be times when you'll be right in the cage with Anja."

"The cage?"

"Yes, the radio booth."

"Oh."

"That's where you'll learn the skills you'll need to fulfill your dream."

"Of course."

"Anja will have Dante send you down to Sal to get measured."

"Measured?"

"Yes, all employees are measured for outfits. You know, for the freebies the designers send over."

My eyes lit up.

"And of course if you're hired, you'll have to sign a confidentiality agreement. Because everything that happens at La Fleur Industries stays at La Fleur Industries."

"Of course."

"So, Chevy, do you have any questions for Anja?"

"What's the pay schedule?"

Crystal

Mama called me at work to tell me that Neville was flying in that evening and would take a taxi straight to my apartment.

"What time is his flight coming in?" I asked, trying hard to keep the irritation out of my voice. I thought I had more time.

"About four thirty."

"Mama, you know I work until six most days."

"Well, baby, he'll just have to wait in the lobby until you get home is all."

"No, no." I jabbed my pen into the middle of a stack of papers that were on my desk. "I guess by the time he clears Customs and Immigration and collects his bags it'll be damn near six."

Mama just stayed quiet.

"I'll be home by the time he gets there. Don't worry."

"Okay." She paused for a moment before going on. "You sound so stressed, honey. I think this visit is going to really help relax you."

"Why would you think that?"

"Think what, sweetheart, that you're stressed?"

"No, that Neville's visit would help relax me?"

"Oh, I don't know. Just an old lady talking foolishness, I guess," she sang.

I shook my head. Sometimes I felt my mother was losing her mind. "So what time is your flight to Vegas?" I asked, moving us on to another subject.

"I'm getting ready to walk out the door now."

I glanced at the small crystal clock on my desk; it was just past nine. "Oh, well, have a safe trip, and be sure to call me when you get there."

"Okay, Crystal. Will do," she said. "And really, you and Neville try to have a good time. Okay? Try to get out and see things. You know Neville hasn't been back to New York in years. I don't think he's even left that island since he moved there."

"Yeah, sure, Mom. Bye."

* * *

I'd just smoothed my hands across the clean sheets of the guest bed when the phone rang.

"Hello?"

"Hey, girl. What's doing?"

"Hey, Geneva. Just putting the final touches on this room."

"What?"

"Oh, I haven't spoken to you recently. Well, Neville is coming in tonight."

"Tonight! Oh, wow. I can't wait to see him. I wonder if he's still got that big ol' jug head!" Geneva laughed.

"Well, you don't outgrow something like that," I said, dragging my finger across the dresser to check for dust.

"I suppose not," Geneva said. "You don't sound excited."

"Well, you know, I just wish I had a little more time to get used to the idea."

"Yeah."

"So what's been going on in your world?"

"Well, girl, I had the most embarrassing moment of my life," Geneva started, then went on to tell me about her early-morning escapade with Eric's manager, Deeka.

By the end of the story I was laughing so hard, my sides were hurting.

"I don't ever want to see that boy ever again in my life!" she ended just as my intercom buzzed.

"Okay, girl," I said, wiping the tears from my eyes, "I think that's Neville. I'll give you a call tomorrow."

"All right, give Neville a hug for me and tell him I'm looking forward to seeing him."

"I will, and listen," I said as seriously as I could, "invest in some pajama bottoms!"

"Oh, you're a real comedian now, huh?" Geneva laughed. "Bye," she said, and the line went dead.

I gave the room another once-over and then headed over to the intercom.

"Yes?"

"A Mr. Neville Gill is here for you."

"Thank you, Joseph. You can send him up."

A few minutes later the front-door buzzer sounded. I took a deep breath, put on my best movie-star smile, and swung the door open.

"Crystal?" a deeply melanated man with shoulder-length locs asked.

"Neville?" I responded.

"Hey, gal. What you saying!" Neville yelled, and bent down and enclosed me in a tight embrace.

"H-hey," I said, more than a little surprised. I gave his back three awkward pats before breaking the embrace. We just stood there for a while beaming at each other. He didn't have a jug head anymore.

"Look at me, forgetting all my manners. Come in, please." I took a step backward, making space for him to enter.

"Wow, this is a nice place," he said as he slipped the green duffle bag off his back and dropped it down to the floor.

"Thanks." I was still at the door, looking in the hallway for more luggage. "Is that all you have?" I asked.

"Yep. All I need." He perused the apartment for a moment before turning back to me. "You've really done well for yourself, Crystal."

"Yeah, I guess I have."

"Don't be coy, gal." Neville laughed, and I noticed that his teeth were so white they seemed to sparkle. "You rich?"

His question caught me off guard; I stumbled for a moment and then recovered with "Rich in family and friends."

"That is the best wealth to have!" Neville laughed again, and brought his hands together in a large thunderous applause.

"Oh, stop it." I blushed. "Sit down, please."

"I really appreciate you doing this for me, you know."

"Neville, please, it's no problem at all, really."

"Oh, before I forget," he said, reaching for his bag, opening it, and digging inside, "I have something for you."

While he rummaged I had a moment to really look at him. He was dressed in a white T-shirt that was thin enough for me to see that he was muscled and firm. Sitting there with his legs open, it was clear to see that God had blessed him more than a few times.

Damn.

"Here you go!" he said, pulling a bottle of rum from the bag and handing it to me. "Just a small gesture. I really appreciate that you're letting me stay in your home."

"Thank you so much, and it's no problem at all. I love the company."

"Well, good."

"Anyway," I said when I found myself staring at him, "over there is your room." I pointed across the living room toward the guest bedroom. "I hope it's okay," I said, standing up and starting across the floor. Neville picked up his bag and followed me.

"It's lovely," he commented, stepping inside and strolling over to the window. "Your mother didn't say how much you were going to charge me."

"Charge? Oh, no. Nothing. I'm glad to do it," I said, waving my hand and trying hard not to focus on the bulge in his pants.

Neville threw his hands up into the air. "Well, *freeness* is not always a good thing, you know."

"'Scuse me?"

"I have to pay you somehow."

I could suggest a few different positions—I mean, ways . . . damn.

"Really, it's not a problem. Don't worry yourself about it." I felt my cheeks begin to sizzle.

Neville nodded his head. "I will repay you in some way, someday."

I just smiled.

"Well, look at us, standing here like we're strangers or something." Neville started toward me. "We've got a lot of catching up to do." Grabbing hold of my hand he piped up, "Come, let's you and me get reacquainted."

It'd been a long time since a man had held my hand.

It felt good. Damn good.

* * *

Before I knew it we had been sitting on the couch, talking for nearly two hours. My stomach was growling, and I realized that the last thing I'd eaten was a Cobb salad, and that was at noon.

Standing up, I started toward the kitchen. "You've got to be hungry, Neville."

"Like a horse!" Neville laughed as he rubbed his stomach and trailed behind me.

"Well, I've got some leftover Chinese food and some salad in the fridge. I'm sorry but I don't get to the grocery store too often; I eat out a lot," I said apologetically.

"You're giving me a place to stay; I don't expect you to feed me too," he said from the doorway of the kitchen. "How about I start thanking you by taking you out to eat?"

I thought about what Mama had said about Neville not having much money. "Oh, no, I couldn't let you do that."

"Please," he said, giving me puppy-dog eyes.

"Okay. What are you in the mood for?"

"Whatever you're in the mood for."

I had been craving steak all week but knew that Neville's pockets wouldn't be able to handle that. "How about pizza?"

"Pizza it is."

"Okay, then. Let me just fix my lipstick and we'll head out."

* * *

We ended up at Ray's Famous Pizza. I ordered a Supreme slice and Neville ordered a Veggie. We both had bottled water and took a seat by the window.

"So do you like being back in New York?" I asked after I'd wiped the red sauce from my lips.

"I always have a good time when I come to New York," he said as he unscrewed the white top from his Poland Spring water bottle.

My eyes popped. "Always?" I asked stupidly, replaying my conversation with my mother in my mind. "When was the last time you came through?"

He eyed me intently as he raised the water bottle to his lips and drank deeply. I watched his Adam's apple bob in his throat. There was something sickly seductive about the movement. I pulled my eyes away. When he'd consumed half the bottle, he lowered it and watched me as he licked his wet lips. "I come here at least twice a year," he said.

I cocked my head to one side and gave him a perplexed look. "I thought you hadn't been here for years."

"Why would you think that?" he asked, taking a bite from his pizza.

"Well, that's what I thought my mother told me," I said, a bit unsure.

"You must have heard her wrong," he said, and looked off toward the glass refrigerator that held the sodas and water. "I'm going to need some more water. How about you?" He pointed to my full bottle.

"No, I'm fine, thanks."

I stared down at my pizza and mentally ticked off all the information Mama had given me about Neville. When he returned to the table, I had a laundry list of questions for him. Without making it seem as if I was giving him the third degree, I casually interrogated him.

"So," I started easily, "have you been anywhere else in the United States?"

"Oh, yes. I've visited Miami a few times. I like that city. I've been to Atlanta, Dallas, San Francisco, and Denver," he said as he counted the cities off on his fingers. "Oh, yeah, and last summer I spent a month at Martha's Vineyard."

"Really?" I said, already feeling angry red heat climbing my neck. My mother had lied to me. "A whole month. What a life," I added sarcastically.

Neville smiled. "Yes, I have a nice life. I can't complain," he said. "I'm supposed to be headed out to England in a few weeks. But that's up in the air for now."

"So you've been to Europe as well." I pretended that the water bottle was my mother's neck and wrapped my hand as tight as I could around its middle. Why would she lie to me?

"Oh, yes. Many, many times. Belgium, Switzerland, France, Holland. I really like Holland."

"All of those countries?"

"Oh, and Italy too."

I was fuming.

"Didn't you like the pizza?" he asked, staring down at my now cold slice. I looked down at it but could hardly see it, I was so angry.

"My appetite just went right out the window," I managed between clenched teeth.

"Are you okay?" Neville asked, his voice filling with concern.

"Fine. Fine," I said, finally releasing the water bottle. "So do you travel for work?" I probed.

A sly smile suddenly appeared on Neville's face, and he looked directly in my eyes and said, "Something like that."

Well, what was it? He was being evasive, which meant that the work he did was probably illegal. Mama had duped me into housing a drug dealer! That knapsack of his was probably filled with reefer!

Well, he did fit the profile. The thick gold chain around his neck, the locs.

I wiped nervously at the corners of my mouth and leaned back into the hard seat of the booth, readying myself for the answer to my next question.

"'Something like that'? What exactly does that mean, Neville?" I said in the sternest voice I could muster.

Neville's head jerked back a bit, and the sly smile turned into an amused one. "Did I say something to upset you, Crystal?"

"I would just like you to answer the question," I said, folding my hands across my chest. "It's evident to me from our conversation that my mother has not told me the truth about you." Then I leaned in and whispered, "You're staying in my house, and I think it's only fair that you tell me who you are and what you do so that I can make a decision as to whether or not I want you to stay."

Neville's face went from amused to serious. He pushed the paper plate aside and leaned in so that our faces were less than an inch from each other. "I am a coastline executive."

"And what is that exactly?"

His eyes wavered for a bit, then he leaned back and said, "I take care of the tourists that come to Antigua."

"Take care of them how?" I probed.

"Well," Neville began slowly, as if he needed to carefully choose his words, "let's just say, I, um, make sure they will always want to holiday on that island."

I smirked at him.

"Okay, I have three Jet-Skis that I rent out and I hire out my BMW as a taxi for island tours and—"

"You have a BMW?"

"An old one, yes. Look, Crystal, I'm the same person you played hopscotch, tag, and hide-and-go-seek with. I'm no drug dealer, murderer, or rapist. I'm a good guy, you don't have to worry. But if you don't feel comfortable, I will leave tonight."

I shook my head. What was wrong with me?

"I'm sorry, Neville. Please forgive me. We New Yorkers have a different mentality."

"I know," Neville laughed. "Trust no one."

I laughed. "That's true. But I'm still confused. Mama made it seem as if you were living in the woods and barefoot. She said you didn't have any money."

"C'mon, you know you don't need money—as long as you've got credit!" he chuckled.

I laughed right along with him, because that was indeed a true statement!

I felt good about him now and ventured into what probably would have been volatile territory for other people, but this was Neville, my childhood friend. My make-believe cousin.

"So this person you were supposed to stay with, was it a woman?" I asked coyly.

Neville grinned and shook his index finger at me. "Nosy," he said.

"Well, was it?" I pushed.

"Yes."

I leaned back. "Girlfriend?" I asked, now more curious than ever.

"Just a friend."

I accepted that, knowing that men were quicker to use the term *friend* than they were *girlfriend*.

"Any other questions?" he said, placing his elbows on the table, leaning in and resting his chin on his hands.

"No, I guess not."

* * *

"He owns three Jet-Skis?" Geneva asked.

"Yeah," I whispered into my cordless phone from my

bathroom. I had the water in the sink running to further muffle my gossip.

"Wow. I can't wait to see him. I can't imagine Neville looking the way you've described," Geneva said, her voice trailing off dreamily.

"Gurrrl, he is fine!" I heard myself say a little too loudly.

Geneva laughed. "Calm yourself. You're celibate, remember?"

"Oh, please, I'm not thinking about doing him." And even as the words came out of my mouth I knew I was lying. I had had a number of one-minute fantasies about Neville ever since he'd walked through the door.

"Uh-huh." I could hear Geneva strike a match and inhale deeply on her cigarette.

"Girl, Neville is my friend. *Our* friend."

"Like friends don't fuck," Geneva said, so matter-of-factly I almost choked.

"Geneva!"

"What?"

"Anyway, I think he's religious."

"Why? Is he walking around quoting scripture?"

"No, but he's got a Bible on the nightstand. It looks like he really uses it. I mean it's worn."

"Yeah, well the religious ones are the worst."

"Oh, stop it, Geneva. You're starting to sound like your mother!"

"Anyway, where is he now?"

"Oh, he's in the living room, watching television."

"Lock your door, girl."

"Oh, please. What do you think he is—some type of murderer?"

"Shit, even though we know Neville, we don't really *know* Neville. You know what I mean?"

I nodded my head. I hated to admit it, but Geneva was right.

"All right, girl, I will."

"Okay, sleep well."

"Wait a minute. Before you go, you heard from Chevy?"

"Nah, not for about a week."

"Hmm."

"Crystal, did you lend her money again?" Geneva asked, her voice stern.

"Well, just because she had to get herself together for this interview with—"

"I don't know how many times I have to tell you not to—"

"Listen, she had an interview with Anja," I said, cutting her tirade off.

"Who the fuck is Anja?"

"Anja the Anaconda."

"The radio host?"

"The very same."

"And you believed her?"

"Why shouldn't I have?"

"You are so gullible, Crystal. Chevy is like a crack addict; she can come up with the most fantastic stories to get your money."

"But, Geneva, I—"

"Remember when she borrowed that five thousand dollars for her boob job?"

"Yes, but—"

"And what did she tell you it was for?"

"Surgery."

"I rest my case."

"It's not like she lied."

"No, and it's not like she told the whole truth either."

We stayed quiet for a while.

"Okay, girl, I'm done preachin'," Geneva said, her voice apologetic. "You have a good night."

"Yeah, you too."

I pressed the end button, then dialed Chevy's number. All I got was the mechanical voice of the answering machine.

"Hey, Chevy. Just checking to see how that second interview went," I said in my most pleasant voice. "Give me a call. And, oh yeah, Neville Gill is here. Okay, call me."

If Chevy had duped me again, I hoped she'd spent the money well, 'cause she wasn't going to get another dime out of me for the rest of her life.

I tightened the belt to my robe, turned off the water, and walked out of the bathroom and into my bedroom toward the door that was open just a crack. Peeking around the entrance I could see that the living room was dark except for the light coming from the television.

"Neville?" I whispered and his head popped up from where he was stretched out on the sofa.

"Yes? Is the television too loud?" he asked, frantically reaching for the remote.

"Oh, no. I just wanted to tell you good night. I have to get up at the crack of dawn, so I'm going to head in."

Neville pulled himself up into sitting position. "Okay, then. Sweet dreams, Crystal."

I gave him a little two-finger wave and then pulled the door closed. Removing my robe and throwing it across the foot of my bed I started to climb in between the sheets when Geneva's warning came to mind, so I climbed back out of the bed and crept over to the door where I gently turned the silver knob of the lock. The click was soft, but in the quiet of my bedroom it seemed as loud as a sledgehammer hitting the wall.

Back in bed now, I would fall asleep with one eye open.

Noah

I had to play it off. Had to act like I didn't know a thing about what was going on over there on 90th and Central Park West. So I was in full character when I got the call from Crystal about Neville.

"You know sometimes, Ms. Crystal, I wonder about you."

"I know, Noah, but you know Mama said that he—"

"I don't care what your mama said; we knew Neville a long time ago. We've all changed. Well, all of us except that crazy-ass Chevy. She's always been a selfish hag. So you say he ain't got that jug head no more?"

"Uh-huh, that's gone. And I gotta tell you, Noah, he is very good-looking now."

"Hmm, someone sounding like they sweet on their new roommate."

"I am not!"

"Why are you screeching, hon? You know what the old people say: 'When you're loud, you're wrong,'" I said, and added two finger snaps for flavor.

"Whatever, Noah."

"Okay, girl. Don't let Neville talk you out of your Victoria's Secrets!"

"You know, I don't know why I call you."

"Ha, 'cause I'm going to tell you the real deal."

"So you say. Hey, by the by, did your new neighbors move in yet?"

"Oh, yes. They're all moved in, and in fact I was over there just the other day with a plate of my famous chocolate chip cookies. A little welcome-to-the-neighborhood gift."

"Cookies? You baking now?"

"A man can pick up a lot of new hobbies when he has time on his hands, Miss Thing."

"Oh."

"Anyhoo, so that Ray-Ray is a fine, tight little scrumptious something!"

"Noah!"

"Look, girlfriend, I'm in a relationship, I'm not dead, you know. I can still observe, admire, and well . . . fantasize!"

"Noooooah!"

"I know my name, Crystal. Damn, stop wearing it out. Anyway, Ray-Ray is Jamaican, but had been living in New York since he was eight years old. He met Aldo in Holland—"

"What was he doing in Holland?"

"No doubt sitting his fine ass up in one of those weed bars, smoking a spliff and dreaming of his childhood on the streets of Kingston!" I wailed with laughter.

"You are so stupid, Noah."

"Anyway, it doesn't seem like he's doing much of anything now except spending Aldo's money. Chile, after we ate a few cookies and drank some champagne—"

"Cookies and champagne?"

"Crystal, dear, please stop interrupting me. Now where was I? Oh yeah, after the cookies and champagne, we went to Harrods, and you'll never guess who we saw there?"

"Who?"

"Whitney Houston and Bobby Brown!"

"Get out!"

"I'm serious, girl. They were acting the fools for that ol' tired show of his."

Being Bobby Brown.

"Uh-huh. We were standing there watching them cut up, and when I looked over at Ray-Ray, he had his arms folded across his chest and his face all screwed up like someone had dropped an egg. Then all of a sudden, Whitney turned around and looked dead at us, and said, 'Ray-Ray, is that you?'"

"Stop. You're. Lyyyyyyyyyyyyyyying!"

"If I'm lying, I'm flying, and, girl, both my feet planted right here on my hardwood floors."

"Whitney Houston knows your new neighbor Ray-Ray? Ray-Ray . . . um . . ."

"Barker. Ray-Ray Barker. Yes, she does. I know you gonna ask me how, but I can't answer that question. I just met the man, for chrissakes. But I tell you this, Ray-Ray ain't even spit on Whitney. He rolled his eyes, rolled his head on his neck, and turned on his heels like she was the one the offensive odor was coming from that got his face all screwed up in the first place."

"I can't even breathe. I can't breathe, Noah. This shit is unbelievable."

"Guuuuuuuuuuuurrrrl, I was there and I still don't believe it. I just followed him, figuring he would share what his beef was with Miss Thing, but he hasn't said a word and that was nearly a week ago."

"So what does Zhan think about them?"

"Zhan hasn't met either one of them yet—you know, with his hours and all. But I'm planning a small dinner party this weekend, and I've invited them over."

"Well, you like them . . . Well, at least you like Ray-Ray, so I'm sure Zhan will like him too."

"Well, I hope so."

"Okay, baby, gotta go."

"Love you, sweetie."

"Love you too, bye."

Geneva

After I'd eased myself down onto the bench in front of my building, I opened up the latest issue of *Vogue* magazine and began lazily flipping through the pages.

Charlie was being entertained by a group of seven- and eight-year-olds as they tried to teach her how to jump rope.

Neville had called me earlier in the day to say that he would be by around six to see me. It was a quarter to, so I lit my cigarette and glared down at the skinny models on the glossy pages of the magazine.

With every turn of a page I could swear I heard the words *Fat, Fat, Fat* floating up from the pictures. It was all I could do not to press the lit tip of my cigarette down into the pretty little faces of the models.

"Stop hating, Geneva," I said out loud before taking a long puff from my Newport.

Looking over at the group of children, I could see Charlie's knock-knees banging together with every leap she took.

"Yeahhhhhh!" I screamed as she jumped five full times before her little feet finally become entangled in the rope.

Charlie beamed and came rushing toward me. "Did you see me, Mommy, huh, did you?" she screamed excitedly.

"Oh, yes, and you were great!" I said, grabbing her little cheeks.

"I'm going to do it again!" she squealed, and dashed back to the group.

"Okay," I encouraged with a smile, before taking another puff of my cigarette and turning my attention back to the magazine.

"Hello, Ms. Holliday." A silky voice floated down to me. I looked up, but the sun blinded me, and I brought one hand up to block its rays.

It was Deeka.

I had fought hard to put that scene from the other night out of my mind. And I was so glad that he hadn't been back to the diner since then. But now here he was, not more than a foot away from me.

"Hey," I said in a small voice, before dropping my eyes back down to the magazine.

"May I?" I heard him say, and saw that his hand was indicating the empty space beside me.

I just shrugged my shoulders.

He stared across the courtyard for a while and then turned to face me. "I have to assume that that's your little one there," he said, pointing at Charlie.

I looked over and then nodded my head.

"She's a beautiful girl. She looks just like you."

I chanced a glance at him. Did he think I was beautiful?

"Thank you," I mumbled.

"What is she—about five?"

"Three."

"Wow, she's tall," he said, surprised, his head swinging back in Charlie's direction for a moment.

"Yeah, she is," I said, lifting my head to admire my beautiful child.

"Um, Ms. Holliday, I really feel bad about the other night and wanted to apologize again."

Oh, God, he had to go there!

"It's okay, really," I mumbled, and flipped a page.

"Well, I'd really like to make it up to you. Maybe take you out to dinner."

What?

My eyes flew up and fastened onto his face. I couldn't have heard right.

"Dinner?" I asked stupidly, then waited for this young, fine thing to give me an awkward look, laugh, and say "Who said anything about dinner?"

But instead what sailed out of his mouth was "Yeah, dinner."

"Errrrrrrrrrrriiicc!" Charlie suddenly screamed, and both Deeka and I looked up to see Eric swinging Charlie through the air.

I found myself sliding an inch away from Deeka, and I could swear that he did the same from me, so that by the time Eric got close to us, there was a respectable distance between us.

"Hey, Ma," Eric greeted me, and then to Deeka, "Hey, man." Deeka stood and they shook hands and bumped shoulders as Charlie stood between them, her head pivoting back and forth on her neck like a wind-up doll.

"Get out of their business, Charlie, and go on back and play," I yelled at her, but she ignored me until I added, "Or we'll go inside." And with that she skipped off back to her friends.

"Fresh ass," I mumbled, and then tried hard not stare at Deeka, who seemed to be trying hard not to do the same to me.

Crystal

I inhaled deeply as I stepped off the elevator. Someone was cooking up a storm. The whole hallway was filled with the aroma of I didn't know what. But it smelled damn good, and my stomach growled approvingly.

I'd had a helluva day and had hardly slept the night before. I hadn't known why I'd let that damn Geneva spook me about Neville. And the morning conversation I'd had at work with Noah didn't help things.

But I'd decided to brush all that nonsense aside and begin afresh with Neville.

I was standing at the front door, fishing for my keys, when the door suddenly swung open. Startled, I stumbled backward on my three-inch-heeled Kenneth Coles. "Oh, N-Neville, you scared me," I stuttered, grabbing hold of my heart.

Neville had on a black tank top; I could see his nipples through the thin material and the curly black hair peeking over the rounded neck of the shirt.

Neville looked just as startled. "Wow, you scared me too."

We just looked at each other for a while.

"I was just heading to the incinerator to throw these fish heads out," he said, and that's when I realized that the fantastic aroma was coming out of my apartment.

"You're cooking?" I said, stupefied.

"Yes, I hope you don't mind."

"No, of course not."

Walking into my apartment, I headed directly for the kitchen. There were three pots bubbling on the stove. A wooden salad bowl, filled with the most colorful salad I'd ever seen, sat on the table.

"You didn't have to do all of this," I sighed when Neville returned.

"I wanted to," he said as he brushed past me, pulled the door open to the oven, and peeked in. "You work hard, you should come home to a good meal."

I smiled. "So what are we having?"

"Baked red snapper with my special secret sauce. Basmati rice." He closed the oven door and lifted the top off one pot. "Callaloo," he said as he lifted another lid. "And I was feeling especially good, so I made a small pot of red pea soup."

"Mmmm," I moaned, rubbing my belly. "That sounds wonderful, and it smells just as good," I said, licking my lips.

"I called Geneva today and told her that I was going to come by and see her, but time just got away from me."

"Oh, I'm sure she'll understand."

"Yeah, I'm going to give her a call now and tell her I'll try to get over there tomorrow."

I started toward my bedroom. "Let me just slip into something comfortable, wash my hands, and then we can sit down to eat," I said, already slipping out of my suit jacket.

"Well, um, I wish I could join you, but I have plans." Neville's voice came from behind me. I turned around and saw that he was propped up against the door frame. Damn, he was sexy.

"Oh," I said quietly, hoping my disappointment wasn't too evident.

"Next time, though, okay?" he said apologetically.

"Yeah, sure, go ahead. I'll be okay," I said, waving my hand at him.

He watched me for a minute before saying, "Well, I could always change my plans."

I wanted to say, "Yes, change your plans and sit and eat with me, and then let's cuddle on the couch and watch a movie, and then . . ."

But I didn't.

"Oh, Neville, this is your vacation. You're not here to babysit me. I'm a big girl."

"You're sure now? 'Cause I will, you know."

"Go on."

"I'm just going to catch a shower, and then I'll leave you to it." He grinned and disappeared down the hall and into his bedroom.

After I'd slipped into a pair of sweats and my favorite HAPPY TO BE NAPPY T-shirt, I returned to the kitchen to find Neville waiting with a dish towel thrown over his arm. "Madam," he said, and bowed his head when I approached. "Table for one?"

I felt myself blush a bit and then looked at the table that had been set for a single diner.

Neville pulled the chair out for me. I sat down, and he dropped a paper towel in my lap. I didn't have any napkins, cloth or otherwise, in the house.

He set a full plate of food as well as a small bowl of soup down before me.

"Oh, this is too much," I said, even though I knew I would devour every morsel.

"Well, eat as much as you can."

"Okay, I'll try," I said, picking up my fork and digging in.

"Enjoy," Neville said, then bowed and walked out of the kitchen. "I won't be back too late," he called as he walked out the front door.

I looked at my plate of food and around the empty kitchen, and for the first time in a very long time, I felt really alone.

Geneva

I stepped a few paces away from the entry door of the diner and lit my cigarette. I was trying to keep my smoking breaks down to one cigarette every two hours, but this Saturday had been exceptionally hectic, so this was my second cigarette in an hour and a half.

I looked up into a blue sky that was quickly vanishing behind an influx of cottonlike gray clouds. "That damn weatherman said sunny and warm all day long," I muttered to myself before tossing the butt down to the sidewalk.

As I reached for the handle of the door, my hand collided with another. Without looking, I mumbled, "'Scuse me," and moved my hand away.

"No, excuse me," a familiar voice replied.

I looked up into Deeka's smoky eyes. Truly surprised, I stumbled backward. "What are you doing here?"

"Brought you these," he said, and pulled a dozen long-stemmed yellow roses from behind his back.

I looked at the flowers and then at him. "Is this some kind of joke?"

"What? No," Deeka said in a wounded voice. "I

brought these for you because, you know, I'm sorry about what happened the other night."

"I told you it wasn't a problem."

What kind of game was this man trying to run on me? Men like him did not buy roses for women like me.

Deeka's face went slack and his eyes swung slowly between me and the roses, and I could tell he was trying to figure out what exactly it was he'd done wrong.

I softened. "I'm sorry," I said, bringing my hand up and wiping the perspiration from my forehead. "I've just had a rough day."

Deeka's face lit up like a Christmas tree. "That's okay. I have bad days too. I know how it is. I hope these will help," he said, pushing the flowers at me again.

"They're beautiful. Thank you," I said as I took them.

A loud tapping sound interrupted us. I looked up at the diner window to see Darlene standing on the other side, hands on her hips, giving me an annoyed look. "We have customers," she mouthed dramatically.

"I gotta go," I said, and then added, "Thanks again," before I hustled past him and through the doorway.

Darlene's eyes were as large as saucers as I scurried in and headed toward the locker room. Once inside and alone, I took a moment to admire the beautiful roses. When was the last time a man gave me flowers? I thought as I pushed my face into the velvet petals and deeply inhaled their fragrant aroma. No time in the past decade, that's for sure.

"Who was that?" Darlene stage-whispered from behind me.

I nearly jumped out of my skin. "Why you always

sneaking up on people?" I barked, and shoved the roses into my locker.

"He looks like one of our customers," she said, rolling her eyes up and to the left. "Is he?"

"Yeah," I mumbled.

"Is he . . . are y-you two . . ." Darlene stuttered, then finally made an offensive gesture with her fingers and laughed.

"Oh please, girl!"

"Oh please, girl, nothing. That man is fine; I know I would be fucking him!"

"Stop it!"

"Who is he?" she asked again, leaning in close now.

"Him? Well, that's Eric's friend."

Her face went blank for a second. "Your son, Eric?"

"Yeah."

Her head swiveled on her neck. "Is it your birthday or something?"

"No."

"Then why the hell is Eric's friend bringing you flowers?" Darlene had a sly expression on her face.

I didn't answer fast enough, and she said, "I knew that man looked too young for you. You robbing the cradle, Geneva?"

"No!"

"Yeah, okay, Mrs. Robinson," Darlene sneered, turning on her heels and walking away.

* * *

At six o'clock on the dot, thunder tore through the sky above the diner and lightning followed each booming clap before rain, like pellets, began to fall from the dark sky.

I stood staring out into the wet evening, sorry that I didn't have the good sense to keep an umbrella at work for these surprise storms.

"You got an extra umbrella?" I asked Darlene, who was adjusting the straps to her plastic rain cap. "Nah, girl. Just this one," she said, holding up a flimsy black umbrella that I knew wasn't going to stand a chance against the strong wind that already had debris frantically spinning out on the sidewalk. Darlene would be soaked through by the time she got to the corner.

"We could share," she said.

"Nah, you go on ahead. Besides, we have to go in two different directions."

"See you Monday, then."

"Have a good one," I said, and watched as she streaked through the door and made a mad dash down the street.

Maybe it will let up, I thought, as I greeted one of the new waitresses who was walking through the door. "It's nasty out there," she mumbled. She made her way past me and slipped twice on the tile floor before carefully tiptoeing her way across the remaining three feet and then through the swinging doors of the kitchen.

"José," I called to the young busboy who was clearing a table nearby, "would you get the mop and clean up the water here before someone kills himself or herself?"

"Sí, Geneva. No problem," he said, and hurried off.

I turned my attention back to the weather. It didn't look like it was getting any better, so I adjusted my pocketbook on my shoulder, clutched my flowers close to my chest, and stepped out into the rain.

* * *

Back in my apartment, my wet hair was wrapped in a towel, my feet were covered in mismatched socks, and what was left of my roses was stuffed into a tall ceramic cup and sitting in the middle of the kitchen table. I was on the couch, Charlie snuggled up alongside me as we watched *The Lion King* for the millionth time.

It was all I could do to keep from grinning every time I looked over at the roses. Who knew flowers could make a woman spin on the inside! But I had to keep it under control. I couldn't let my fantasy life spill over into my real life. Deeka was probably just really sorry for what had happened and was working overtime to make it up to me. I mean, he did want to manage my son and I was Eric's mother, so who best to kiss up to, right?

That was all it was. He was just trying to get close to me to keep Eric. He wasn't a bit more interested in me than I was in the neighborhood crackhead.

The lock turned and the doorknob shuddered as the door creaked open and Eric walked in. "Hey, Ma. Hey, squirt."

"Hey, Eric," Charlie and I said in unison.

"Where you been?" I asked.

"Practice."

"Oh."

"You washed your hair?" He posed the question as he flipped through the mail that was on the table.

"Nah, got caught in the storm."

"Yeah, it really came down, huh?"

I nodded my head.

"If I had a car I would have picked you up," Eric said as he grabbed hold of my terry-cloth turban. "Well, if everything goes the way Deeka says it will, I might have one before the summer is over."

I sat up slowly and looked deep into my son's eyes. I knew about dreams that never came true. Shattered hopes. "That's nice, baby. But what do you really know about this Deeka guy? How do you know that he won't just use you and the other guys and then toss you aside for something better?" I asked, knowing full well I was expressing my own personal fears.

"I don't," Eric said as he started toward his room. "I just have to take that chance."

* * *

I felt a hand on my shoulder, shaking me awake. "Geneva." My name came through the remaining wisps of a dream. Turning over, I sat up and reached for the switch on the lamp. "Huh?" I mumbled as the soft yellow light illuminated the room.

"Hey," the voice came again.

My eyes flew open and Deeka was standing over me. "What the hell are you doing here?" I screamed, snatching the covers up over my bare breasts. "How did you get into my apartment? In my bedroom!" I screeched, snatching the extra pillow from beside me and holding it up like a shield.

"I needed to see you."

I shook my head, trying to clear my mind so that I

could understand what was happening here. "Where's Eric?"

"Ever since I first saw you, I haven't been able to get you out of my mind," he whispered, coming to sit on the edge of the bed.

I inched backward until my back was pressed against the headboard.

"Geneva, I'm not here to hurt you. Why are you so frightened of me?"

"I'm dreaming, right? This is a dream?"

"Shhhhh." Deeka hushed me and reached for the pillow. "I asked God for you, Geneva, and he brought you to me."

"What?"

"Shhhhh," he whispered, and reached over and pressed his index finger against my lips. As he inched closer to me, I could smell his cologne and feel the heat streaming off his body. Everything inside of me was suddenly alive and thumping. I hadn't felt that way in so long!

His fingers moved slowly across my face, caressing my cheekbones, stroking the lobes of my ears, then moving to my chin before dropping down to my neck. Both hands now, caressing, stroking.

I moaned loudly, and then his lips were on mine, his tongue probing.

I was limp with lust and fell effortlessly back against the headboard, my arms flailing at my sides.

"Geneva," he moaned, and climbed on top of me, his hands pulling the comforter down, revealing my naked breasts.

"Don't," I said, ashamed of their size and how, now at this age and after two babies, they'd lost their perkiness and slid like cowards down into my armpits.

"Why? They're beautiful. You're beautiful," he said, and gathered up my double-Ds and began to plant tender kisses all over them.

I was dizzy with desire, and my hands grabbed hold of his head, my fingers stroking the short stiff hairs on his head as he hungrily sucked on my nipples.

When I knew I couldn't take much more, I forced his mouth back to mine and we kissed passionately.

"Ma?" Eric's voice echoed off to my right.

"Ma!"

My eyes flew open, and I was blinded by the white fabric of my pillowcase.

Throwing the pillow off my face, I looked up to see my son giving me a bewildered look. "What are you doing?"

What did it look like I was doing? I was making out with my pillow!

"Nothing, why?" I said in my best mind-your-goddamn-business, I-pay-the-fucking-bills-in-this-piece mother voice.

Eric made a face and then hit the snooze button on the clock radio, bringing Barry White's sweet serenade to an abrupt end.

Eric gave me a knowing smile before walking out of the room.

I lay there for a while, pissed off that it had been a dream, but even more pissed off that I hadn't had a chance to get to the good part!

Noah

The dinner party I threw went off without a hitch. Aldo and Ray-Ray were our guests of honor, so I'd called in two caterers, one for each of their individual palates. I had Italian hors d'oeuvres that included antipasto, toasted ravioli, black olives in brine Riviera, and so forth. For Ray-Ray, I had miniature beef patties, jerk chicken, oxtail, and rice and peas. And of course a big green salad. And yes, loads and loads of wine!

We had a ball, and Zhan and Aldo really hit it off. They were holed up in the corner most of the night, engaged in what looked like to me an intense political conversation.

Ray-Ray really let his hair down—well, he sports a baldy—you all know what I mean. He was just a-singing and a-dancing, twirling around in the middle of the floor like one of those colorful spin tops from my childhood. I looked at him and found my eyes misting.

"What's wrong, Noah?" one of Zhan's office mates asked when she caught me wiping at my eyes.

"Watching Ray-Ray dancing around like that is making me homesick."

The woman, a petite blonde with radiant blue eyes,

considered Ray-Ray for a minute and then looked back at me. "Why is that?"

"Well, him dancing around like that—with all that energy—is reminding me of my days at the Garage."

The girl—Mimi, I think her name was—just gave me a quizzical look, patted me on the shoulder, and walked away.

I knew she was far too young to know anything about the Garage. The baddest nightclub New York City ever had! I had my first sexual experience at the Garage, right in the bathroom stall. It was glorious!

Ahhhh, memories.

The evening lasted until four in the morning and after we'd bid our guests goodbye, Zhan and I fell into bed with every intention of making love, but somehow, all that ended up happening was a few sloppy, wine-soaked kisses and then we passed out.

When the phone rang, my head rang right along with it, and I grabbed up the receiver, muttered something that sounded like "Hello," and "Yes, I'll accept the charges," and then Geneva was off and running her mouth.

"Stop yawning in my ear, Noah!"

"Well, what do you expect when you call me at this ungodly hour?"

"Noah, it's just after two o'clock in the afternoon there."

"I had a late night, Geneva."

"Oh, please."

"Go on, Geneva. You were fucking your pillow when Eric walked in and—"

"I was not fucking the pillow; I was kissing it."

"Same difference."

"Well, and I can't stop thinking about him either. I mean, I think about him all the time."

"So what's wrong with that?"

"He can't be much older than Eric!"

"Well, is he legal?"

"Yeah."

"Then he's not too young for you."

"I don't even know why I'm stressing. I mean, it's not like he's really interested in me."

"You said the boy brought you roses and offered to take you out to dinner, right?"

"Yeah."

"Sounds like he's interested to me."

"I don't know."

"Stop selling yourself short, Geneva."

"I know."

There was a marching band playing in my head, and they'd brought along a drill team and some knock-kneed cheerleaders. I couldn't listen to any more of Geneva's insecure whining.

"Okay, well, I gotta run. I have a colonic scheduled for three o'clock."

"A what?"

"You know, I gotta keep the pipes clean."

"What?"

"Oh, Geneva, I don't have time to explain. Ask Crystal. Anyway, before I go, you heard from Chevy lately? I been calling that bitch for days now, but I just keep getting the machine."

"No, Crystal told me that she was up for some job with Anja the Anaconda."

"The radio diva?"

"The very same."

"Interesting. Well, I hope she gets it so that I can get my damn rent money."

"Well, it's your own fault, allowing her to stay there when you're halfway around the world—"

"Blah, blah, and fucking blah, Geneva, damn!"

"Okay, Noah, you win. Go on and get your colon thingy done."

"Thank you, Jesus! And one other thing, baby girl."

"Yes, Noah?"

"Don't call me collect again, okay?"

Chevy

I waited by the phone for the rest of the week and through the weekend.

Crystal called three times to see if I'd heard back from La Fleur Industries. Noah called too, but I wasn't even trying to speak to him. I knew the only conversation he had for me was about the rent money, and I wasn't trying to have that talk . . . again.

I took that phone with me everywhere, even when I went to the bathroom to take a shit!

And finally, on Monday, it rang, and Dante's voice came through the other end, shouting, "Chevanese, congratulations! You're hired!"

I did a little jig right there in the middle of the living room and silently promised God that I would not fuck up!

"Thank you so much," I said to Dante.

"Can you start tomorrow?"

"Of course I can."

* * *

I arrived at La Fleur Industries dressed in my sharpest Burberry suit. My hair was so slick a fly could have ice-skated across it. Of course I'd called Noah and begged and pleaded for him to wire me some money ASAP. I had to listen to a lecture, which included him calling me every kind of bitch there was. I had to swear on my mother's life that I would start paying him the back rent I owed him as soon as I got my first paycheck, and he even wanted me to promise to name my first child after him. "Fine," I said, 'cause I knew I wasn't making no babies!

* * *

When I stepped off the elevator, I already had my shoes off and handed them over to the waiting geisha girl.

Jheri, the receptionist, greeted me with a hug and said, "Welcome to the family," before she pressed the magic button beneath her desk that opened the secret door.

I floated down the hallway toward Dante's office. He was waiting outside it, the palms of his hands pressed into his cheeks as he beamed like a proud parent. "Welcome to the La Fleur family, sweetie," he squealed, then wrapped me in a tight embrace.

I wasn't used to all of this affection, especially not in the workplace, but I guessed that I would become accustomed to it in time. I hugged him back.

"Now your office is right across from me," he said as he took a few paces across the hall and pushed the door open. It was small but comfortable. The walls were soft yellow with white moldings around the doors and windows. There was a glass desk and a leather swivel chair.

Next to my flat-screen computer monitor was a small bunch of gardenias. I walked over and plucked the card from between the leaves. "Congratulations, Chevy. I'm looking forward to a long, wonderful working relationship. Anja."

There was a potted palm near the row of floor-to-ceiling windows, a flat-screen television on one wall, and a chaise lounge against another.

The floor was covered in ecru-colored shag, and, somewhere, incense was burning.

"Behind that door is a walk-in closet," Dante said, pointing. "And in here"—he sashayed across the room toward the other door—"is your bath suite."

As I pushed the door open, my eyes were treated to the most beautiful bathroom I had ever seen outside of a magazine or *MTV Cribs.* "Wow," I said as I walked into the suite.

I knew before I even touched them that the walls and the floor were marble. I took in everything: the toilet, bidet, sauna, and Jacuzzi tub.

"All the fixtures are gold," Dante said proudly.

"Really?" I said as I ran my fingers down the neck of the sink faucet.

I didn't understand why it was I needed a full bathroom suite or a walk-in closet. But who was I to complain, right?

"Anja is in Los Angeles right now; she should be back tonight. She's hosting a party at Siboney at eleven. Do you know the place?"

My eyes popped. Who didn't? Everybody who was anybody knew Siboney. It was the swankiest private club in New York City and sat right in the belly of Harlem. Rumor had it that former president Bill Clinton was one of the people who had backed it. But that had never been proven.

"Sure, I do," I said, already feeling the excitement build.

"Well, there are some last-minute things you must tie up before tonight. Anja has emailed you a list. Your sign-on and password are on your desk."

"Okay."

"Of course, you'll be at Siboney tonight as well."

Yes!

"It's a white affair. Your outfit is in the closet."

"'Scuse me?" I said. This was really too good to be true.

Dante smiled. "We take care of most everything for our employees here at La Fleur."

I just grinned. This was going to be the best fucking job ever!

"So I'll leave you to it," Dante said, and turned to leave. "Oh yeah, lunch is at noon. I'll pick you up and take you to the cafeteria," he threw over his shoulder before walking out and pulling the door shut behind him.

God had really come through for me this time. I was the luckiest woman in the world.

Crystal

I'd called the apartment three times already. Three times, and each time I got my goddamn machine. Where was he? I picked up the phone again and hit the redial button. After listening to my outgoing message, I yelled: "Neville, if you're there pick up. Neville!"

Nothing.

I slammed the phone down and thought of how sick this was.

He'd been there for little over a week, cooking and cleaning for me, massaging my feet, entertaining me with his around-the-world stories, and then leaving me every evening to "just hang out," he said.

The man had been a perfect gentleman, hadn't even attempted to make a move on me, and here I was acting like a jealous wife!

I felt so possessive of him, and I didn't understand why that was. Maybe he was just stupid; because it was apparent that I was throwing myself at him like a cheap rag! Walking around the apartment in the skimpiest, sexiest outfits I could dig out of my wardrobe, and sometimes I had even started sleeping with my bedroom door open. Wide open!

And still he hadn't made a move.

I know he didn't think I was ugly. He told me every day how beautiful I was. Well, come to think of it, maybe he was just being nice?

I snatched up my pocketbook and pulled out my compact. Staring at myself in the mirror, I tried to see what it was that disgusted him so.

There was a small pimple forming on my chin. My eyebrows did need a touch-up and—oh, my God!—was that a whisker growing out of the side of my face!

I snapped the compact closed, picked up the phone, and called Elizabeth Arden. I needed a facial and quick!

As the phone at the spa rang, a small voice whispered at the back of my mind, Maybe he's just not that into you.

Geneva

"What would you like?" I asked the three white men who were sipping coffee and gawking across the room at Darlene's ass as she bent over to pick up a box of stirrers she'd dropped.

"Her," one of them mumbled, and the other two broke out in laughter.

"She's not on the menu, sir," I said in a dry tone.

The men realized that I wasn't going to join in their chauvinistic amusement and hurriedly cleared their throats and gave me their orders.

"Thank you," I snapped as I snatched up their menus.

"Assholes," I murmured under my breath as I made my way behind the counter and shoved my order at Arthur. "Make sure you spit in this," I said loud enough for the men to hear.

Arthur threw them a look and shook his head. "She's just kidding!" he yelled at them, and then to me, "Are you trying to get this place shut down?"

"Men are shit," I growled, spinning around and almost colliding with Darlene.

"That one with the yellow tie is so cute," she said, giving Yellow-Tie Man bedroom eyes.

"Yeah, if you think mules are cute."

"What's with the bad attitude, girl?"

"Nothing," I snorted, and walked over to a table filled with teenage girls.

"Can I get you something to drink?" I asked as I set down four glasses of water.

"Um," one girl with a neat blond ponytail, flawless skin, and striking blue eyes began, "yeah, can I get a bagel, lightly toasted with cream cheese, and a cup of black coffee?"

My eyebrows climbed at the "black coffee" part of her order.

"You sure you don't want hot chocolate?" I suggested in my best motherly voice.

"Uh, miss, if I wanted hot chocolate I would have asked for it," she reeled off in perfect Valley Girl vernacular.

I clutched the order pad tightly, willing myself not to bring it upside her head. "And you?" I asked, turning my attention to the biracial girl who had a curly Afro and light brown eyes. "The same," she tossed without looking up at me.

"Okay," I muttered, and swung my eyes in the direction of the mousy-looking girl. She adjusted her oval-shaped eyeglasses and said, "Can I have two scrambled eggs, grits, and a side order of bacon?"

I scribbled it down. "Something to drink?"

"A chocolate shake with whipped cream."

I didn't know where she was going to put it all—she was as thin as a rail—but I kept my comments to myself and turned to walk away, almost walking right into Deeka.

"Oh!" I yelped as he caught hold of my shoulders.

"Sorry."

I looked quickly across the restaurant at Darlene. Her back was turned as she flirted scandalously with Yellow-Tie Man.

"What are you doing here?" I whispered as I grabbed him by the elbow and ushered him toward the counter.

Deeka positioned himself on a stool and reached for a menu. "I've come in for a cup of coffee."

"Just coffee?" I moved behind the counter, passed my order to Arthur, and reached for the coffeepot with the red handle.

"Is that decaf?"

"No."

"Decaf, please."

"Oh, can't take the real stuff?" I teased, and wondered why it was I was allowing myself to play a word game with this little boy.

Deeka's face contorted a bit, and his eyes narrowed. "Oh, I can take it."

And we both knew he wasn't talking about the coffee.

I placed a blue cup down in front of him and began pouring the steaming black liquid. "Cream?"

"Just a bit."

I obliged and tilted the small glass carafe until the cream spilled into his coffee. The whole time I could feel his eyes on me.

"Sugar?" I asked, trying hard not to grin.

"Are you offering to dip your finger in it?" he said with a sly smile.

I thought this must be another dream. So I reached up and pinched my cheek.

"What are you doing?" Deeka laughed.

"What are you trying to do to me?" I retorted as I rubbed the pained skin of my cheek.

"Trying to get you to go out with me."

"Why?"

"Because there's something about you."

"Me?"

"Yes."

"I think you're going through some pubescent crisis," I laughed.

His face suddenly turned serious. "I'm a man, Geneva. Don't let the date on my birth certificate fool you."

I was stunned mute by his statement.

"Think about it," he said, before dropping five dollars down beside the coffee cup, getting up, and strolling out.

Crystal

I rolled over and blinked at the purple dawn slipping through the slats of my miniblinds. I sure didn't feel like going to work.

The red digital numerals on my bedside clock told me that it was 5:40 a.m. In five minutes I would hear Steve Harvey and the rest of the WBLS morning team yukking it up.

I rolled over onto my side, turning my back on the offensive red numbers, and willed myself five more minutes of sleep when suddenly I heard a strange sound.

Umph, umph, umph.

What the hell?

I raised my head up off the pillow and listened a bit more intently.

Umph, umph, umph.

Easing myself out of bed, I crept to my bedroom door and pressed my ear against the cool white wood.   .

Umph! Umph! Umph!

Was Neville having sex?

No, he did not bring some heffa in this house to screw when I was right here, willing and more than able!

I swung the door open, biting back the four-letter

words that marched to the front of my throat as I sped down the hallway toward his room. How dare he bring some skank ho back to my home to screw when all the pussy he needed was right here!

I was halfway down the hall when I screeched to an abrupt halt. What the fuck was I thinking? This was not supposed to be about me; well, it was about me in some ways. I mean, it was about respecting my home, respecting me. It was not about him not making a pass at me, not propositioning me. No, no, of course not.

I started forward again. The door to his room was ajar; I pushed it open and rushed forward.

"Neville!" I screamed at the top of my lungs.

"Yes, Crystal?"

I blinked. He wasn't in the bed and neither was anyone else. The bed was empty. Slowly my eyes moved down to the floor, and there he was hunched up on his fists in mid-push-up.

Push-ups?

I felt like an idiot. A complete fool.

"Crystal?" he said again. "Is there something wrong?" he asked, coming down flat on his stomach and then rolling over onto his back.

I looked down into his fine face. He was shirtless, and it just made my day to see that broad beautiful chest and rippling six-pack beneath me.

He was wearing a snug pair of gray cotton shorts. I could see the curve of his penis, and it looked bigger flaccid than any erect dick I had ever had.

Damn!

I shifted my eyes back to his face. "Um, I thought I heard the smoke alarm going off," I lied miserably.

"Really?" he said, giving me a quizzical look. "I didn't hear a thing."

"Oh, sorry, I must have been—" I didn't even finish the statement; I just abruptly changed the subject. "So you work out, huh?"

Neville's face remained puzzled, and then he let go a small laugh and said, "Yeah, I try to do about three hundred and fifty push-ups and sit-ups a day."

"Wow," I marveled, understanding how he got that chiseled upper body. "You do it every morning?"

"Yep!"

"That's impressive," I said, sounding like a smitten teenager. "I usually run five miles a day, but I just haven't been motivated lately."

"Well, I would love to run with you."

Here was my chance to spend some time with Neville. "Well, I'm taking a personal day today. We could go for a run this morning . . . well, if you don't have any plans."

That last part of my statement had a tinge of sarcasm attached to it, so I quickly batted my eyes and offered a sweet smile to take the edge off it.

"Sure, I'm all yours," he said.

* * *

I showered as quickly as I could and doused myself in Sung before I spent ten minutes looking for the cutest, sexiest jogging suit I owned, which happened to be a slick black outfit made by Baby Phat. I pulled my hair back into a prepubescent ponytail and even had the nerve to tie a pink bow around it.

My diamond studs, a little MAC lip gloss, and I was ready to go.

"Wow!" Neville exclaimed when I walked into the living room. "Are we still going running?" he said, standing back and folding his arms across his chest. "You look beautiful."

I blushed, waved my hand at him, and said, "This old thing? *Pullleeze.*"

* * *

Once inside Central Park, I kept the pace slow enough that I wouldn't work up too much of a sweat. We were at the beginning of our second mile when it happened. It was a sharp uphill turn; Neville was slightly ahead of me, and I took advantage of the opportunity to snatch a peek at his legs and that wonderful rock-hard ass of his, and when I looked up again, a young woman on Rollerblades was coming right at me. Startled, I veered right to avoid colliding with her, but my feet became entangled and down I went.

Blam!

"Owwwwwww!" I screamed as I lay writhing in pain on the ground. I'd landed on my right hip in an effort to try to break my fall, and I'd scraped my hand, most of my forearm, and my elbow.

"Crystal! Crystal!" Neville cried as he rushed back to me. "What happened?"

"Clumsy," I muttered as he gently helped me back up onto my feet. I rubbed my hip and moaned.

"Look at you!" Neville exclaimed as he examined the scrapes on my arm and elbow. "C'mon. Let's get you back home," he said, pulling off his T-shirt and wrapping it around my bloody arm.

Looking at those well-defined pecs almost made me forget about my pain.

He wrapped his arm around my waist, and we started back toward my apartment.

Damn, he felt good against me.

It took us about thirty minutes to get back to the apartment, and once inside, I collapsed onto the couch. The effort it took and all the pain I was in had taken a toll on my appearance. I had caught sight of myself in the wall-to-wall mirrors in the lobby of my apartment building. What a sight!

My hair was a mess, my track pants were torn at the hip, and one leg was covered in road dust. And there were half moon–shaped sweat stains in the armpits of my T-shirt.

"Okay, now let's get you fixed up," Neville said, and he slapped his hands together. "Do you have any alcohol around here?"

"Yes," I said weakly. He was still shirtless and seemingly very comfortable with it. And I have to admit, so was I. "In the medicine cabinet in my bathroom."

Neville darted off and was back before I could blink. In his hand he had a bunch of cotton balls, a bottle of alcohol, and a few Band-Aids.

He unwrapped his T-shirt from my arm and examined my wounds. "Hmm, well, the bleeding has stopped," he said. "Now brace yourself, this will sting."

I watched him as he undid the lid to the alcohol and then drenched the cotton balls with the clear liquid. "Are you ready?" he asked, holding my arm with his hand, while the other held the cotton balls just an inch from my lacerated skin.

"Wait, wait," I whispered as I grabbed one of the throw pillows and pressed it against my mouth. I nodded at him that I was ready.

The first dab sent an icy spike through my brain; the second brought tears to my eyes; and the third was the worst: I screamed bloody murder into that pillow.

"Sorry, sorry, baby. I just got to make sure the wound is properly disinfected," he cooed.

Did he call me baby? I grinned into the pillow.

When he was done, he examined my arm again and blew warm air onto it.

"Does it feel better?" he said, turning those beautiful brown eyes on me.

"Uh-huh." I nodded, even though it was still stinging.

"Now let's get a look at that hip," he said, and reached for the waistband of my track pants. That move took me off guard, and my hand automatically went up to fend his away.

"Oh, I'm sorry," he said quickly, shaking his head apologetically. "What was I thinking?" He was obviously very embarrassed.

What the hell was I thinking? Damn instant reactions!

"That's okay," I muttered. Both of us averted our eyes for a moment. "Um," I started, and then realized I didn't know what to say.

Neville cleared his throat and said, "So I'm going to go jump in the shower, okay?"

"Yeah, yeah. Go on ahead. Me too. I mean I'm going to take a shower too."

"All right, then."

"Thanks for everything," I said as he turned away.

* * *

"What's wrong with you?" Geneva asked after I barely eked out a hello. "I called your job, and they said you took the day off. You sound horrible."

"Oh, I'm groggy because I just took some Tylenol PM and it's just starting to kick in."

"Migraine?"

"No, I fell while I was running in the park yesterday."

"Oh, no. Did you twist your ankle?"

"No, but I banged up my arm and hip pretty badly."

"Do you need me to come over and do anything for you?"

"No, no. Neville is here," I said a little too quickly.

"What do you mean 'here'?" Geneva whispered wickedly. "You mean in your bed *there*?"

"Oh please, Geneva."

"Uh-huh, the man has been here for nearly two weeks, and I haven't seen hide nor hair of him. What—you got the brother on lockdown or something?" she laughed. "Keeping him as your sex slave!"

"You are so stupid."

"Yeah, okay. I hope you're feeling better by this weekend 'cause Eric is playing at some dinner club and I need you to help me go shopping."

"Yeah, I should be okay by Saturday."

"Okay, then. Are you sure you don't want me to come over?"

"No, I'm fine, really."

I hung up the phone and continued listening to the *umph, umph* sounds coming from the next room as Neville did his push-ups.

I turned over and hugged my pillow tightly; I sure did envy that floor.

A few minutes later, I was out like a light and dreaming about Neville giving me my very own private strip-tease show, when the phone rang and rudely interrupted my wet dream.

I angrily snatched the receiver off the base and groggily barked, "Hello?"

Chevy

"Guess where I am," I whispered happily into my headset.

"Who the hell is this?" Crystal responded, as if I'd woken her from a deep sleep.

"It's me, Chevy—now guess where I'm calling you from!"

"Chevy?"

"Yes, Crystal! I've got gold fixtures in my bathroom—gold fixtures!"

"Wh-what are you talking about, Chevy?"

"I got the job at La Fleur!"

"Oh, oh, that's nice, Chevy." Crystal didn't sound excited for me at all. Bitch.

"And Crystal, I'm going to Siboney tonight."

"Really, um, that's nice."

"Anja is hosting a party there and I have to assist her," I nearly screamed with joy.

"Yeah, yeah. Look, Chevy, I took some—"

"That place is supposed to be amazing. I heard that Denzel Washington is a regular."

"Well, I wouldn't know, but—"

"Hey, why aren't you at work?"

"Oh, is it my turn?" Crystal said spitefully, sounding fully awake now.

"Can't I just have my moment, Crystal? Damn. You always raining on my parade."

"I don't mean to, Chevy. It's just that I took some Tylenol PM, and I'm really only half hearing what you have to say. You know, the way you do all the time."

"Ha-ha. Very funny, Crystal."

"Okay, I'm happy you got the job." Crystal yawned. "Just try to hold on to this one, okay?"

I could tell this was going to lead to a lecture, so I said: "Got another call, gotta run," and pressed the end button on the phone.

* * *

It was already after ten and I hadn't even signed on to the computer. I was too busy flipping through fashion magazines, dog earring pages of outfits I planned to purchase with my first paycheck.

"Okay," I said out loud as I finally turned on the computer, "let's get down to work."

I signed on and was surprised to see emails from more than a dozen people. All of whom worked at La Fleur and wanted to welcome me to the family. Most of them said they were looking forward to meeting me at lunch.

When I opened Anja's email, I almost fell off my seat. It was a three-page detailed letter, instructing me on all the things that I needed to take care of. Most of which were supposed to have been done by nine a.m. I looked at the clock; it was ten twenty.

"Oh, shit," I mumbled as I heard Crystal's warning reverberating at the back of my mind.

* * *

Ten things were supposed to be taken care of by nine. Three of them I was able to get done quickly. Call Marcia Platt at Interscope Records to confirm that 50 Cent would be at the party tonight and then call Peter Rodgers at Interscope to make sure that the Game wouldn't be.

I then had to contact Myles Coshi at Emblem Entertainment to secure Venus the snake dancer. Myles was out of his office, so I blew up his cell phone until some out-of-breath woman answered, "Who the fuck is this?"

"Um, this is Chevy Cambridge. I work with Anja, and I'm—"

"You done called here thirty fucking times, don't you get it? Leave a message, and he will call your impatient ass back when he—"

At that point there was a grappling sound and a sleepy voice came on saying, "Yeah, this here is Myles. Whadya want?"

In the background the woman was still ranting and raving, "I hate them damn queens over there." She was yelling loud enough for me to hear.

Queens?

Maybe she thought she was talking to Dante. I shook away the insult.

"I say, who dis?" I looked at the phone. Surely this wasn't Myles Coshi. Not *the* Myles Coshi?

"Mr. Coshi?"

"Yeah, speak, man, damn."

"Um, this is Chevy Cambridge. I work with Anja, and she wanted me to confirm with you that we had Venus the snake dancer for tonight."

"Mm-hmm," Myles hummed, and then sucked something out from between his teeth. I heard the woman chuckle loudly in the background and then say something like, "You so nasty."

I didn't want to imagine what he'd removed from between his teeth.

"Yeah, well, I told Anja that she couldn't have her for less than five Gs and I ain't seen no five Gs, so I guess Venus won't be bringing her python tonight."

My lips flapped and my eyes darted to the email I'd printed out. All it said was to reconfirm. It didn't say I had to negotiate a price. What to do?

"Can I put you on hold, Mr. Coshi?" I said quickly, and pressed the button before he could respond. Then I hit the button above the white label that said DANTE and tapped the table nervously with my fingertips while I waited for him to pick up, but his phone just went into voice mail. Panicked, I jumped up from my desk, swung my door open, and dashed out into the hallway, nearly bumping into Dante.

"Dante, thank goodness," I said, never so happy to see someone. "I have a situation and I—"

"Handle it," Dante threw at me without looking at me. "I'm late for a meeting." He swished his way down the hallway, leaving me standing there with my mouth hanging open.

Fucking Jekyll-and-Hyde motherfucker.

I slowly moved back into my office and stared at the blinking hold light on the phone. It was my first day, and already I was going to lose my job.

I had to think fast.

I took a deep breath and took my seat again. I pressed the receiver to my ear and released the hold button.

"Mr. Coshi?"

"Yeah, I was about to hang up on your ass."

"Sorry about the wait. I've consulted with Anja, and she said that if you don't stick to the terms that you originally agreed to, then she would have to, well, you know, do what it is she does best."

"What?"

"Mr. Coshi, you and Anja have a long history together, and I don't think you'd want any of it aired on national radio, would you?"

Now I didn't know Coshi from a hole in the wall, but I figured that Anja had dirt on everybody, so why wouldn't she have some on a lowlife talent agent like Coshi?

I held my breath, crossed my fingers, and waited.

"That's low. She said that?" Coshi sounded wounded.

"So will Venus be there tonight or not?" I said in my most pleasant tone.

"Yeah, damn," Coshi said, and the line went dead.

My hand was shaking by the time I hung up. Thank God I could think on my feet.

Now on to the other tasks at hand.

* * *

By the time Dante knocked softly on my door, I was halfway through with the morning emails. Since then, Anja had sent three more emails with instructions, each one as detailed and as lengthy as the last.

I'd spoken to so many people that my voice was hoarse.

"Come in," I croaked.

"Are you ready for lunch?" asked Dante.

I was still wounded from his reaction this morning and really didn't much feel like dining with him. But my stomach was growling, and I was so hungry, I didn't think I could even muster the strength to go outside and look for something appetizing to eat.

"Sure," I said as I pushed my chair back from my desk.

* * *

The cafeteria was on the twenty-fifth floor. It didn't look like any cafeteria I had ever been in. I expected nice, but this was luxury.

There were chandeliers, and white-gloved waiters waiting to pull out our high-backed, red suede chairs. Linen tablecloths and silk napkins. Silk!

There was a grand piano in the corner that was currently being played by an elderly white gentleman.

"Sit down, Chevy," Dante coaxed as I stood ogling the room.

"Oh," I finally said, my trance broken. The waiter pushed the chair in beneath me, took the silk napkin up from the table, and placed it in my lap.

"I know it can be a bit overwhelming at first," Dante said as he lifted his menu.

I nodded and reached for my own.

"Today," the waiter began, "our specials are potato-leek soup à la Thailand and sweet potato–filled ravioli with a cucumber-cognac sauce as well as a poached lobster with down-home collard greens and pecan rice."

Was he serious?

"Thank you, Craig," Dante said without looking at the man.

"Can I get you something to drink?" the waiter asked.

"I'll have a Perrier," Dante said. "And you, Chevy?"

What I really needed was vodka on the rocks after the morning I'd had. I looked across the room and saw that there was a bar and there were people seated at the bar, so that meant there was liquor.

"A white wine, please," I said quietly, then looked at Dante to see if there would be a reaction, but there was none. He just kept perusing the menu.

"I think I'm going to keep it simple," Dante started as he closed his menu and laid it down on the table. "What about you?"

I made a face as I allowed my eyes to continue to scroll through the list of appetizers and entrées. There were no prices alongside the offerings, so I assumed this was another perk to working at La Fleur Industries.

"Uhm, I think I'm going to have the steak and potatoes au gratin," I said, flipping the menu closed.

"Good choice," Dante said as the waiter returned with his water and my white wine. "The steak here melts in your mouth." He leaned in and whispered, "The chef has been a visiting chef at the James Beard House as well as at the Ritz in Paris and Le Sirenuse in Positano."

"Really?" I said, very familiar with all of the establishments.

Dante was right, the steak was out of this world; it had melted in my mouth like butter.

After I'd finished two glasses of wine and had had more than a dozen introductions to other members of the La Fleur family, Dante stood up and announced that it was time to get back to work.

When I entered my office, there was a silver pot of what I knew was green tea resting on the side table near my chaise lounge. My head was swimming from the wine, and the steak and potatoes au gratin had brought on niggeritis, so I flipped on the plasma television, stretched myself across the chaise, and promised myself that I would allow myself only twenty minutes. That was at one twenty in the afternoon.

* * *

At four o'clock my eyes flew open. I looked at my watch and it told me that I was a dead bitch.

"Oh, shit!" I yelled as I leaped off the chaise.

"Stupid! Stupid! Stupid!" I screamed, wiping the drool from the corners of my mouth and the crust from my eyes. I turned on my monitor and saw that there were now twenty more emails from Anja.

I scrolled through them as quickly as I could, trying hard to pinpoint which ones were priorities and which ones could wait until the next day.

There were none that could wait.

Shit!

Crystal

"I'm coming over," I said into the receiver of the telephone. It was a little after one, and the effects of the Tylenol PM had worn off. I wasn't completely alert but knew that, after a cold shower and something to eat, I would be.

Neville had gone out, leaving the sweet aroma of his cologne in the air, and his sexy-ass black silk briefs thrown across his bed. It was all I could do not to snatch them and take a huge sniff!

Yeah, I was losing my mind, so I had to get out of that apartment!

"Okay," Geneva said happily. "I got some corn bread in the oven, and my stories are getting ready to start."

"I don't want to sit up in the apartment, Geneva. I want to go out," I said as I moved into my walk-in closet and pulled a pair of 7 jeans from the wooden hanger.

"But the corn bread—" Geneva started to whine.

"Oh please, Geneva. We'll get a salad while we're out. See you in fifteen," I said, and hung up the phone.

* * *

It took some convincing, but Geneva finally got me to wait through at least the first half hour of *The Bold and the*

Beautiful as well as two slices of corn bread, though I refused the sweet butter and strawberry jam that she'd generously spread on her portion.

We decided—well, really I decided—that we should spend the rest of the day shopping for new outfits for Eric's big performance next weekend at Lola's Bar and Restaurant.

When we finally did hit the streets, Geneva had a hard time keeping up with me. I guess I'm not sensitive enough to the fact that Geneva's legs are shorter and stouter than mine, not to mention the fact that I'm in better physical condition than she is.

There must have been ten people between us before I finally realized that I was talking nonstop to a stranger.

"Geneva!" I yelled as I turned back to look at her, waving my hand for her to hurry along.

Thirty-fourth Street was crowded with spring shoppers and tourists walking along with their heads tilted toward the sky. I tried my best to keep my temper as I navigated around them.

So as not to have a repeat performance of Geneva's tragic outfit episode from brunch a few weeks earlier, I suggested that we pay a visit to the women's section at Macy's.

Once inside, we dawdled in the perfume section on the main floor. I guess I spent more time than usual testing the men's colognes. I was toying with the idea of buying Neville a bottle of Calvin Klein, but then I looked up and saw that Geneva was giving me that "What's this all about?" look.

"You got a boyfriend I don't know anything about?" she said after balling her fists and pushing them into her wide hips.

I retorted with an "Oh please, Geneva" before abruptly setting the bottle back down onto the glass counter.

"Or are you spraying cologne on your pillows and pretending that there's a man in your bed?"

I just gave Geneva a bored look and moved on.

"It's okay if you do," she laughed. "I been doing it for years."

I shook my head and laughed as I grabbed her hand and started toward the bank of elevators.

Fifteen shoppers, including Geneva and me, squeezed into the elevator.

"You still have that rash?" Geneva stage-whispered to me.

I just smirked. I knew where she was going with that question. It was part of a game we'd been playing since grade school.

"You know, the one that the doctor said he wasn't sure was contagious or not?" she continued.

The corners of my mouth began to twitch as I fought hard to control the laughter that was building up inside of me.

Meanwhile the other passengers on the elevator began to shift uncomfortably where they stood.

"Well, I just wanted to know, because I think I may have it too," Geneva said, her voice rising as she scratched vigorously at her neck. "That cream working for you?"

The doors opened, and even though six different

buttons had been pressed, most everybody filed out. The two people who remained were standing so close to the back wall that they almost became a part of it.

"You're sick, girl. You need some serious help," I hissed at Geneva as we stepped off on five.

We were met with the blank expressions of the shapely plastic dummies dressed in colorful bathing suits. Beach balls and real sand lay at their feet. Geneva closed her eyes and walked past them.

"Girl, we need to get to the beach this summer."

"Yeah, right," Geneva laughed, and continued across the floor.

"Look, Geneva, this one is real cute." I had snatched up an orange and green striped bikini that looked more like a mess of strings than a bathing suit.

"You're joking, right?" Geneva's bottom lip hung dramatically low as she eyed me like I had five heads.

Geneva

An hour and a half later, and we still hadn't found anything that I could afford.

Crystal looked down at her watch. "Well, we still have a few hours before the stores close. Do you want to go to Lane Bryant?"

"I went in there yesterday," I lied. It was bad enough I was in the women's section of Macy's; I hated going into the fat-girls' store to shop. At least at Macy's I could fool myself into believing that everyone in the store was the same size. In the fat-girl store, that fantasy was impossible.

Crystal sighed, and then something went off in her eyes. "Uhm, I don't know why I didn't think of this before," she said excitedly.

"What?"

"I know this woman in Brooklyn. She runs a boutique out of her apartment. She makes one-size-fits-all kind of stuff," Crystal rattled on as she started toward the escalator.

"Brooklyn?"

"Yeah, she's really nice. Fanta is her name."

"Like the soda?" I said as I followed her.

"Yeah."

"Do we have to go to Brooklyn?" I whined.

"Well, that's where she is, Geneva."

"You know how I feel about Brooklyn," I said, and stepped onto the escalator.

* * *

The taxi pulled up to a dilapidated apartment building that sat on the corner of Pine Street and Pitkin Avenue. The street was strewn with trash, and a group of old men sat playing dominoes on a makeshift table that was really just a square piece of plywood resting atop an old crate.

On the other side of the building's entrance, a young boy with a durag on his head and three cell phones clipped to the waistband of his jeans pressed himself against a young light-skinned girl, who I assumed had spent the better part of the morning combing and sculpting the so-called baby hair around her face.

"You sure this is the place?" I said warily.

"Yes, this is it."

Crystal gave the money to the driver, told him to keep the change. The taxi screeched from the curb and disappeared down Pitkin Avenue.

"Ooooh, I wouldn't mind a ride on that donkey!" one of the old men screeched as we walked by.

"He's talking 'bout you, girl," Crystal laughed as she poked my behind with her index finger.

"Stop it," I said, and self-consciously tugged the hem of my T-shirt down over my ass.

"Shake like jelly, don't it?" I heard another man say

just as I pushed the door open and stepped into the white-and-black-tiled lobby.

Inside, the heat was stiff. The hallway was clean, but the walls had been marked up in pen, marker, and spray paint.

"Death to Osama!"; "Maria loves José"; "Ziggy007."

"Why do these kids do this shit?" Crystal commented as she started toward the staircase.

"What floor she on?"

"Third, why?"

"Can't we take the elevator?" I said, pointing at the ancient maroon door with the brass handle and cracked window.

"That elevator hasn't worked in years."

Unbelievably, I stabbed at the black button and waited for the sound of the machinery to echo back, but nothing happened. I stabbed again and then peered into the broken window. All I saw was blackness.

"I told you," she said, and started up toward the second floor.

It seemed as if everybody had decided to cook dinner at the same time. I could make out the curry chicken, the fried porgies, and even the pot of collard greens coming from behind the door of 3C. But when we stopped in front of 3A, the aroma that greeted me was foreign.

Crystal pressed the bell and waited. "You'll see, you'll like her and the clothes."

"Coming!" a voice rang out from behind the door. "Who is it?"

"It's Crystal Atkins."

The door flew open and a short, ebony-colored woman

with an Afro, plump lips, and excessively large breasts greeted us.

"Oh, sister-friend!" she squealed, and rushed forward, throwing her arms around Crystal's waist. "Long time!"

"Yes, Fanta. Too long. This is my friend Geneva," Crystal said, pointing at me.

"Welcome, friend of sister-friend," Fanta said, and suddenly her beefy arms were wrapped around me. "Come in, come in."

The space was warm; three fans whirled loudly from different corners of the room. Colorful bolts of fabric were propped up against the wall, and three sewing machines sat in the middle of the living room. There were two mannequins draped in fabric, and incense burned on a small glass table near the open window.

To the left was the kitchen, which held a square wooden table littered with pages from fashion magazines, spools of thread, and packages of synthetic hair. On the stove a pot bubbled, and on top of the beige refrigerator a small radio spewed the midafternoon news.

"Sit, please," Fanta said as she shoved fabric aside to reveal a worn brown love seat.

"Fanta," Crystal began as we settled ourselves, "Geneva needs an outfit. Something elegant, not wedding or banquet elegant, but elegant just the same."

Fanta considered me. "Stand up, please," she said as she placed her hands on her hips.

I stood.

"Turn," she instructed, and made a twirling movement with her fingers.

I turned around slowly, my arms sticking out awkwardly like broken wings.

"Uh-huh," Fanta affirmed. "You are an African man's dream," she laughed as she reached forward and patted my behind. "Plenty of cushion."

I threw Crystal a mean look.

"Well!" Fanta announced, "I have many, many things for you. But what is the occasion?"

"Her son is in a band. He'll be playing at a very upscale restaurant."

"Music? How nice." Fanta beamed. "The child of myself"—Fanta pointed to a dozen haphazardly hung framed pictures on the wall—"plays the piano."

The child of myself?

"Oh, that's nice." I smiled.

"I have some pieces in the back room," Fanta said, and disappeared down the hallway.

"The child of myself?" I whispered to Crystal, who just shrugged her shoulders.

Fanta returned, her arms laden with dresses, skirts, and tunic-style tops.

The next hour was spent with Fanta and Crystal dressing me in different outfits. Nothing was made with a zipper or a button. Everything was fastened on with ties.

After some time we mutually decided on three outfits. Two of which were full-length skirts with side slits that climbed up to my thigh. One all black, one black with goldish green stripes. The other was a brilliant white linen dress that came down to my ankles with a daring split up the back. The top was sleeveless, and the square collar edged with a gold braid. That outfit was my favorite.

But I didn't want to say so, even though I knew that that was the outfit I liked best—because wearing all white would make me feel that I looked as big as a whale.

"So which one do you like the best, friend of sister-friend?" Fanta asked.

"I guess the black one. So how mu—"

"You don't really like the black one, Geneva," Crystal huffed, snatching the black skirt and fingering the material. "Not that it's not lovely," she said to Fanta before turning back to me. "But I saw the light in your eyes when you put that white number on."

I hated that she knew me so well.

"Yeah, but—"

"Yes, yes, friend of sister-friend. The white one brings out your lovely complexion."

"Thank you, but—"

"That it does," Crystal added, nodding her head vigorously in agreement.

I wasn't going to win here. "Yes, I do like the white one the best," I conceded. "So how much?"

"For you, friend of sister-friend, two hundred and twenty-five dollars."

I looked at Crystal whose expression told me that the price was a bargain. "Oh," I moaned, knowing full well that I had budgeted only seventy-five dollars for this Friday night soiree. And that included getting my nails done and buying some protein gel to slick my hair back with.

"I—I can't afford—"

"That's fine, Fanta. We'll take it," Crystal jubilantly cut me off, and reached into her purse and pulled out her checkbook.

Back down on the street, dress in hand, I was feeling mad. "Thank you," I barked at Crystal as I dug into my purse for my cigarettes.

"What the hell is wrong with you?" inquired Crystal as she turned on me.

"It's not that I don't appreciate this, and believe me, I will be paying you back, even if it takes me three months to do so, but I hate that you treat me like some kind of charity case."

The hurt on Crystal's face was immediate. "I'm sorry that you think of it that way, Geneva. I thought I was treating you like the friend I love and care for."

I puffed on my cigarette and just watched her. I was stumped for words and felt like a complete idiot. What the hell was wrong with me?

"I—I didn't mean to sound like an asshole," I mumbled before I took another puff from the cigarette and tossed it to the ground. "I just . . ." I began, but couldn't grasp hold of the words I needed to express myself so I just settled on "I'm sorry, Crystal. I must be PMSing."

Crystal's face softened a bit. "It's okay, girl. I know you haven't had any in some time, and that alone can make a woman cranky." She laughed as she started toward the corner and the cab that was waiting there. "Believe me, I know."

Chevy

By nine thirty I had addressed all of the emails that I thought were pertinent. The rest of them would have to wait until tomorrow. Stretching my arms above my head, I let out a loud yawn.

I'd been up since five thirty that morning and was in no way feeling like partying the night away, but I didn't have a choice; partying was now part and parcel of my job description.

So I shook the cloud from my head and pulled myself out of my chair.

With all the excitement, I hadn't had a chance to look in the closet to see what that night's outfit looked like. It was probably because I didn't have a thing to worry about. Anja had great taste. I had seen her in many an outfit that I would have worn myself.

I opened the closet, and the first thing my eyes fell on was a plastic silver-and-white clothing bag. Nice, I thought, and was about to reach for it when I spotted the shoe box sitting on the floor beneath it. "Hmm," I mused. I had a weakness for shoes.

I bent down and retrieved the box, which was labeled

DOLCE & GABBANA on the outside. "Oh, yeah!" I screamed as I snatched the lid off and threw it aside.

They were the most beautiful pair of shoes I'd ever seen. Metal-colored raw-silk stilettos covered in Swarovski crystals.

I hurriedly pulled my pumps off and slipped my feet into them. They were a perfect fit. "I love this fucking job," I screeched as I hungrily reached for the clothing bag.

I eagerly unzipped the bag and peeked in. Everything was white, as I expected. First I pulled out the white silk pants and matching white T-shirt.

T-shirt?

Well, okay, whatever, I thought as I removed the T-shirt from the plastic wrap.

I freed myself of my clothing and pulled on the pants. They were a cigarette cut and fit my body like they had been tailor-made for me. My ass has never looked so good, I thought, as I twisted my body left and right to see.

Unfolding the T-shirt, I caught sight of black letters across the front. When I held it up to eye level, I couldn't believe what it read: ANJA'S BITCH.

What!

I threw the T-shirt down.

That bitch was crazy if she thought I was wearing that! This was some bullshit—some total bullshit! I was nobody's bitch, least of all Anja's!

Rushing over to the door, I angrily swung it open and stepped out into the hallway. In my haste, I forgot I didn't have a shirt on, but to tell you the truth, I really didn't give a good goddamn!

My mission to go off on a tirade was aborted when a group of women who were walking down the hallway and dressed in white silk pants and T-shirts that read ANJA'S BITCH gave me a strange look before giggling and hurrying on.

I cleared my throat and stepped back into my office.

Well, at least I wasn't Anja's sole bitch, I told myself as I retrieved the T-shirt from the floor.

* * *

Siboney was all that I'd imagined it would be, and more. It was set up like an oversized loft, with massive columns and exposed brick walls. There were three levels, each with a different type of music pumping from the speakers that had been embedded in larger-than-life-sized nude mannequins that were so anatomically correct, groups of people stood transfixed before them.

Me, Dante, and this Asian Afro-American chick from Special Services named Kunta shared a limo from the office to the club. Once inside, Kunta saw a group of people she knew and hurried over to them. I was about to make my departure too, when Dante grabbed me by the elbow and said, "Here," and presented me with a headset that was connected to a walkie-talkie. "Clip the walkie-talkie on your waist."

I studied it for a moment and then put it on.

"Anja will communicate with you on it."

"Is she here already?" I asked as I adjusted the headset.

"Oh, yes, I'm quite sure she is," Dante said, and then, "Where is your pen and pad?"

I gave him a stupid look and said, "What?"

"Your pen and pad!" he screamed over the thunderous music.

"I—I didn't bring one."

"Oh, brother," he said, and snatched the headset off my head, taking along with it one of my silver hoop earrings.

"Ow!" I exclaimed, and brought my hand to my ear to check for blood. Dante just gave me a bored look as he pressed the button on the walkie-talkie and said, "Magda, I'm on the first level near the naked black woman with Z-cup tits, and I need a pen and paper, pronto!"

He flung the headset back at me and searched the crowd expectantly. A small woman with a blond wig suddenly appeared. She gave me a quick, disgusted once-over before presenting Dante with a pen and yellow pad. He snatched both from her and shoved them toward me. "Here," he barked, and the little blond-haired lady disappeared into the crowd. "*Always, always,*" he stressed, "have a pen and paper. You are on the clock!"

I nodded my head.

"Now," he said, switching back over to his Dr. Jekyll personality, "let's go get a martini."

I hadn't had a meal since noon, so the first three sips of the martini went straight to my head. I was grinning and bopping my head to the music when I heard a voice in my head.

"Chevy? Chevvvvvvvy, are you there?" I looked around frantically for Anja.

"What's wrong with you?" Dante inquired with a mild look of concern on his face.

"Do you hear her?" I said, turning my head this way and that, trying to locate Anja.

"She's on your headset, silly," Dante advised in a bored tone.

"Oh," I said, and grinned stupidly. "Hello, Anja," I said very slowly into the mic of my headset.

"Press the button, Chevy," Dante said, his voice filled with annoyance as he pointed to the black button on the walkie-talkie. "Press this to talk and release to listen."

"Oh," I said again, and pressed the black button. "Hello, Anja."

"Yes, Chevy, Anja needs . . ."

Anja began to reel off two dozen things she would need done by ten a.m. the following morning. "Ta-ta," she ended, and the connection went dead.

I realized that I had not written one thing down, so while my head spun and the music thumped, I tried in vain to recall the laundry list.

* * *

Dante found me at about three a.m. "I'm out," he said, yawning. He held the hand of a young wide-eyed white boy who I was sure was just off the bus from Wisconsin. "I'll see you in the a.m.," he said, and turned to leave.

The party was still pumping, and from the looks of it, there was no end in sight. "I was thinking about leaving too," I called after him.

Dante turned on his heels and marched back to me.

"Did Anja say you could leave?" he said, and gave me a tight look.

"N-no," I meekly responded.

"You leave when Anja leaves. Understood?"

I nodded my head.

"Okay, sweetie. Try to enjoy yourself. You're at Siboney!" he sang, throwing his hands up and turning around and dancing away from me.

At five a.m. I got the call. "Chevy? Chevy, are you there?"

I pressed the black button, stifled a yawn, and said in my brightest voice, "Yes, Anja, I'm here."

"Oh, my," Anja giggled. "Anja is just pulling into the driveway."

Anja lived in a suburb of Philly over an hour and a half away from New York.

"Anja totally forgot to tell you it was okay to leave," she said, and the line went dead.

It was five o'clock; I had to be at work by seven; it just didn't make any kind of sense to go home.

Now I understood why there was a walk-in closet, bathroom suite, and comfy chaise lounge. Once you signed on with La Fleur Industries, you would never see your family, friends, or home again.

* * *

I was up and at my desk by nine a.m. My head was pounding, and my eyes were swollen from lack of sleep. I turned on my computer and saw that in addition to the instructions Anja had given me the night before, there were also three new emails listing still more duties for me to perform.

This woman is straight-up crazy, I thought as I reached for the phone to make the first call of the day.

I decided that if this is how every day was going to be, seventy-five thousand wasn't nearly enough.

* * *

What I wanted to do on my first day off was sleep. I'd been working for eleven days straight. Anja seemed to have an event every night and that included the weekends. I'd slept in Brooklyn only two nights since I'd started the job.

But Crystal knew that that Friday was payday for me, so bright and early Saturday morning she was blowing up my phone, telling me I better come straight to her apartment and give her some money before I give it all to my friends Barneys and Saks.

I started to blow her off and roll over and go right back to sleep, but I thought I'd better try to stay in Crystal's good graces. I've fucked her over about money in the past, and everybody's patience and kindheartedness runs out sooner or later—so I pulled myself out of the bed, caught a shower, slipped into my Apple Bottom jeans, this rust-colored halter top I picked up from Urban Outfitters, and some three-inch-heeled mules, and I was out.

"So how's the new job?" Crystal asked as she opened the door to let me in. Geneva was already there, preparing a salad for lunch.

I didn't want to talk about La Fleur or the fact that when I got my first paycheck it was short $250!

When I called Accounting on Friday to let them know that there must have been a mistake, I was informed by Samantha that "No, there wasn't a mistake, the two hundred and fifty dollars was for the lunches."

"I thought those were free!" I screamed.

"Oh, no, Ms. Cambridge. If you read your hire letter, you would see that any meals taken in the cafeteria are automatically deducted from your paycheck."

I was so excited about getting the job that I hadn't read the fine print.

"But two hundred and fifty dollars!"

"If you like, Ms. Cambridge, I'll email a list of your meals and their prices."

"You do that!" I'd screamed before banging the phone on my desk three times and then slamming it down onto the base.

Before I could take a breath there was a *ping* sound on my computer. I glanced at the monitor, and looking back at me were large yellow letters that announced: YOU HAVE MAIL, CHEVY!

The email was from Samantha; as promised she'd sent a detailed breakdown of every meal I'd consumed in the cafeteria. I was so enraged; I picked up the phone and called Accounting again.

"Samantha. May I help you?"

"Samantha," I began, my anger boiling over, "this just doesn't seem right. I mean there aren't any fucking prices on the menu . . . Had I known that a side order of mashed potatoes was ten dollars, I wouldn't have ordered it . . . It's not fair, and I shouldn't have to pay because I didn't know . . . There aren't any prices and—"

Samantha was silent for a while as I ranted and raved until finally she cut me off and said, "True, there aren't any prices on the menu, because we here at La Fleur believe in the old adage: 'If you have to ask, then you can't—'"

I hung up the phone on that bitch before she could finish her sentence.

Now, under Geneva and Crystal's scrutiny, I just decided to lie. "It was fine," I said, and took a deep breath as I mentally cleared my mind of the last two weeks. "So where is Neville?" I asked, desperately wanting to change the subject.

"Yeah, where is Neville?" Geneva chimed in as she plucked a cherry tomato from her bowl of salad and popped it in her mouth.

"I don't know, out visiting friends," Crystal said with an air of disinterest that I knew was forced. "Are you going to come down to Lola's tonight to see Eric play?" she said, totally changing the subject.

"I dunno yet," I said, and then blatantly I asked, "Have you fucked him?"

"Who, *Eric*?" Geneva yelped, her eyes popping.

"No," I said, staring Crystal right in the eyes, "Neville."

"No! Why would you say something like that?" Crystal shouted, her voice filled with surprise.

"You ain't fooling me, Miss Thang," I threw at her.

"Are you?" Geneva pressed, moving closer to Crystal.

"No!" Crystal shouted again.

Crystal

Had I fucked him?

That lazy morning last week, while under the magical spell of Tylenol PM and listening to Neville doing his push-ups, I found myself touching myself. Stroking my clitoris with one hand and rolling my nipples between my fingers with the other. I was fantasizing about Neville, imagining his strong muscled body on top of me, his soft lips pressed against mine, and before I knew it I was swallowing a scream as my body shook with a thunderous orgasm!

I lay there, breathless, my body begging for more and cussing me for having slapped his hand away earlier.

I needed to be touched, caressed; shit, I needed to be fucked in the worst kind of way, so I jumped out of the bed and went to the bathroom, brushed my teeth, ran my fingers through my hair, smeared some scented oil over my body and marched out into the hallway. I was about to go toward the guest bedroom when I saw that the television was on in the living room.

"Hey," I said softly as I approached the back of the sofa. Neville was stretched out there, watching Nickelodeon.

"Did I wake you?" he said, turning apologetic eyes on me.

"No, no, just came out to make some tea," I said, and started toward the kitchen. "Would you like some?"

"Yes, thank you," he said, and sat up. "But you're the patient, let me handle it."

He was shirtless again, dressed only in a pajama bottom, and as I watched him approach, I could swear to God he didn't have briefs on. That big ol' dick of his was just a-swinging!

He put the kettle on the stove and turned the flame on beneath it. Me, I sat down in the chair.

"So how are you feeling?" he said, his eyes full of concern.

"Oh, still a little sore, but I'll be okay."

"Hmm," he said, and looked up at the ceiling.

I saw that I was going to have to force his hand. "I think I cleaned up the wound on my hip pretty well, but I'm not quite sure. Can you look for me?"

A quick look of surprise spread across Neville's face. "O-okay," he said as I rose from my chair and hiked my slinky nightgown up and over my waist. I was wearing a pair of black silk French-cut panties. "Can you see it?" I asked.

Neville hadn't moved from his place near the stove. "Well, can you?" I pressed, eager to have more than his eyes on me.

"Um, yeah," he said as he stepped closer. "It looks like you cleaned it up fine," he added as his fingers came to rest on the side of my exposed thigh. I shuddered a bit; his fingers seemed to be shooting electric bolts. He was on his knees now, his face close to the bruise on my hip, his fingers were kneading my flesh, and I could feel the warmth of his breath on my skin.

My eyes fluttered and I felt myself begin to swoon. Could a woman want a man more than this?

Just his breath against my skin was sending me into a sexual frenzy, and just when I thought I couldn't take it anymore, he stood up, patted me on the head, and said, "Looks like it's healing just fine."

Gee, thanks!

"You think so?" I said with as much coyness as I could muster.

"Oh, yeah. I'll go out later and get you some aloe vera, so you can smear the jelly of the plant on the bruise. That'll ensure that you won't scar."

"Oh, okay," I said as he turned to leave. "Thanks for looking at it for me."

"No problem," he threw over his shoulder as he left. I heard the kettle on the stove start to whistle as he went.

Had I fucked him? Well, no, I hadn't, but I sure as shit wanted to!

Noah

"Well, why won't you just throw yourself at him?"

"I can't do that, Noah, please!"

"What happened to women's lib and all that good shit?"

"I don't know, I just couldn't."

"You sound like a prude, Crystal. Just walk into his room in the middle of the night, stick your head under the covers, take his dick out, and put it in your mouth!"

"You're disgusting, Noah! I am not going to do that."

"Well, it always works for me and Zhan."

"Maybe he just doesn't find me attractive."

"What's Geneva say about all this?"

"I haven't breathed a word to Geneva. We're supposed to both be celibate, so I don't want to get her off track, you know."

"Uh-huh, so you're doing the buddy-system thing, each-one-helps-the-other type of shit, right?"

"Yeah, something like that. So I really hope these conversations remain between the two of us, okay?"

"Of course they will, honey. Don't worry."

"Okay, gotta run."

"Me too."

"Kisses."

"Kisses."

I hung up the phone and was about to trudge into the kitchen to heat up some leftover Thai food when I heard the elevator in the hallway kick on. I don't know why I did it, because I'm not a nosy type of man, but I sauntered my behind right over to my front door and peered out through the peephole. The elevator door was just open-ing and who did I see stepping out but Aldo and two very good-looking young men.

"Humph!" I said out loud, and then threw my hand over my mouth. It was early afternoon. I knew Aldo and Ray-Ray entertained a lot, but so early in the day and in the middle of the week?

I watched until they disappeared from sight. The apartment door opened and then closed.

Maybe Aldo was bringing clients home for lunch?

But Ray-Ray wasn't home, and I knew that Aldo had two left hands in the kitchen. Ray-Ray was the cook in the relationship.

Hmm.

Well, maybe Ray-Ray had prepared the meal the night before and all Aldo had to do was heat it up.

Yeah, that was it.

But still something in the pit of my stomach just didn't feel right. I walked over to the far wall. The wall our apartment shared with Ray-Ray and Aldo's. I pressed my ear against the wall, but all I could hear was low mum-bling. Disgusted with myself for eavesdropping, I moved to the couch and flopped down onto the blue and white brocade fabric. I'm ashamed to say that I wasn't there for long, because before I knew it, I'd run into the kitchen, grabbed a glass, and was back at that wall!

I still couldn't hear perfectly, but what I did hear sounded a lot like sex!

Geneva

I was so excited to see my baby boy in his big coming-out performance that I'd smoked nearly a whole pack of cigarettes in less than three hours.

After I'd slipped into the white Fanta original and spent fifteen minutes in the mirror staring at myself, trying to decide if the outfit really suited me, Charlie walked in and made an *ooooh*ing sound before declaring, "Mommy, you look soooo beautiful!"

Well, if my baby girl thought I looked beautiful, I guess I did.

I dropped Charlie off at my mother's and headed to Crystal's apartment. I'd managed to wash my hair and slick it back. I would have to cut the ends next week, but for now it looked okay. No time to do my nails, so I just removed the chipped polish and went au naturel.

When I arrived, Erykah Badu's "Love of My Life" was playing on the stereo and there were scented candles burning everywhere.

"Hey, girl," I said when Crystal opened the door.

"Geneva, you look gorgeous!" Crystal shrieked. "Girl, I knew that outfit had your name all over it!"

"And don't count yourself out, Miss Crystal. That out-fit is hot!"

"Why, thank you!" Crystal laughed and did a little *America's Next Top Model* runway for me.

Her shoulder-length hair was loose and flowing. She wore an off-the-shoulder camel-colored dress that hugged her size-eight figure like a glove.

I looked around. Something about Crystal's space was different. The vibe was real mellow. I wondered if it had something to do with Neville.

"Is Neville coming?" I asked as we moved into the kitchen.

Crystal shrugged her shoulders. "Maybe, maybe not. He's out with friends, but I gave him the information."

"Oh."

"First off," Crystal said as she handed me a glass of champagne, "I'll clean up those wild eyebrows of yours."

"What's wrong with my eyebrows?" I asked, self-consciously running my index fingers over them.

"Well, you look like you've been living in the jungle for five years, that's what's wrong with them." We started toward the bedroom.

"That's a little extreme, don't you think?" I said as she guided me into the bathroom and plopped me down on the toilet seat.

"No, it's not. Look," she said, and turned my head toward the professional makeup mirror that showed every pore, crease, and crater in my face.

"Oh, shit," I moaned; my eyebrows did look out of control.

"Yeah. Oh shit is right," Crystal laughed, and picked the tweezers up from the vanity. "Now hold still."

It was a painful ten minutes, but when she was done I looked 100 percent better.

"Do you want me to do your makeup too?"

"You know I don't wear that shit."

"I think tonight you can put on something other than lip gloss," Crystal said, already plucking out mascara, eyeliner, and shadow from her massive makeup bag.

"No," I wailed as she started toward my face with the eyeliner.

"Oh, come on, Geneva, live a little. It's your son's big night; look the part of the glamorous mother."

"I'm far from glamorous," I said, swatting her hand.

"That's because you don't want to be."

I sighed. "Okay, just a little."

Another fifteen minutes passed, and when I looked at myself again, I almost didn't recognize the person staring back at me. "Oh, this is too much!" I screamed, and reached for the box of tissues.

"It just seems that way, because you never wear makeup," Crystal said, quickly confiscating the tissue box and hiding it behind her back.

"Are you sure?" I said, leaning in and examining the new me a bit closer.

"Would I lie to you?" she said, and that's when I caught sight of the washcloth thrown across the silver pole of the shower.

"Maybe not about this," I said slyly.

Crystal just gave me a baffled look.

"Are those the shoes you plan on wearing?" Crystal

gasped when I pulled the beaten gold and white sandals out of the crumpled brown paper bag I'd brought
with me.

"Yeah, it's all I have that matches."

"Oh, Geneva, I asked you if you had shoes, and you
said yes!"

"And I didn't lie, these are them!" I yelled back defensively.

Crystal snatched the shoes from my hand and tossed
them to the floor. "Those shoes are horrible," she said in
disgust. "What size do you wear again?"

Crystal had stepped into her huge walk-in closet and
was sifting through the dozens of shoe boxes that were
neatly stacked on the floor.

"Ten," I muttered, flopping sloppily down onto the
bench at the end of her bed.

"Ten?" Crystal turned on me, a surprised look resting
on her face. "Since when?"

"Since Charlie," I said, chewing absently on the cuti-
cle of my thumb.

"Oh," Crystal said. "I wear a nine, so I don't think
that—oh, wait a minute!" Crystal snapped her fingers,
turned, and darted out of the room. On her return, she
had a dusty white box in hand.

"What's that?"

"Stop biting your cuticles," she warned as she approached. Lifting the top off the box, she pulled out a
pair of gold sandals.

"I even think those are ugly," I said, making a face
like they stunk too.

"Yeah, but they're a ten and in better shape than those things you got."

They were in better condition, but God, they were something awful to look at, with thick, rubberized soles and garish gold-foiled leather.

"Why do you even have these?" I asked, taking them from her.

"Now promise me you won't go crazy when I tell you."

I had already slipped one on my foot. "Where did you get them from?" I asked, holding the remaining sandal in my hand.

"Promise first."

"Okay, I cross my heart and hope to die," I said as I quickly made the sign of the cross with my free hand.

"Aunt Wanda, when she came to visit that time."

I ran the name through my memory bank. "Dead Aunt Wanda?" I said quietly.

Crystal nodded her head.

"Are you crazy?" I said, throwing the shoe across the room and kicking off the one on my foot.

"Geneva!"

"It can't be good, wearing a dead woman's shoes!" I hissed.

Crystal put her hands on her waist. "Better than showing up at your son's show in those things."

"I'd rather go barefoot," I said defiantly.

"Well, that's how you will go, because I refuse to be seen with you in these!" she screamed, and snatched up my battered shoes and ran out of the room. I just sat there for a while, shaking my head, until I heard the front door open and it dawned on me what it was she was going to do with them.

"Noooooooooo!" I screamed, and bolted from the room.

It was too late. By the time I hit the hallway, Crystal was coming back from the incinerator and looking very proud of herself.

"I can't believe you did that."

"It was for the best," she said as she trailed past me and back into the apartment.

"Bitch," I grumbled as I followed behind her.

"Takes one to know one, sweetie."

"Now what am I going to do?"

"You're going to wear Aunt Wanda's shoes; that's what you're going to do."

I stood at the bedroom entryway, staring at the shoes. "Maybe if we pray over them, it'll be okay?" I wondered aloud. "Burn some incense, maybe?" I walked slowly toward them. "Got any holy water lying around?"

* * *

It didn't take any time to get a cab. On the ride down, I kept adjusting the top of the dress. "Stop it!" Crystal screamed, and slapped at my hands.

"Don't you think it's too much?" I said, indicating the amount of cleavage that was showing.

"No," Crystal said pointedly. "Some of us don't have any to show and wish we did. Those babies need to be put on display."

I wasn't so sure about that.

By the time the taxi pulled up to the curb, I was so

nervous, I had sweated through the material of the dress. It felt mighty damp down between my legs.

About twenty people stood in small groups, laughing, talking, and smoking. That's just what I need to calm my nerves—a cigarette, I thought as I started digging in my purse. Well, the purse that Crystal had lent me.

"Later, girl," Crystal said, and pushed the pack back down into the black silken cave of the purse.

A tall, burly-looking gentleman with a nice smile and a football player's wide shoulders opened the door for us. "Have a good time, ladies," he said in a cavernous voice.

Crystal giggled like a schoolgirl, and I just grunted.

We made our way through the tight clusters of beautiful people sipping apple martinis, toward the back of the restaurant where the female maître d' smiled up at us expectantly.

"Name?"

"Holliday."

The woman scrolled through the computerized list. "Oh, yes, Holliday. Two, right?"

"Yes," Crystal said.

"Oh, are you Eric's mother?" the girl squealed with delight. "It's so nice to finally meet you. I'm Julie," she said as she extended her hand to Crystal.

I looked the girl from top to bottom. She was cute. Not cute enough for my son, but cute enough I supposed. A tiny thing, cedar-colored with large dark eyes and a mess of long silky hair that hung down her back.

"I'm Ms. Holliday," I snapped. Crystal turned and gave me a sober look. I just rolled my eyes and then bored them into Julie.

"Oh, I'm sorry." Julie smiled and moved her hand in my direction. "Ah, yes, I see it now. You and Eric have the same eyes."

Was she trying to butter me up?

I looked at her hand but didn't extend my own.

"Well," Julie continued, seemingly unscathed, "we have a table for you right up front."

And she was right; we were right in front of where the band's instruments had been set up.

"A waitress will be over soon to get your drink order." Julie gave Crystal and me menus, smiled sweetly at us, and wished us a good time before turning and walking off. On her retreat, I saw why Eric was interested: she had an ass as wide as a football field!

"Uhmph, ho," I mumbled.

"No, Geneva," Crystal scolded as she leaned over the table. "You need to stop acting like that. Eric is your son, not your man!"

I ignored her as I perused the menu.

She continued, "There was no reason for you to act like that with that girl."

I closed my menu and looked at her. "I'm just trying to protect my child."

"He may be your child, but he's also a man."

"Oh, please," I said, really not wanting to hear the truth. "He's far from a man; he can barely wipe his ass right. Believe me, I know. I still do his laundry."

"TMI, Geneva, TMI," Crystal said as she shook her head and looked down at the menu.

"Well, it's true."

"Whatever. Let's move on to something else." Crystal's tone was exhausted, and then suddenly she piped up, "This place is really nice. I liked the spot they had in Chelsea, but this new Soho location is fabulous."

I had to admit, it was very nice. I hadn't been out in so long that I had trouble keeping my mouth closed as I gazed at the people that moved fluidly around us.

"Hello, ladies, and welcome to Lola's," a young woman with auburn locs said as she placed a square napkin in front of each of us. "What can I get you to drink tonight?"

"Um," I said as I reached for the specialty-drink menu.

"I'll have a raspberry martini," Crystal said.

"Excellent choice," the young waitress responded before turning her smiling face on me.

"Um," I said again, unable to make a choice, even though I really truly wanted to have a Corona, but I didn't want Crystal to flip out.

"Two," Crystal finally said, holding up two fingers and then turning to me and saying, "You'll like it, trust me."

"Okay."

When Eric finally arrived, I was busy trying to shove my feet and the ugly shoes I had on as far under the table as I could, and hoped and prayed to God that I wouldn't have to get up and go to the bathroom. I wouldn't be able to deal with the whispers and finger-pointing these ugly shoes would attract.

"Hey, Ma!" Eric said, leaning over and embracing me. "Glad you made it."

"I wouldn't miss it for the world," I said, beaming.

"Hey, Auntie Crystal."

"Hey, big man," Crystal said as she embraced her godchild. She was cheesing so hard that I had to cover my eyes against the glare.

"Is the table good enough for you?"

"Perfect," Crystal and I said in unison.

"Well, we're going to get started in about ten minutes, okay?"

Crystal and I nodded.

Eric started to walk away, but I caught him by the elbow and indicated with a nod of my head for him to come closer.

"Yeah, wassup?"

"Uhm, I met your little friend," I whispered in his ear.

"Who?"

"Juuuuuuuuulie," I sang.

Eric blushed and pulled himself erect again. "Oh, yeah?"

"Yeah," I said, and folded my hands across my bosom.

"A'ight, and?"

I didn't have to say anything, the smirk I gave him said it all.

"Oh c'mon, Mom, gimme a break," Eric whined.

"Go on, Eric," Crystal interrupted. "Meditate, pray, or whatever it is you musicians do before a gig. Don't pay your crazy mama any mind."

Eric seized the opportunity and fled. I shot Crystal a hard look and said, "Can't you mind your business?"

"No," Crystal laughed, and started bopping her head to the music that was swirling out of the speakers.

The waitress returned with the drinks, set them down,

told us that her name was Sugar, and said to let her know if we needed anything else.

"Sugar," I said when she was out of earshot. "What kind of name is that?"

"Sound like a stripper's name," Crystal commented between sips of her drink.

"You think her mama gave her that name?"

Crystal shrugged her shoulders.

"Shit, sound like a name for a whore."

"Yeah, it does. In fact, I think I read a book by the same title."

"Sugar?"

"Yeah, and in the book the woman was a whore."

"Get out!"

"Uh-huh, I think I got it at home. I'll lend it to you if you want."

"Sure, why not?"

We sat sipping and people watching for a while, and I have to admit, once I'd sipped half of my drink, I started feeling comfortable.

"Oh, damn, that brother is fine," Crystal breathed as she leaned in. I followed her eyes and saw that she was looking at Deeka.

"Oh, that's um, Eric's manager," I said nonchalantly.

"Oh, really? Well, girl, he is gorgeous!" Crystal said, her eyes crawling hungrily over him.

"Yeah, he's all right, I guess."

Crystal made a face at me. "All right? The boy been blessed about five times over."

It was true; Deeka was a specimen.

"If I were a few years younger . . ." Crystal moaned, and licked her lips. "They just didn't make them like that when we were that age." Crystal laughed and tilted her drink to her lips.

"They sure didn't," I agreed.

"The brothers we grew up with couldn't keep their hair combed—"

"Or cut for that matter!"

"Shit," Crystal whispered as she leaned in close. "I'm not saying that I'm a freak or anything," she began, and I nodded my head. "But I can sort of understand why some of these teachers are dipping in the honey pot, if you know what I'm saying."

I did know. But who the hell wanted to admit that out loud? Some of these sixteen-year-old boys looked like twenty-one-year-old men. Women were facing the dilemma that men had been knee-deep in for years.

"You ain't saying nothing but a word, girl," I said, and we gave each other some dap across the table.

When I looked up, Deeka was standing over me.

"Good evening."

"Hi," Crystal sang, her eyes rolling seductively over him.

"Hello, Deeka," I said, barely looking at him. "This is my friend Crystal Atkins."

"Ms. Atkins," Deeka said, taking her hand in his and shaking it.

"Deeka. That's a very different name."

"Well, it's common in the Caribbean."

"Really? So you're from the islands. Which one?"

"Well, my parents are from Tobago."

"Tobago. Oh, the sister island to Trinidad."

"Oh, you've been?"

Was she hitting on my man—I mean, my son's manager?

"No, but I've seen pictures and it looks beautiful."

"It is. You should really plan on visiting sometime."

"I will."

"And you must bring Ms. Holliday with you," Deeka said, resting his palm on my shoulder. The heat from his hand was so intense, I had a hard time not squirming in my chair.

Crystal's eyebrows climbed. "Oh, I'll be sure to do that."

"Ms. Holliday, I have to say, you look beautiful."

"Oh, thank you," I responded, still not looking at him.

"I think you are the most beautiful woman here tonight," he added, and those words finally got me to lift my head. When I looked into his eyes, they were warm and sincere.

"Thank you, Deeka."

We just stared at each other until Crystal made a sound in her throat, breaking the trance.

"Well," Deeka said, as he slapped his large palms together, "the band is about to get started, so I'm going over to wish them good luck."

Crystal and I nodded.

"Anything you ladies require before I go?"

"I'm fine. You, Geneva?" Crystal said.

"I'm good."

"Okay, then. See you after the first set." Deeka tipped an invisible hat at us and then moved off.

"Whew!" Crystal said as she dramatically fanned herself with her hand. "He is one suave, good-looking brother."

I just smiled.

"Girl, and I think he got it for you."

"Got what?"

"The hots!"

"I'm old enough to be that boy's mother."

"He don't look like no boy to me, Geneva."

"Look, I thought we were off men."

"Oh, yeah, yeah, but it don't hurt to dream, do it?"

A few minutes later, a tall woman with vicious curves and fire-engine-red hair walked to the front of the restaurant and took the mic. "Esteemed guests, you're in for a treat tonight. Lola's has the immense pleasure of welcoming Soiree to the stage. Let's give them a loud Lola's welcome!"

The crowd around us applauded enthusiastically as the band members, Eric included, made their way from the back of the restaurant and took their places behind their instruments. The lead singer was a short, brown-skinned man with bulging eyes and tiny lips. It didn't look to me like he could hum a decent note, but when he opened his mouth and began his rousing rendition of Marvin Gaye's "Let's Get It On," I knew I'd better stop judging people by their appearance.

An hour passed, and the singer belted one soulful song out after another. I'd gone through two cocktails by the time the lead singer announced that the band would be taking five.

"How'd you like it?" Eric asked as he stood beaming over me. His face was drenched in sweat, and he was rapidly flexing his fingers as he stood waiting for my response.

"Oh, baby, it was wonderful!" I said, jumping up out of my chair and giving him a big hug.

"You were wonderful. The best one in the entire band!" Crystal squealed, clapping her hands together like a two-year-old.

"Ma," Eric said, a little embarrassed as I behaved like the proud mother I was and covered his face in kisses. "Come on, now. Not here," he said as he gently pushed me back down into my seat.

"Okay, okay," I gushed as I held on to his hand. This was my baby. My son! I wanted the world to know that. "I won't embarrass you in front of your friends," I said as the band members filed past us, grinning.

"We've got one more set and then we're done. Do you think you can hang out for another hour and a half?"

"Of course we can," I chimed.

"Good. I'm going to get me some water," Eric said, looking toward the bar and the crowd of people who congregated around it. "Y'all need anything?"

"I'll take another one of these raspberry things," I said.

"Me too," Crystal added as she lifted her glass and drained the remaining sweet liquid.

"A'ight," Eric said, and started toward the bar where

Julie was waiting with open arms. I watched as she hugged my baby so tightly, I felt my breath steal away.

"Umph!" I said.

"Stop it, Geneva!" Crystal warned.

By the time the band ended their last set, my head was swimming and my legs felt petrified. I wasn't sure if I was going to be able to stand up.

Crystal's elbows were on the table, her hands folded beneath her chin as she tried hard to look alert, but it wasn't working, her eyes were slits.

"They were great, weren't they?" she said through a yawn.

"Uh-huh," I yawned back. We laughed. "It's contagious," I said, putting my palm against my mouth, stifling the one that followed.

"Yeah, and they hit in sevens, like waves," Crystal said as she covered her own mouth.

"Hey, hey, what's all of this yawning about?" Eric laughed as he approached.

"Tired, boy, what you think?" I smiled and grabbed his hand. "We're not as young as we used to be."

"Speak for yourself," Crystal said in mock defense.

"Hey, man." Deeka seemed to appear out of nowhere. "Y'all were off da hook!" he said, slapping Eric on the back.

"Did you have any doubt?" Eric said.

"Not one bit, man. In fact, the owner wants to talk to me about booking you on a regular basis, starting in September."

"A regular gig here!" Eric was astounded. "You shitting me, man, right?"

"Hey, hey, watch that language, boy," I warned.

"Sorry, Ma." Eric gave me puppy eyes before returning his attention back to Deeka and saying, "Are you serious, man? I mean, on the real?"

"Dead serious," Deeka said.

Eric jumped a foot off the floor and then threw his arms around Deeka, embracing him in a great big bear hug. "Man, this is fantastic!"

Eric and the rest of the band members followed Deeka to the back of the restaurant, where the owner sat waiting to congratulate them. Eric advised me that he would just be a moment, but after fifteen minutes, my eyes were starting to burn and Crystal's head was rolling on her neck as if she were a heroin addict.

"Let's get out of here, girl," I said, gently tapping her hand.

"Huh? What?"

"I said, let's go. I'm tired."

Crystal had a dumbfounded look on her face, like she wasn't sure exactly where it was she was, then the light returned to her eyes. "Yeah, it's late, let's go."

Just as we gathered ourselves to leave, Eric approached. "Sorry"—he touched my shoulder—"it took so long."

"It's okay, baby. We're going to head home. You want to share a cab with us?" I slung my purse over my shoulder and slapped at my numb thighs.

"What's wrong, Ma?" Eric asked, concern clouding his face.

"Raspberry cocktails is what's wrong with her," Crystal laughed as she stepped around us and started toward the door.

"You know I can't do anything stronger than a Corona," I said sheepishly, and started off behind Crystal. Eric followed, making his way beside me and grabbing hold of my elbow. "Hey," I said, snatching my arm from him, "I'm not a gray-haired old woman. I can walk."

"Okay, Ma, dang."

"So you coming with us?"

"Nah, I gotta pack up my drums," he said as he pushed the door open and then stepped back to let Crystal and me pass through.

"Eric, we still on?" I heard a soft voice float from behind us. When I turned around, Julie was standing there.

"Yeah, give me a minute," Eric said.

"Did you have a good time, Ms. Holliday?" she asked sweetly.

I just nodded my head at her and then gave Eric a sly smile and said, "Drums, huh?"

We stood on the sidewalk among a throng of people who'd filed out of the restaurant. Some of them milled around, engaged in conversation; others stumbled drunkenly up the street on to their next destination; and those remaining, including Crystal and me, stood near the curb, our hands thrown up in the air desperately trying to hail a cab.

"Can I give you ladies a lift?"

Crystal and I turned around to see Deeka standing there.

"No—" I started, but Crystal cut me off by saying, "Yeah, sure."

"Okay, let me just go get the truck from the lot and bring it around."

"You got 'em, Deeka?" Eric asked.

"Don't worry, dawg, they're in safe hands," Deeka said, and patted him twice on the shoulder as he started off down the block.

I watched him until he hit the corner, took it, and disappeared.

"Okay, then," Eric said, his eyes bouncing between me and Julie, who was engaged in a conversation with one of the waitresses.

"Uh-huh," I said, and gave Eric a hard stare. "I hope you protecting yourself because—"

"C'mon, Ma, dang," Eric said. "I'm not a little kid anymore, Ma." His voice was filled with pleading.

"Okay, okay," I surrendered, tilting my cheek toward him. Eric leaned in and pecked me on the cheek.

"See ya, Aunt Crystal."

"Okay, baby, you stay safe."

"Not too late, okay?" I couldn't help but add, and Crystal quickly reached over and pinched me on the hip.

"Enough, okay?" she said.

Deeka's black truck pulled up alongside the curb. Snoop Dogg was spilling loud and raw from the car speakers.

"Hmm, nice ride," Crystal muttered under her breath.

"They call it a whip now," I commented as Deeka rounded the front of the truck and opened the passenger-side front door and then the back.

Once inside, Deeka turned the music down to a

bearable level and asked, "So, Crystal, where do you live?"

"Just a block away from Geneva. Ninetieth and Central Park West."

"Buckle up, please," Deeka said as he expertly maneuvered the truck into the thin line of traffic.

Before Deeka could get the car up to twenty-five miles an hour, Crystal was knocked out. Her head lolling on her neck, and her mouth open as she snored loudly.

Deeka and I both turned around and shot her surprised looks.

"Too many martinis," I quietly said, embarrassed for her.

"Yeah, I guess," Deeka laughed.

We rode along in an uncomfortable silence for a while before Deeka turned to me and said, "Um, Crystal's address sounds familiar to me. What was it again?"

I reeled off Crystal's address.

"Oh, yeah, yeah, I do know that building!" Deeka said, snapping his fingers.

"Really?"

"Yeah, I used to date this girl who lived there."

I felt a stab of jealousy.

"Oh."

"Yeah, Crystal may even know her," he went on.

"Yeah, maybe," I said flatly, and turned my head to look out the window.

"Yeah, hmm, Sunny Joseph," he mused, like he was remembering something tasty.

"Sound like a white girl," I spat, then laughed to cover

the spite in my voice. I was acting like a fool, like this man—man-child, I should say—was mine.

"Yeah, in fact she was," Deeka laughed. "But that was a long time ago," he said as he waved his hand through the air, "when I was young and foolish."

"Really, and what are you now? Old and wise?" I said with a smirk.

"Something like that," he said, and gave me a sly look.

"Yeah, well, when I was twenty I thought I knew it all too."

"Well, I'm actually twenty-three. And I do know a lot, but I'll be the first to admit that I still have some things to learn."

"You can say that again," I said, and snapped my fingers twice for effect. I was acting like an ass but couldn't seem to help myself.

Deeka just laughed and scanned the radio stations from a button on the steering wheel until he found a station playing grown and sexy music—Rick James and Teena Marie doing "Fire and Desire."

"You like this song?" Deeka asked. We were stopped at a red light, and my eyes were focused straight ahead. I loved that song; it was one of my favorites, and I had to resist croaking along to it.

"Uh-huh," I murmured without turning to look at him. But I could feel his eyes stroking my cheek.

"Me too," he said as he stepped on the gas. "It's one of my all-time favorites."

I nodded my head, but remained quiet.

"That song reminds me of how I feel about you."

His words hit me like a ton of bricks, and my head spun around on my neck so quickly I thought I'd have whiplash the next day. First I looked at him and then I turned to see if Crystal was still sleeping.

"Don't say things like that!" I hissed at him, before pressing my index finger against my lips and giving him the evil eye.

Deeka gave me an incorrigible smile before saying, "Well, it's the truth."

I cut my eyes at him and folded my hands across my chest like a vexed two-year-old. "Stop it."

"Not until you go out with me."

I turned my head and threw another wary look over my shoulder at Crystal. We were just pulling up to her building. "I'm not going to go out with you."

Deeka smiled, and then turned around; reaching his arm over, he stretched his hand toward Crystal's knee. "Let's see what Crystal thinks about all of this," he teased.

I hurriedly slapped at his arm. "Stop playing!"

Crystal stirred and her eyes fluttered open. "What's going on?" she asked, bleary-eyed as she wiped the spittle from the corners of her mouth.

Deeka opened his mouth to speak, but I cut him off. "Just wanted to let you know that we're at your apartment."

"Oh, damn, I fell asleep," she said, still in a daze. "Was I snoring?" she asked sheepishly.

"Nah," Deeka said. "Not at all."

"Oh, good." Crystal gathered herself to leave. "Thanks

so much for the lift, Deeka, and it was so nice meeting you," she said, extending her hand over the front seat.

"Same here." Deeka took her hand and kissed it. "Can I escort you upstairs, Crystal?"

"No, no, but thank you." She blushed and then turned to me and said, "Well, what a gentleman he is; they sure don't make them like that anymore—huh, Geneva?"

I just shrugged my shoulders.

"Okay, then. Let me head on upstairs. Talk to you later, girl," she threw at me as she hopped out of the truck.

Deeka and I sat in silence, watching Crystal through the plate-glass windows until she disappeared into the elevator.

"So are you hungry, Geneva?"

I turned slanted eyes on him. "No, I'm tired and just want to go home."

"Aw, c'mon now. I know this great place just a few blocks from here that serves the best chicken and waffles in town."

Hmm, chicken and waffles.

"I think it's too late for a meal that heavy," I said, even though my mouth had started watering at the mention of it. "And I've been wa-watching my figure," I blurted out stupidly.

"I've been watching it too, and it looks fine," Deeka said as he pulled off.

A few blocks ended up being somewhere in the Bronx in the basement of a house. Some illegal after-hours spot named Ruby's.

A three-piece band played softly while a girl that

looked no more than twelve years old belted out an old Dinah Washington tune.

I had to admit, the space was cozy. The brick walls were painted a muted purplish red, and long sheer silver scarves were draped from the ceiling.

The space held ten square tables that each seated four. There were a few people standing along the walls, holding plastic cups filled with wine, and the scent of chicken and waffles being cooked somewhere in the back part of the basement wafted through the air.

"This is a cool spot, right?" Deeka said as he pulled a chair out for me. I was a little hesitant to sit down. The chair looked a bit fragile, and all I needed was for the legs to give way and me to end up on the floor.

"What's wrong?" Deeka asked when I remained standing.

"Oh, nothing," I said as I gently eased my behind down onto the edge of the chair, shifting most of my weight forward.

"Hey, D!" shouted a buxom woman who looked very much like the actress S. Epatha Merkerson. She was dressed in a black sequined tube dress. I immediately knew that Crystal would say that that wasn't a dress for me, and Chevy would just call it ghettofied. But I liked it, and this woman who I would find out was Ruby was just as big as I was and looked fabulous!

"Hey, Ms. Ruby!" Deeka said, standing up and greeting her with a bear hug.

"Where have you been hiding your fine self?" Ruby said, rolling her eyes up and down Deeka's body like a steamroller.

"Oh, working, you know."

"Uh-huh. Working what, though?" Ruby said, imitating Mae West.

"This is my friend, Geneva," Deeka said, ignoring Ruby's flirting.

"Hi."

"Hi?" Ruby mocked me. "You better get on up here and give Mama Ruby a big ol' hug!"

"Oh, um, I—"

"That's the problem with black folks; we don't know how to show one another any love!" she roared, and pulled me into her. Our supersized breasts collided; the impact was not pleasant.

Pulling back, she wailed, "Ooooh, you a big ol' gal, ain't ya!" Ruby laughed as she slapped me on the ass with one hand and then tweaked my cheek with the other. "Corn-fed southern girl, huh?"

"I was actually born—"

"Shoot, good thing you ain't fall into this skinny-white-girl shit that all these chirren is fallin' into. Starving themselves and walking around here looking like them poor chirren in Africa; hip bones sticking out so far, if you rub against them you'll cut yourself, I swear!"

Ruby was talking so rapidly, it was clear that neither Deeka nor I was going to get a word in, so we just stood politely by and let her ramble.

"I ain't never been on no goddamn diet! Not me, I'ma still eat my swine and my carbs! You know what I'm saying, girl?" she said, poking me on my shoulder. "I say I'ma keep putting butter on my bread and sugar in my collard greens. I'm gonna keep on doing what I been doing, 'cause it makes me happy and keeps me healthy, no matter what dem white people at the FBI say."

"FDA," Deeka mumbled.

"Whoever!" Ruby said, and started to say something else, when a young boy sidled up beside her and whispered something in her ear.

"Lord Jesus, can't I leave you all to do the right thing at all?" she bellowed, and started off behind the young man without even a goodbye.

Deeka and I just stared at each other for a moment. I felt like I'd just been through a hurricane.

"I know, I know," Deeka said, shaking his head. "Ruby can be a bit much."

* * *

A plate of waffles and three Coronas later, I couldn't seem to remember how it was Deeka had moved from sitting across the table from me to sitting right beside me. But he was there, and his hand was thrown across the back of my chair as he bopped his head to the music in between whispering sweet nothings in my ear.

"You're so beautiful, Geneva," he murmured.

"Thank you," I uttered, realizing that I had become too comfortable with the whole scene, completely forgetting about my big ass and the scrawny chair I was seated in. Slowly, I tried to straighten my back so that I could move my weight to the edge of the chair again, but Deeka's hand was suddenly pressing down on my shoulder.

"When you gonna stop trying to get away from me, Geneva?"

What was I supposed to say? Yeah, I like the fact that

you're whispering in my ear, because I haven't had a man do that to me in some time, but I need to sit up and lean forward because I think this chair is going to break?

"I'm not running," I squeaked as I eased myself erect. "It's just that I'm, uhm, getting a little tired, and besides it's so late. I need to get home."

"Oh, okay," Deeka said, still pressing his hand down on my shoulder. "We'll go after this set. But I'm still waiting on an answer."

"An answer to what?" I said, turning to him. His face was so close to mine that our lips almost brushed. I jerked my head back in surprise, and then I blushed.

Deeka smiled slyly. "I asked if you thought you were beautiful."

Well, I knew I wasn't a dog; I just didn't feel beautiful all the time. I sighed. "Well, I think I'm beautiful tonight," I whispered, and was instantly struck by my honesty.

"Just tonight?" Deeka said, his eyes widening with surprise.

"Well, the new clothes, the makeup, and the hairstyle helped." I grinned. "But I'm sure the first time you saw me at the diner, beauty wasn't what came to mind."

Deeka leaned back, a look of amazement on his face. "That's not true, Geneva. I saw beauty the first, second, and twentieth time I walked into that diner and laid eyes on you. You're beautiful to me all the time."

That was the most wonderful thing a man had ever said to me while we were sitting up and fully clothed!

We just stared at each other for a while, and then his hands were on my face pulling me to him. I didn't even try to resist, and before I could take a breath, his lips were pressed against mine and every fantasy I'd ever had about him exploded in the pit of my stomach. The heat was on as our tongues explored each other's mouths.

We kissed like we were hungry for each other, and if Ruby hadn't come along and interrupted us, I swear we would have ended up on the table dry-humping each other!

We continued our "exploration" outside. Deeka had me pressed up against the car, and our hands crawled all over each other's bodies. We looked like two lovestruck teenagers. Or at least *lust*-struck!

Finally, when I thought I couldn't take much more for fear of giving myself over to him right then and there, I pushed him off me and asked, "What do you want from me?"

Deeka looked deep into my eyes and answered, "I want you. All of you."

"This has got to be some type of joke," I said, digging into my purse for my cigarettes. I hadn't had one in hours, and truthfully, hadn't thought about having one until that moment. "You must be crazy," I said as I popped the Newport into my mouth and lit it.

"I've been called worse," he said, taking a step toward me. I took two steps away from him.

"I'm almost old enough to be your mother," I said, blowing a plume of smoke over his head. "And I smoke. Men don't like women who smoke. And I can tell by your body that you're probably a health nut."

"Oh, God!" Deeka screamed as he threw his hands

up into the air. "What do I have to say or do to make you believe that this is real?"

He walked in circles for a minute, apparently having a conversation with himself before walking over to me, putting both hands on my shoulders, and saying, "I don't care about your age, age is just a number, and you'll stop smoking when you're ready to, I know that. I will say that you should stop sooner than later, because I want to have you around for a long, long time."

I looked around for the movie cameras; surely I was being "punk'd" by Ashton Kutcher!

"Give me a chance, Geneva, please."

"I—I just don't know," I mumbled. Deeka bit down hard on his bottom lip and turned his head toward the moonlit sky. I swear I saw a tear in his eye.

I took a deep breath, flicked my cigarette down to the pavement, and moved toward him. "Deeka?"

Deeka looked down at me, and I examined his face, his eyes, the soft curve of his bottom lip for some flaw, some tic that would tell me this was all some cruel joke. But there was nothing. Not a trace of insincerity.

Besides, I'd been involved with a number of different men who hadn't ever begged and pleaded for my company the way Deeka just had. As ludicrous as it all seemed, I had to admit that somewhere deep inside of me it felt right.

"Okay," I said.

Noah

"Well, Miss Thing, it seems all of y'all across the pond got the fever," I said in the middle of yet another one of Geneva's pity-party, woe-is-me tirades. Shit, I had my own problems and wasn't really feeling like counseling Geneva—yet again!

"What?"

"Everybody's fiending for one thing or another, it seems," I said nonchalantly.

"Everybody like who, Noah? Something like what?"

"Oh, girl, just everybody, the world, but go on with your story. He took you out and . . ." I said the last bit with little interest, but that went right over Geneva's head, so in typical Geneva style, she continued.

"We just had a really great time, and I don't know, but I just can't get past his age and my weight. . . ."

We were on the weight thing again? I wanted to scream, but instead I said, "Blah, blah, blah . . ."

"I hate when you do that, Noah. It's very rude, not to mention infantile."

"Look, Geneva, I know you don't have money to waste to call me and tell me the same thing over and over again, right?"

"Well, yeah, but—"

"So we talked about this already; he don't have a problem with your weight and your age and your tired-ass hairdo—"

"I never mentioned my hair—"

"Whatever. The point is, he likes you for who you are and that's what's important."

"Yeah, I guess—"

"I'm sure Crystal has told you all this—"

"No, I haven't told Crystal a thing, 'cause we're off men. You know, power in numbers."

"Uh-huh."

"So don't tell her any of this—okay, Noah?"

"Yeah, sugar, my lips are sealed," I yawned.

"Promise?"

"Cross my heart and hope to go straight." Something I felt sure was worse than death!

We talked a little longer, me not really hearing what Geneva was saying; my mind was all turned around with what I thought was happening with my neighbors next door. For three days straight I'd seen Aldo coming home in the afternoon, always accompanied by two men and always during the time when Ray-Ray was off for his two-hour strength-training session at the gym.

Each time I pressed the glass to the wall, and each time all I could hear was moaning and groaning!

Aldo was cheating on Ray-Ray, I was sure of it!

I liked Ray-Ray, he seemed like a good guy, full of life and very much in love with Aldo. I wanted to tell him what was going on but felt that our friendship was still too new for me to say anything. And besides, Aldo and

Ray-Ray had been together for damn near ten years, and really, who the hell was I?

I hadn't even confided what I'd been seeing and hearing to Zhan. I mean, if he knew we had a philandering gay man next door, he might start thinking that I would be Aldo's next victim.

As forgiving as Zhan had been three years earlier when I confessed my infidelities to him, I knew he hadn't forgotten. I'd seen him watching me for a reaction on more than one occasion whenever we were out and a good-looking woman walked by. I guess if the shoe were on the other foot I would behave the same way. A gay man does not quickly get over the fact that his lover went on the "down low" with women.

So for the time being, I kept my secret to myself, but I didn't know how long I would be able to.

Chevy

I felt bad that I wasn't able to go to Lola's last week and see Eric play. I had every intention of going, but I was so tired, all I did was sleep the weekend away. On Monday, goddamn Anja had me on a train to Connecticut at the eleventh hour to meet with some new rapper named Loose Change so that I could pick up a copy of his yet-to-be-released CD.

Anja was the queen of the "exclusive," whether it was gossip or a much-sought-after cut from a CD that wouldn't be released for another month.

"Anja would send you in a private car, Chevy, but you know there are spies all over the place, and Anja can't risk having you followed."

"I don't understand," I said stupidly on the phone.

"What don't you understand?"

I flipped the phone the bird, then said brightly, "Will there be anything else, Anja?"

"No, just make sure you don't miss the train; it's leaving in exactly twenty minutes."

Click.

I looked at the phone for a while, amazed that someone had actually given birth to someone like that. And when I finally looked at the clock, I realized I had been sitting there for two full minutes! I now had eighteen minutes to get to Grand Central Station.

Snatching the printout of the information from my Lexmark, I scooped up my Louis Vuitton bag and ran out of my office, barely avoiding a head-on collision with Dante.

"Hey, hey, what's the rush?"

"I gotta catch a train," I said as I moved swiftly past him.

Out in the hallway I jabbed the down button for the elevator twenty times before the bell chimed and the doors opened. It was packed with people, hardly enough room for a small child, but I squeezed in anyway, as I ignored the annoying hisses of air from the person I was pressed up against.

Once out on the street, I practically ran down the middle of Sixth Avenue as I waved my hand frantically for a taxi. At least five passed me by, and that's not because I was black, it was because I looked crazed!

Finally, this brother wearing a kente-cloth tunic stopped. I jumped in and said, "I'll give you twenty dollars over the meter if you get me to Grand Central in three minutes or less!"

Who knew in this administration that twenty dollars had the same effect on a person now that it would have had during Clinton's reign?

I buckled my seat belt, tucked my tongue behind my teeth, closed my eyes, and braced myself as the cab tore off.

When we hit 42nd Street, he made a sharp turn and screeched to a stop.

I thrust the money at him, leaped out, and when I found the train and rushed on, I had exactly thirty seconds to spare.

Out of breath and shaking like a leaf, I eased myself down into the seat. I pressed my hand against my heart and found that it was galloping fifty miles a minute. I was sweating profusely, and my mouth was as dry as the Sahara.

Looking out the window at the scenery that sped by, I wondered if this job and the money was worth all the aggravation.

Crystal

I was sitting at the kitchen table, going over the minutes of a meeting, when Neville walked in.

I hadn't really seen him much over the past week. It seemed as though when I was coming in he was going out.

There was always a delicious meal waiting for me, and in the three weeks he'd been at my place, I was sure I'd gained six pounds.

I'd been working hard at bringing the fantasies I was having about him to a halt. It didn't make any sense to me to keep thinking about him in that way, when it was clear he wasn't interested. I mean, at first, I thought he was. Well, with the dinners, the flowers, and the foot massages, and even the little notes he left me that he closed with x's and o's . . .

But now I knew that he was just being his sweet self. And besides, I doubted that he was going off sightseeing every evening. I was sure that what he was seeing was some beautiful woman.

"Hey, gal. Still working?" Neville said as he opened the refrigerator and peered in.

"Yeah, it seems like it never ends," I said without even looking up at him.

"Hmm," he said, and then I heard the fridge door close. "You need to take it a bit easier, you know. I think you need a vacation."

"Yeah, I guess I do. It has been a while."

"Too long from what I can see," he said, and then his hands were kneading my shoulders. "You are so tense."

I was tense. Bottled up, to be truthful. His fingers seemed to make magic as I felt my muscles become Jell-O beneath his touch.

He moved from my shoulders to the base of my neck.

"Does that feel good?" he asked.

"Oh, yeah, it does. Where did you learn how to do that?" I inquired, allowing my head to fall forward so that he could massage deeper.

"Ah, I am a man of many talents," he breathed into my ear as he leaned down. His breath was minty-Scope-fresh!

"Yes, that's what it seems." I laughed. I was enjoying the massage, but my mind was still on work. Just when I was about to stop him and shoo him away, he made a tempting suggestion.

"If you'd like, I could do this to your whole body."

Now there was an offer that I did not want to refuse. But as much as I wanted that man's hands all over my body, I wanted everything that could come after that. And like I said, I just didn't think he was into me like that.

"I don't know, Neville. I have all this work to do," I said, reaching for the papers strewn out on the table.

"Come on now. I will not take no for an answer," he said, his hands under my armpits pulling me up from the chair.

"I'm ticklish!" I screamed, wiggling away from him.

"Now, you know you shouldn't have told me that!" Neville laughed and began tickling me all over.

I got away from him and ran laughing through the apartment, with Neville close behind. We circled the couch, giggling like schoolchildren. It felt good to laugh like that!

Catching me, he pulled me down onto the couch and tickled me until there were tears in my eyes.

"Okay, okay, I can't take much more, I'm going to piss on myself!" I wailed, fighting to get away from him.

He let me go, exclaiming, "No, don't do that! Wouldn't want you to ruin this beautiful sofa!"

I'd barely made it to the toilet before my urine started trickling out. Sitting there, I was struck with a fit of giggles.

"What's so funny?" Neville yelled from the living room. "Can I see too?" he said, and I could tell he was grinning.

"Don't you dare come in here!" I warned between bouts of laughter.

When I was done, I sauntered back into the living room with a huge grin planted across my face. Neville, who was seated on the couch, remote in hand flipping through the channels, turned and looked at me.

"Did you wash your hands, young lady?" Neville said in a gruff voice.

"Yes," I said, holding up damp hands. "All clean!"

"Are you ready for your dessert, then?"

Where were we going with this? I didn't know, but I continued to play along.

"Take off your clothes and wait for me on the bed. I'll be there in a minute."

I blinked. "Take off my clothes?"

"Don't talk back to me, young lady. Just do as I say!" he bellowed so loud that I jumped where I stood.

Was this a game? Was he serious? I wasn't sure but turned and obediently went into my room.

Sitting on the edge of my bed, not knowing what I should do, I listened as the television went off and the stereo came on. I could hear him in the kitchen, doing something, but I didn't know what.

Should I get up and lock the door? Call Geneva? Call the cops?

Suddenly he was at my doorway. "Are you still dressed?"

I nodded my head guiltily.

"You have thirty seconds to take off those clothes, or there will be no dessert for you tonight."

I just stared at him.

"Oh, and this is for you," he said, stepping into the room. From behind his back he pulled a tall glass of something that was reddish in color.

"What's that?" I asked meekly.

"Rum punch, to help you unwind," he said, and flashed me a huge smile.

Unwind? I wasn't sure I should drink it. Suppose he'd put some type of sex drug in it. Geneva was right, I really didn't know him.

I took the glass. "Thanks," I said, barely looking at him.

"Are you okay, Crystal?" he said now in his regular voice. "What's wrong?"

I shook my head and forced a smile as I looked up at him. "It's just that, you know, you told me to take off my clothes and that tone—"

"Crystal, I was role-playing with you. You know, like we used to do when we were kids."

I shrugged my shoulders; I guessed I was being silly.

"And how am I supposed to give you a full-body massage if you're dressed in jeans?"

"That would be difficult, huh?"

"But if you're not comfortable with it, I understand."

"No, no. I am, it's just my imagination started running away with me."

He gave me an incredulous look before saying, "You sure?"

"Yes, yes," I said, really smiling now. "Just let me enjoy my drink, and I'll be ready."

"Okay," Neville said, and waltzed out of the room.

I took a tentative sip of the drink and found my mouth drenched in pleasure. This rum punch was really good. I took a few more sips and then finally guzzled it.

When Neville returned with a small bowl of heated baby oil and a hand towel, I was laid out on my stomach, almost naked—I'd kept my panties and bra on.

"Okay, now, let's get to it," he said, resting the bowl down on the nightstand. He'd changed out of his jeans and was now in a pair of loose-fitting cotton shorts.

"Move to the center of the bed," he instructed, and I did.

"Um, Crystal?"

"Yes?" I murmured. That rum punch had me very mellow.

"The bra has to go, love."

"Oh?"

After a moment I told myself, What the hell, right? So I reached my arms behind me in a lackluster effort to undo the hooks when I felt Neville's hands on mine. "Let me," he cooed, and with the flick of two fingers, my bra fell open.

I eased myself up onto my elbows and pulled the straps down my arms. I was sure he got a nice view of my breasts. Good for him!

Tossing my bra aside, I rested my head on my pillow and waited for his fingers to do their magic.

I don't know what I expected, but his climbing onto the bed and sitting on the back of my thighs wasn't it!

"What are you doing?"

"Well, since you're not on a table, this is the best way I can massage you."

I didn't know about that.

"Am I hurting you?"

"No, no."

"Well, if you become uncomfortable at any time, just let me know, okay?"

He started with my shoulders and then moved to my neck before sliding his hands down my back and working the area around my spine.

"Does it feel good?"

"Oh, yes," I moaned.

After pouring more baby oil onto my skin, he began

working on my lower back. "You may feel some sensation here," he said. "I'm massaging your kidneys."

And he was right; it felt as if there were sharp stones beneath my skin. Lower still, his hands traveled until his fingers found my apple bottom. I stiffened.

"Crystal?"

"Yes?"

"Are you okay with this?"

Yes, I was, but his touching me there, like that, was going to make me want this to lead to . . . other things.

"Yes, I am."

"Well, then relax."

It took some time, but finally I did.

I think about forty minutes had passed by the time he said, "Okay, turn over."

"Turn over?" I repeated stupidly as I lifted my head and began searching frantically for my bra with my eyes.

"Yeah, turn over, gal. It's not like you got something I haven't seen before." He laughed and slapped me playfully on the ass. "Or do you? Hmm, does Crystal Atkins have a third nipple?" he joked.

I managed a small laugh but still did not move, even when he climbed off me.

"C'mon, Crystal, now."

Slowly I turned over onto my back, careful to keep my eyes planted on the ceiling and one arm thrown over my breasts.

"Okay, now," he said as he climbed back on top of me. "You have to put your hand down. I won't laugh at your third nipple, I promise."

Slowly I lowered my arm.

"Well, look at that, no third nipple!"

I couldn't help but grin, and finally I looked at him and found him staring directly at me. "You're one beautiful woman, you know that?"

I just grinned.

When he brought his hands down on my shoulders, I closed my eyes while he worked, and when his hands fell on my breasts I kept them closed and just enjoyed the fire his fingers sent through my body.

I felt movement against my thigh, a small jerk, and then three more. My eyes slowly opened, and Neville was grinning sheepishly. "Um, sorry about that. That doesn't usually happen," he said as his hands massaged my stomach.

"It's okay," I breathed as I felt warm moisture fill the space between my legs.

We watched each other, while his hands worked my stomach and his dick bounced happily against my thigh. I found my hand reaching out for him, my fingers pulling at the waistband of his shorts. I was sitting up now, my lips brushing against his as my hand found the rounded tip of his swollen member.

"Crystal, Crystal, we shouldn't," he murmured, but I quieted his objections with my tongue.

His dick was fully engorged; I could feel the wavy impression of the veins pulsating through the skin. I stroked him while we kissed passionately.

He pushed me back down and jumped off the bed, stripping himself out of his shorts while I struggled to remove my panties.

Suddenly, there it was: long, strong, and beautiful!

I shuddered in awe. It was just as I had fantasized it would be.

He was on me again, eating me up with his kisses, his hands moving over me, his mouth sucking and licking, and then he dropped down and roughly pushed my legs open.

Before I could object, his tongue was flicking over my clitoris. I grabbed hold of the pillow while he teased it.

This boy knew his stuff!

Just when I thought I would burst, his hot mouth devoured my entire womanhood! Oh, the pleasure!

I grabbed hold of his head while he sucked. I grabbed hold and hung on for dear life as I rode his mouth like it was a prizewinning stallion!

In no time, I exploded and let off a long strangled cry of pleasure before my body fell limp.

We lay there for a moment, Neville's head resting against my thigh, my body jerking with tiny electric bolts.

"You taste so sweet," he whispered.

"So do you," I managed, still having the taste of his tongue in my mouth.

"I want to make love to you, Crystal Atkins."

"And I want you to, Neville Gill."

Geneva

It had been days and I was still walking on air.

"Geneva Holliday, what the hell is wrong with you?" Darlene kept asking me.

"Nothing. Can't a girl smile?"

"Not like you been smiling," Darlene stated, and then leaned in and gave me a hard look before pulling back and slapping her hands over her mouth. "Geneva Holliday, you got some dick, didn't you?" Some customers looked up from their meals at us.

"Lower your voice," I said, grabbing on to her arm and dragging her to the far end of the diner. "I did not."

"Yes, you did. I can tell."

"You can't tell nothing, now stop it." I blushed.

"Hmm, you can't fool me. I know what a woman looks like when she gets some dick, but then again . . ." She trailed off, then gave me another penetrating glance. "Humph, it could be an I'm-in-love look too," she said, screwing her face up and scratching her chin.

"I ain't get no dick and I'm not in love," I said, turning my head away.

"You got something or in something. You hit the number?"

"Darlene, leave me be, okay?" I said, and sauntered away from her toward the counter.

I was humming when he walked in, humming and thinking about those words, his lips, that night!

He took his regular table. "You got a customer, Geneva," Darlene called over to me, and then nodded in Deeka's direction.

I looked over and my heart almost exploded. But I contained myself and took my time walking over to him.

I poured some coffee in his cup and asked, "What can I get you?"

"A tall cup of you, with a side order of you." He grinned at me over the menu.

"Shhh," I giggled.

I hadn't seen him since that night, but we'd been talking on the phone until all hours of the morning. Once we almost got busted when Eric picked up the extension, but luckily Deeka didn't breathe a word until he heard the phone hang up.

"I need to see you," Deeka whispered. "Tonight."

"I don't know if I can," I whispered back, trying my best to look nonchalant.

"Try. I'll pick you up at ten."

"At night!" I screamed, and I could see Darlene's radar go up from the other side of the diner.

I gave her a nervous smile and scribbled some nonsense down on my pad while I spoke from the side of my mouth. "I can't go out at ten o'clock. What am I going to do with Charlie?"

"Can't your mother—" he started to say, but I ended that with a quick shake of my head.

He looked down at his menu. I could see his mind was working at a solution. He looked back at me. "I wouldn't mind her coming out with us."

Men just don't get it, do they?

"It's ten o'clock at night, Deeka."

"Well then, I'll just have to come there."

My eyes popped. "Are you crazy? What about Eric?"

"Eric has a gig tonight at nine. I'll pop in to make sure they're all set up and then pop out and come uptown to hang with you for a while."

"I don't know about that."

"It'll be fine."

* * *

Charlie was fast asleep with her Pooh tucked protectively under her arm by the time Deeka called me from his cell phone. "Coast clear?"

"Yeah."

"Then open the door."

I had spent most of the night putting on and taking off clothes, messing with my hair and gargling with mouthwash after each cigarette. Finally I decided on a pair of black leggings and a T-shirt that Chevy had brought back for me from a trip to the Bahamas. It was a cheery pink with a large green and purple palm tree on the front. And it was large enough to not make my gut so noticeable.

"Hey," I said when I swung the door open.

"Hey," he responded, and walked in planting a long, lingering kiss on my lips. Stepping back, he held up a large paper bag. "I brought champagne and sushi."

Sushi?

"Oh, baby, I've already eaten," I said, not wanting to chow down on raw fish and seaweed.

"Really? I should have checked with you first," he said, spreading everything out onto the table. "Well, at least you can try one roll."

I folded my hands and nodded. "Maybe just one." I guess my face was screwed up because when he turned to look at me again, he said, "Oh, you don't like sushi, do you?"

"Well, I don't think I do. I've never had it, on account it's raw fish."

"Hmm," he mused as he picked up a pair of chopsticks and poked at one of the rolls. "Try this one, it's a California roll."

I made a face.

"No fish, just imitation crab, cucumber, avocado, and rice."

Dipping it into soy sauce, he made an airplane sound as he guided it toward my tightly pinched lips. "C'mon now, open up."

I did, but reluctantly. I braced myself as I bit down, and you know what, it wasn't bad, wasn't bad at all.

Chevy

I looked at my computer screen again, and still my inbox remained empty. Could it be true? Could the gods actually be smiling down on me today?

It was five thirty and not one email since four o'clock!

I would wait until six, just to be sure, and then if there was nothing in my inbox, I was going to be out of there like a bat out of hell!

I busied myself with tidying up my desk. I so wanted to go home and sleep in my own bed. I'd been sleeping at the office for three straight nights.

Flipping my compact open, I saw that I had circles under my eyes and that my skin was beginning to break out with blackheads.

"Fuck!" I yelled to my walls as I snapped my compact closed. This job was sucking the life out of me. Fuck it. Six o'clock or no six o'clock, I was leaving.

Snatching up my purse, I didn't even bother to make a pit stop in the bathroom; I just hauled ass out toward the door.

Just as my hand hit the knob, the phone started to ring. I didn't even look back. Fuck Anja, I thought as I turned the knob.

* * *

Outside, I sucked in the evening air. I wanted to spread my arms out at my sides, throw my head back and scream as I spun in circles in the middle of the sidewalk, but I refrained from doing so. I didn't want to be hauled off in a straitjacket, so I just grinned like a lunatic as I rushed down Sixth Avenue.

I felt like I had just been released from prison! I needed to celebrate. I needed to kick back and get loose! I needed a frickin' drink and some conversation. I needed my girls!

Digging into my pocketbook, I pulled out my cell phone and quickly dialed Geneva.

Crystal

I didn't want to go out; all I wanted to do was head home and get some more Neville Gill loving. We'd been doing *it* every night, and by God, it seemed it just got more intense each time.

I was having the time of my fucking life!

Not even those asshole bosses of mine or the number-crunching anal-retentive accountants could dampen my mood—at the end of the day, I knew what I was going home to! So this is what good dick did to a girl? Well, goddamn!

Just as I was gathering myself up to leave, my phone rang. But I just ignored it. Wasn't nobody or nothing going to keep me in that office past six o'clock. I sat on the corner of my desk and folded my legs diva-style as I carefully applied my lipstick and thought about how all of a sudden men were falling all over themselves to get to me. It was as if I were sending off some kind of signal, scent, or vibration that indicated that I was screwing again.

Brothers were beside themselves: passing me slips of papers with telephone numbers, trying to rub up against me on the train—it was out of control. One guy was trying to rap to me so hard that he walked into a telephone pole!

I laughed at the thought of it and then heard my cell phone vibrating in my pocketbook. Hmm, I thought, maybe that's Neville, wanting me to bring home some more whipped cream; we'd finished off the can I'd brought home last night!

I didn't even check the number, I was so sure it was him. I flipped the cover, pressed the phone to my ear, and practically yodeled, "Yes, lover!"

"Crystal?"

I recognized Chevy's voice instantly, and in a panic flipped the cover to the phone closed again. Shit! I'd sworn Neville to secrecy. I didn't want anybody knowing what it was he and I were doing up in that apartment every night. Well, Noah knew, but I didn't want Chevy to know, and I certainly didn't want Geneva to find out. She'd think I'd abandoned her and our cause.

The phone vibrated again, and I let the call go to voice mail, but then when it started up for the third time, I answered it.

"Hello?" I said in a tired voice.

"Crystal?" Chevy sounded panicked. "Did I just call you?"

"Call me? No," I said, sounding bewildered.

"Oh, I must have dialed wrong. Some woman answered and said—well, anyway that's not important. I need to get out."

"So go."

"No, I mean with the girls."

"Is this Chevanese?"

The Chevy I knew would never make a request like that. Chevy was a loner and didn't need anybody to hang out with her—especially women. She never wanted the competition, even though she always reiterated that Geneva and I weren't competition.

"Yes, it's me, now stop playing. Can we get together?"

I looked at the phone and thought that all I heard about working for Anja the Anaconda was true. You went in one way and never came out the same, if you came out at all.

"Let me just make sure; this is Chevanese Cambridge, right?" I teased.

"I said stop playing!"

"Okay, girl, okay."

"Let's meet at Ida Mae's."

"All right, I'll call Geneva and see if she can—"

"I already called her; she'll be there at seven," Chevy said, and the phone went dead.

Geneva

Deeka would drop me off to meet the girls at Ida Mae's, so I met him two blocks away from the diner. We'd been meeting like that for more than a week. Sneaking away during my lunch hour so that we could neck in the car like lovesick teenagers!

I used to meet him around the corner from the diner, but I had to change that because, one day, just when I was about to put my hand on the door handle, something said to look up, and who did I see but that nosy-ass Darlene! She was pressed up against the wall, like I wouldn't notice that bleached-blond hair and bright red lipstick!

"Hey, girl!" I yelled at her, waving as I swerved away from the truck and continued down the block.

Deeka knew to follow me to the corner.

Tonight, we sat two blocks away from Ida Mae's, holding hands and talking as the rain poured down around us.

"I hate that we have to sneak around like this, 'Neva."

Deeka had taken to calling me 'Neva, his pet name for me. I liked it.

He squeezed my hand and turned sorrowful eyes on me. "I want everybody to know that I love you."

My heart stopped. Love?

Now it was one thing for me to be kissed and felt up

by this twentysomething hunk of a gorgeous man. I mean, I'd seen *The Graduate* fifty times, and Benjamin sure didn't end up with Mrs. Robinson! So I was prepared for this whole thing to go to hell in a handbasket. I had had a long talk with myself and had convinced myself that I would keep my emotions in check; just have a good time while there were good times to be had. Nothing more and nothing less. Simple.

So where did this love shit come from?

I was enjoying the attention. He wasn't pressuring me for sex—even though all I could think of was jumping his bones—and he was genuinely a nice guy who I enjoyed being around.

But love? I'd been to that place too many times before, and while it was a pleasure getting there, the stay often went sour and the leaving almost always killed me.

"Did you hear me, Geneva?"

I nodded my head.

His hand squeezed mine again, and he placed his other hand gently on my cheek and turned my face toward him. I thought he wanted an answer, but I had none to give him. Luckily all he did was kiss me.

"Okay, I've got to go," I said, eager to get out of that space.

"Okay, what time should I pick you up?"

"Don't worry. I'll share a cab with Crystal."

He was hurt. I could tell from the look in his eyes that he wanted to hear me say I loved him too.

"Well, I'll call you later, then," Deeka said.

"Later, then," I said, and waved at him as I started down the block toward the restaurant.

Crystal

"So who's watching Charlie?" I asked after I gave Geneva a kiss on her cheek.

I caught a whiff of cologne. That was strange.

"Oh, Eric is," Geneva said as she pulled out a chair and sat down.

She was still dressed in her blue and white waitress uniform. Some customers stared openly at her, and even the waitress gawked for a moment when she came over to take our drink orders.

I wasn't going to say anything about it. If she was comfortable with it, I was too.

"Um," Geneva said as she scanned the drink menu, "do you have a late-harvest Riesling?"

My mouth almost dropped open. Geneva almost always drank Corona beer, and on the rare occasion that she didn't, it was usually a rum and Coke, but wine? And calling it by name? Who was this woman?

"And you?" The waitress turned to me.

"I'll have a rum punch," I said before I could catch myself. I saw Geneva's eyebrows climb her forehead, but she said nothing.

"So you're wearing a new scent?" Geneva had been

a Jean Naté girl since she was ten years old, so this masculine-smelling perfume she'd adopted seemed to be out of character for her.

"No," Geneva responded, surprised. "Why?"

"Oh, you smell like you have something on that's kind of, I don't know, woodsy."

"Woodsy?"

"Well, to be truthful it smells like a cologne that Kendrick used to wear."

Geneva's face looked confused, and then I swear I saw a lightbulb go off in her head.

"Oh, oh, yeah, I remember now," she laughed guiltily. "I squirted on one of Eric's colognes this morning."

Lie!

I gave her a hard look. She wasn't being truthful; I could tell because she'd answered me without looking up and now she was fiddling with her napkin.

"Uh-huh, and why would you do a thing like that?" I probed.

"'Cause I'm grown," Geneva spat, and snatched up her menu.

I just blinked.

I was about to prod further when Chevy breezed in.

"Hey, hos!" she yelled happily.

"I told you I don't like that. It's just as bad as referring to us as bitches," I grumbled.

"Oh, Crystal, loosen up," Chevy chastised, and then threw Geneva a slanted glance. "What is this, a new fashion statement or something?" she said, flicking the collar of Geneva's uniform with the tip of her index finger.

"Don't start with me, Chevy. You called me at the last

minute and demanded that we all be here by seven—I didn't have time to change. And here you are strolling in late."

"As usual," I said. "So what's the emergency?"

"Nothing, really, I just needed to be with my girls," Chevy said as she snapped her fingers in order to get the waitress's attention.

Geneva and I exchanged looks.

"So how's the new job?" Geneva asked in between sips of her wine.

Chevy opened her mouth and then closed it. "Are you drinking wine, Geneva?" she asked in amazement.

"Yes. And?" Geneva rolled her head on her neck.

Chevy just made a face and then turned and looked at me and then down at my drink. "And what the hell is that?"

"Rum punch," I mumbled.

Chevy's eyes rocked between us. "Am I high? None of these things is right. You don't like fruity drinks with umbrellas," she said, pointing to me before swinging her finger to Geneva. "And you certainly don't drink wine!"

Geneva and I said nothing.

"What's going on here?" Chevy asked, leaning back in her chair and folding her arms.

"Nothing," Geneva and I said at the same time. We exchanged glances; we knew something was certainly going on with the other, but what?

Chevy

I eyed both of them.

Something was going on here, and I was missing out on it because I worked for a task master.

"Well?" I pressed.

"Oh, Chevy, please," Crystal said and waved her hand at me. "Ain't nothing going on but the rent, child."

Geneva laughed and raised her wineglass in salute before tipping it to her mouth. I swear her pinky finger was sticking out. Had she become proper overnight? I looked at her waitress uniform, and that reminded me that she hadn't.

"So tell us what it's like to work for Anja!" Geneva squealed.

"The Anacooooonda!" Crystal added in a heavy whisper.

I leaned forward in my chair and ran my index finger around the rim of my champagne flute. I wasn't going to tell them the real deal. I couldn't, it was too embarrassing. So I proceeded to do what it was I always did. I lied.

"Gurrrrl, it is a dream-come-true job. I mean, I'm making big bucks, and I have this fabulous office with the most fantastic view you could ever hope for. Did I tell you about the gold fixtures in my bathroom?"

"Real gold?" Geneva gasped.

"Real gold, girl. I mean the bathroom itself is gorgeous, marble this and marble that and a Jacuzzi tub."

"Jacuzzi tub?" Crystal muttered.

"And we have a real dining room—like a restaurant—no grade school cafeteria shit. Tablecloths, bone china, and silk napkins. I'm talking white-glove service!"

Geneva's eyes popped. "So what about Anja? Is she the bitch everybody says she is?"

"Oh, she's tough all right—but not with me. She just loves Chevy!"

Crystal screwed up her face and said, "Well, that's a first."

"What?" I said defensively.

"Um," she began as she leaned in and propped her elbows up on the table, "you've never had a boss who loved you. In fact, you've never had a boss who even liked you, Chevy."

She wasn't telling a lie, it was true.

"Well," I countered, "Anja and I are very much alike."

"Egotistical and selfish?" Geneva laughed.

"Ooooh, you learned a new word, huh, Geneva?" I barked at her. "No, we are both movers and shakers, and we just don't take shit, and nothing is wrong with that."

"Oh," Crystal responded, "so you've been going to a lot of club openings and hip celebrity parties?"

"Oh, yes. And I'm meeting so many people. The other night I was at the press party for Carol's Daughter. Lisa Price is taking her stores national, you know?"

"Carol's what? Lisa who?" Geneva piped.

"Carol's Daughter is the name of the natural skin- and hair-care products Lisa Price created. Her flagship store is in Bed-Stuy," Crystal informed Geneva. "Hey, aren't Jada and Will Smith backing her or something?"

"Yep, and they were there too. Will Smith is even better-looking in person!"

"He is fine," Geneva said, and licked her lips seductively.

"Calm down," I said to Geneva. "He is too good-looking for the likes of you. But I tell you something, he was watching my booty all night long!" I fell into a fit of laughter.

Well, I had to make it sound good. I couldn't say that I didn't get within spitting distance of him. And even if I could have, I wouldn't have wanted to—not dressed in that friggin' ANJA'S BITCH T-shirt.

"Wow, sounds like you have landed the dream job, Chevy. I'm proud of you," Crystal said.

Noah

I opened the door to find Ray-Ray standing there with a bottle of wine in his hands. Aldo was standing behind him. They were both grinning and a bit flushed in the face.

I was taken off guard. Of course I was always happy to see Ray-Ray, loved that we could kick back together and talk about some of the favorite haunts we visited as we grew into our queer identities. It was always amazing to us that while we had frequented the same gay clubs and lounges, we'd never met each other. Although we did find out that we had some acquaintances (and former lovers) in common.

We always fell quiet during some part of our reverie when our minds stumbled on the thought of the amount of friends we'd lost to AIDS over the years. We had remained infection-free by the grace of God. 'Cause Lord knows we had taken some stupid risks over the years.

"Hey, guys," I said brightly. Even though just seeing Aldo standing there, with his hand affectionately resting on Ray-Ray's arm, made my stomach churn.

"Are we interrupting your supper?" Ray-Ray asked as he stepped in.

"No, not at all."

Zhan was seated in his leather recliner, sipping a cup of peppermint tea. He had the paper open in his lap. Miles Davis filled the background and there was a lavender-scented candle burning on the windowsill.

"Well, hello." Zhan peered at Aldo and Ray-Ray over the rims of his reading glasses.

We were dressed in baggy T-shirts and loose cotton shorts—our normal evening attire—while Aldo and Ray-Ray were wearing silk shirts and linen slacks. "Are you guys headed out?" I asked when I closed the door.

"No, no. We've just come back from dinner, and Aldo wanted us to stop by and maybe have a few glasses of wine with you two before we turned in for the night," Ray-Ray said as he moved into the kitchen and set the bottle down on the butcher-block top of the center island.

"Oh," I said. "That was nice of you."

Zhan nodded approvingly when I held the wine bottle up for him to see. "A very good year indeed!" He clapped his hands together and then looked over at Aldo and said, "You have very good taste, old man."

"Grazie," Aldo said.

I opened the bottle and pulled four crystal wine-glasses out of the cabinet. "Let it breathe for about ten minutes," Aldo instructed.

"Okay," I said, and then went for the water crackers in the pantry and the brie we always kept at the ready on the dairy shelf in the fridge. "I wish I had some grapes," I complained under my breath.

"It's okay, darling," Zhan called over to me. "The cheese and crackers will do."

Ray-Ray chose to sit in Aldo's lap. I made myself comfortable on one of the floor pillows nearest Zhan's chair. The three of them fell into an easy conversation. I remained mostly silent, amazed at how natural Aldo could behave when he was screwing around on his man!

It wasn't until after we'd smoked some hash that I felt relaxed enough to actively participate in the conversation. By then my head was clouded, and I couldn't care less about mostly everything.

Zhan had said something really funny, and I was laughing so hard my sides were beginning to ache. When I finally got myself under control, and lifted my glass to drain the last drops of the Pinot Noir, Aldo cleared his throat and Ray-Ray dropped the bomb.

"We were wondering," he began as he seductively stroked the back of Aldo's neck, "if you guys ever swapped."

"Swapped?" Zhan and I questioned in unison.

"Swapped what?" I said.

"Keys." Aldo's voice was low.

"Keys? I don't understand," Zhan said.

Ray-Ray was curling himself up tight in Aldo's lap. He planted a kiss on his cheek and then looked back at Zhan and me—both of us confused.

"You know, you give me the key to your apartment and we give you the key to ours."

Like a ton of bricks, it hit me. I knew exactly what they were talking about. My high went right out the window and I felt my back go rigid.

"You mean, like, for emergencies?" Zhan said, still not understanding.

A throaty laugh emanated from Aldo and he levied hefty slaps on Ray-Ray's behind. "Is that what you call it?" Aldo grinned.

Zhan had a foolish smile on his face when he looked down at me. "Do you know what they're talking about?"

I slowly nodded my head.

Zhan and I had shared our fantasies with each other. I wanted to make butt-naked love in the middle of an open field, and Zhan wanted to have a threesome. He'd obliged my fantasy one night in Prospect Park and I'd told him that I would do the same for him, whenever he was ready. Well, that was before I knew I wanted to spend the rest of my life with him. Now, I didn't want him to even look at another man, much less fuck him!

"It's late," I abruptly announced, and pulled myself into a standing position. The look on Zhan's face wavered.

"What's wrong, Noah?" he said to my quickly retreating back, and then to Aldo, "Please explain to me what it is that you two are talking about."

Ray-Ray opened his mouth, and I flew back into the living room and parked myself in between Ray-Ray and Zhan. Bending over, I gave Aldo and Ray-Ray a good view of my tight ass. My face was an inch from Zhan when I said, "They're talking about swapping partners. You fuck one of them and one of them will fuck me, or we can all get together and do a ménage à quatre!"

Zhan's eyes bulged and he strained his neck to look around me at Aldo and Ray-Ray, who were sitting there with their eyebrows raised.

"Really?" Zhan said, the confusion in his face replaced with curiosity.

I went erect and placed my hands on my hips. "Oh, no, you didn't!"

"I don't see anything wrong with talking about it," Zhan said as he leaned forward and used his hand to gently move me aside. "You've done this before, have you?" he asked Aldo.

I'd been dismissed. Ignored. Pushed aside like a jilted lover!

"Yes. Many, many times."

"I've always been interested in, you know—" Zhan started, then stopped when he glanced my way and saw that my eyes were throwing daggers at his throat.

"It has saved our sex life," Ray-Ray said, and then leaning in, he whispered to Zhan, "Let me talk to him," and nodded in my direction.

There wasn't anything to talk about. It just wasn't going to happen!

"Walk with me, talk with me," Ray-Ray said as he gently took me by the elbow and led me across the floor to a quiet corner.

"Now look, Noah," he said in a soft voice, "it's nothing for you to get upset about. We like you and Zhan and would love to share this glorious experience with the two of you." He murmured this as if our fucking one another was as natural as the four of us sharing a pupu platter. "What are your fears?"

I had plenty. For one thing, Zhan might really like it!

"I'm not afraid—" I began to lie.

"Hush," Ray-Ray said, and pressed his index finger against my lips. "Don't lie to me," he breathed before cocking his head to one side and eyeing me. "I was afraid too, the first time. It was about three years ago. I didn't want my man sleeping with anyone but me. But I also wanted to make him happy, so I allowed it. It was a friend of ours, just as you and Zhan are friends. His name was Darryl. I had always been attracted to him, and I guess Aldo had seen that."

I opened my mouth to utter something obscene, but the look Ray-Ray gave me caused me to clam right back up.

"It was . . ." Ray-Ray's eyes rolled back in his head, and then his eyelids fluttered wildly. It looked as if he were having an orgasm right there in the corner of my living room. That or a seizure.

". . . magnificent," Ray-Ray finished.

He seemed to need a minute or two to compose himself before he went on. There was a light film of sweat on his forehead, and it took everything in me not to reach over and wipe it away. "You have no idea what it's like to unleash yourself sexually with another man while your mate watches and then participates. It's—It's heaven."

I just blinked at him. The skin on Ray-Ray's arms was goosebumping and his cheeks had suddenly developed a twitch. Damn, I thought, that shit must have been good, because the memory alone is getting this man all hot and bothered.

I licked my lips. Suddenly my throat was dry, and there was heat pushing up from my groin. Was *I* getting hot and bothered?

I looked across the room and whatever it was Aldo was saying to my man had Zhan all red in the face. No doubt, Aldo was sharing the same story.

"Just think about it," Ray-Ray said, and patted me on the shoulder.

* * *

That night, Zhan and I lay in bed together, pretending of course to be sound asleep. We hadn't spoken about Aldo and Ray-Ray's proposal, but lying there in the dark, the sounds from the street floating up and filtering through our open window, I knew that we were both thinking about it.

Geneva

It was just past ten. Charlie was sound asleep and Eric was sprawled out on the living-room couch, talking on the phone with Juuuuuuuuuuuuulie.

Me, I was in my bedroom in front of the mirror, trying to pull myself together after having the shock of my life a few moments earlier while sitting on the toilet. I'd barely looked down there . . . you know, at my vagina. I mean, everything I needed to do to it, or for it, was so automatic—washing, wiping—it was just something that's done without any thought, but for some reason as I was sitting there daydreaming, my eyes moved down to that vicinity, and I saw what I thought was a stray thread from my underwear, but when I pulled it, to my horror, I found out that it was attached!

It was a gray hair! On further examination, I found that it had family! I counted six!

When had this happened? I didn't have not one gray hair on my head, so why the hell were they invading the space around my pleasure palace?

Oh, the shame.

So I found myself standing in front of the mirror, looking at the sad state my body had fallen into. I cursed myself as I glared at my reflection. Was that me, dressed in a pair of washed-out pink drawers complete with tattered waistband? Was that my gut? So large and protruding that my sagging titties used it as a shelf?

I looked a mess. A complete and utter mess!

Who was I fooling? Deeka couldn't possibly want that, I thought as I pointed an accusing finger at my reflection. Chevy's comment about Will Smith being too good-looking to want me rang in my ears. The truth always hurt, didn't it?

Deeka was young and good-looking—better-looking than Will Smith, so if Will wouldn't want me, why the hell would Deeka?

He was on the road to success, and I was sure that in the next few years he would be walking somebody's red carpet, and would I be the one to be at his side? I doubted it—shit, I was no Jada Pinkett!

Shutting off the light, I climbed into bed and told myself that that was it. I wasn't going to allow this fling to go any further, because the natural next stop would be sex. And there was no damn way I was going to spread my thirtysomething-year-old legs for a twentysomething-year-old man and have him fall off the bed with laughter when he spotted those gray hairs of mine!

Chevy

I felt good when I walked into my office the next day. I even drank the green tea that was waiting for me on my desk. I really needed those few hours I'd spent out last night with the girls. And to finally sleep in my own bed again! Ahhhh, that alone made me feel like a new woman!

I was musing on the fact of how happy I was to have slept in my own bed, when a soft knock came at my door.

"Come in."

Dante pushed the door open. Even though it was just forty-five degrees outside, Dante was dressed in baggy white Bermuda shorts that almost looked like high-waters on his minuscule frame. On his feet he wore open-toed brown Birkenstocks and a white buttoned-up blouse that had frills cascading down the center.

I didn't get it—but, hey, that was Dante for you.

"What's up, Dante?"

Dante smirked at me. He had a file in his hand, which he tossed onto my desk from where he stood in the doorway.

I slowly put my cup of tea down. "What's this?"

"Well, Miss Honey," he started as he rolled his head

on his neck and pursed his lips, "it seems that you will be accompanying Anja on the Look-See this year."

"The *Look-See*?" I repeated slowly. "What's that?"

My ignorance did nothing but infuriate Dante. He stepped inside my office and slammed the door behind him. "Don't play coy with me!" he yelled, waving his index finger in the air. "I don't know what you did to get me booted, but I will find out and when I do—" Dante took that moment to use his index finger as a knife and dragged it across his neck while he made a ripping sound with his mouth.

"Dante," I said as I cautiously reached for the file, "I don't know what the hell you're talking about."

"Oh, really, Miss Backstabber!" he bellowed, and then turned on his Birkenstock heels, swung the door open, and stormed out.

I sat there for a moment trying to digest what had just happened. None of it was making sense, so I picked up the folder and opened it.

It was a memo from Anja to Dante with a CC to me.

To: Dante
CC: Chevy

The Look-See this year will take place June 1–June 5 on the beautiful island of Virgin Gorda, which is located in the British Virgin Islands.

We will be staying at the exclusive Little Dix Bay Resort!

Please check your email for travel information.

Chevanese Cambridge will be accompanying me this year. Dante Whitaker will be her backup while she's off-site.

Anja

I read and reread the memo and still didn't know what a "Look-See" was. Oh, well, I laughed to myself as I leaned back into my leather swivel chair, I was going to Virgin Gorda!

Noah

"Look, Miss Drama, I am sick and tired of talking to this goddamn answering machine. I know you're there, so pick up! Pick up!

"Okay, it's like that, huh?

"I know you're working, Miss Thing. It's all over the wire, so I better get my rent money and soon. What do you think? The house is paying for itself?

"And send my money Western Union; I don't want to hear no shit about the check is in the mail.

"In fact, fuck that, deposit my money in my account, take your little narrow ass right down to Citibank and deposit my fucking money!

"CHEVY!

"I don't know why I let you take me there. Why do you take me there? All you have to do is—"

Beeeeeeeeeeeeeeep.

I was so disgusted, I threw the phone across the room and it shattered on impact against the wall, then fell to the floor in a crumpled heap of plastic, wire, and microchips.

I was mad, mad as hell, and not at Miss Drama!

I had agreed to do it. And as soon as I agreed, I regretted that I had. Zhan just seemed too goddamn happy!

"When should we do it?" he asked, beaming at me across the room.

"You're an eager little bunny," I snapped.

Zhan didn't say a word. He knew that if he even looked at me wrong, I would use that as a reason to start an argument and then I could renege on my agreement!

"I don't care," I finally said, when Zhan didn't bite.

Now the date was set for next Friday at the Savoy Hotel.

What had I done?

Crystal

"Where are we going?" I laughed as Neville dragged me by the hand down the sidewalk.

"I told you, it's a surprise," he said as we rounded the corner and headed for the subway.

Neville had called me at work earlier in the day to tell me that he would be meeting me after work. When I asked what he had planned, he just said, "You'll see."

Really, I didn't need to go anywhere but to bed with him. I feared that I'd become a nympho! It seemed as though my appetite was insatiable, but thank God, I'd found a man that could keep up with me. Sometimes we found ourselves doing it two or three times a night!

Once down in the subway, the platform was packed tight with people. We managed to squeeze ourselves into the first car of the number 4 train. Pressed up against each other and other people excited me, and I could tell that Neville was getting a rise out of it as well, because his dick was like solid rock against my stomach.

He bent down and pecked me on the lips, then whispered, "Behave yourself, Crystal," as I'd started grinding myself against him. "Behave yourself or else," he warned again.

"Or else what?" I teased as I pushed myself closer to him.

"Or else I'm going to tickle you."

That was enough for me. I backed down.

We exited the train at Union Square and climbed the stairs with the throngs of people heading who knew where. Shoot, I was one of them.

"Can't I just get a hint?" I said as Neville walked a bit behind me, his hand pressed into the small of my back as he guided me through the sea of people.

"Nope."

We rounded the corner and stopped briefly to stare into the dressed windows of the ABC Carpet store. "There's a dresser in there I've been wanting for a long time," I commented. "Can we go in?"

Neville looked at the black-and-white Swatch watch he wore on his wrist and said, "No, we don't have time." Grabbing me by the wrist, he gently pulled me down the street and around the corner.

"Here we are," he said, his voice hardly able to contain his excitement.

Where were we? I was looking at a six-story building badly in need of a paint job.

"What's here?"

"The surprise," he said, and bounded up the five stone steps. "Come on." He pushed the glass door open and walked into the lobby.

The lobby was small with a black-and-white marble floor. The doors, which I assumed opened into apartments, were all painted white.

Maybe he had a friend here he wanted me to meet?

"We have to go upstairs to the top floor."

"Where's the elevator?" I asked, spinning around in a circle.

"There is none."

I let off a heavy sigh. My idea of a surprise did not include climbing five flights of stairs.

"Crystal, you're a runner; these little bit of stairs are not going to kill you."

"I was a runner," I said, dramatically throwing my hands on my hips. "But that was before I started fucking you. Now I do all my best work on my back!"

Neville grinned and said, "I love it when you talk dirty!"

Yes, I'd become quite comfortable playing the filthy-mouthed sex kitten.

I followed him up the stairs. Once on the top floor, I looked to see just one lone apartment door. I was sweaty, partly from climbing the stairs and partly from the heavy petting that went on between us on the landings.

"This better be worth it," I breathed as Neville gave me a sly look before walking over to the door and knocking.

Geneva

When Deeka called that night, I picked up the phone, said hello, then said, "Hold on," before I yelled for Eric, even though I could hear Deeka saying, "No, no, 'Neva, I want to talk to you!"

After that, I spent the whole week avoiding him. I even called in sick a few days so that I wouldn't run into him at the diner.

But that had backfired on me when Deeka walked in there and asked Darlene point-blank where I was, and, as Darlene relayed it to me, when she asked, "Who the hell wants to know?" Deeka said, "Her man, that's who!"

"Giiiirrrrl, I knew you were robbing the cradle!" Darlene screamed into the phone when she called to tell me what had gone down.

So now I knew my business was all in the street. Darlene was like the *Daily News*! I was down and out. I mean, really depressed; not having Deeka around was like having a gray cloud over me. I couldn't believe that I had grown so used to him in such a short time.

Not even Charlie and her corny jokes and mispronounced words could drag a smile from me, and it was so bad, Eric, who hardly ever noticed anything, noticed.

"Ma, what's got you looking so down lately?"

I was curled up in my bed, watching television but not watching television, you know?

I just shrugged my shoulders and muttered, "Nothing."

Eric sat down on the side of the bed and patted my arm. "You know, whatever it is, you can tell me. Maybe I can help."

I looked up and gave him a sad smile. I wished I could tell him, but I knew in my heart of hearts that my nineteen-year-old son would not understand my having an affair with his manager, his *boy*.

"Oh, baby," I moaned, "Mama's just tired is all."

"Just tired?"

"Yeah, just tired," I repeated, and turned my eyes back to the television.

"Well, I guess you would be. You and Crystal and Chevy been running the streets pretty hard lately," he laughed.

They'd been my excuse for my nights out with Deeka. My luck had been good. Crystal was distracted with who knew what, and Chevy, for the first time in her life, was bogged down with work, so neither of them called me as much as they usually did. And I never said exactly who I was out with. All I ever told Eric was that I was out with the girls and he automatically assumed it was Crystal and Chevy.

"Yeah, that must be it," I yawned.

"Well, maybe you're getting a little too old for that," Eric innocently commented, but the damage was done. There was that word again. *Old.*

Chevy

Well, I'd found out that a Look-See was what Anja referred to as an on-site inspection. Once or twice a year, she traveled to a luxury resort for the purpose of deciding whether she would holiday there over Christmas with thirty or forty of her closest friends.

The resort, eager to please and of course confirm a large party of upwardly mobile celebrity types with cash to burn, always comped Anja and her staff.

From what I heard around the water cooler—which actually dispensed green tea—was that Dante had been on the last four Look-Sees and had just assumed that he would continue traveling with Anja for the next twenty or so more years. Now I had come in and changed all that.

"You better watch your back, Chevy," one girl with limp brown eyes and a baldy warned me. "He'll slice you and dice you, and we'll never even find your body," she said, and then made hissing sounds with her mouth before turning her fingers into claws, swiping at the air in front of me, and scurrying away.

I just laughed it off, even though the baldy hadn't cracked a smile.

In the dining room, I ate alone while Dante held court at the twelve-seater table, talking loudly about what horrible things could befall a backstabber.

Me, I did my best to ignore his stupid ass, but I have to admit, the hairs on my neck were at attention, and I was on guard.

If I could just get through this last week, I would be off to sunny Virgin Gorda.

Friday would begin the long-awaited Memorial Day weekend. Anja was hosting a huge party at Babalu's for the rapper Loose Change, the very same artist I had traveled all the way to Connecticut for. I would be there to assist and then I was off until Tuesday! I just had to watch my back for four more days.

I looked cautiously over my shoulder. Dante was staring right at me; I stared back as I bit down into my ten-dollar tuna sandwich.

Noah

"H-hello?"

"Noah?"

"No, this is Zhan . . . Who the hell is this?"

"Sorry, Zhan. It's Crystal. Is Noah there?"

"Well, where else would he be? Hold the line. Noah, Noah, wake up; it's one of your bloody American girlfriends. Bloody Christ, can't they ever call at a decent hour?"

"Hello?"

"Noah, I'm so sorry. Did I wake you?"

"Crystal? What in the world is wrong?"

"I just have to talk to you about something."

"Miss Thing, it's—it's five o'clock in the morning."

"It is? I'm sorry. I just can't get the time thing right. It's just midnight here."

"So what's the problem this time?"

"I—I did something that I'm not really proud of."

"Girlfriend, you already confessed to me that you were boning Neville. What could be worse than that?"

"I told you, Noah, he doesn't look anything like he did when we were kids."

"If you say so. So what did you do?"

"Well, I, um—I just don't know how to tell you this."

"Spit it out, spit it out."

"Well, I just came in from a . . . a . . . a . . ."

"Come on, you can do it. You came in from an abortion clinic. I told you to make sure that man covered his dick. He could have given you something worse than a baby if you know what I—"

"Noah, no!"

"Well, what can be so bad?"

"I just came in from a swingers' party."

"A what?"

"What did she do this time, baby?" Zhan whispered from beside me.

I didn't even want to tell Zhan, seeing the day for our little sex quartet was quickly approaching and I was still trying to concoct a way to get out of it. Why the hell was she calling with this information now?

"Um," I started, then quickly blurted out, "Crystal went to a swingers' party."

Zhan's eyes lit up. "Really? Oh, well, let me run in the other room and pick up the extension. I've got to hear this!"

"No, no. Tell Zhan not to, please," Crystal said.

I caught Zhan by the elbow and tugged him gently back into the bed. "Zhan, I will relay all the details when I'm finished," I whispered after covering the mouthpiece with my hand.

I couldn't believe Neville had gone that far. I wondered if Peyton knew that he'd taken her daughter to a swingers' party. Well, I wasn't going to mention it, if she didn't. But for the moment, I had to play ignorant.

"How in the world did you end up at a swingers' club? Did Miss Drama take you?"

"No, Chevy didn't take me. Neville did."

"Didn't I tell you he was a freak?"

"Yes, you did."

"Well, go on, unload, tell me all about it."

"You see what had happened was . . ." Crystal began, and over an hour she divulged all the sordid events of that evening.

* * *

"After Neville knocked on the door, a gorgeous woman dressed in what I thought was a fashionable red silk dress and matching floor-length duster opened the door—I would realize later that it was a high-end set of lounge wear. We walked into the apartment, which actually took up the entire sixth floor—at least three thousand square feet.

"The woman introduced herself as Cookie, but I doubted that that was her real name. Long black hair, with high cheekbones and deep dark eyes. She looked Cherokee to me, but I never asked.

"Neville introduced me, then took my hand as we followed her down a long hallway. The walls were painted red, and there was incense in the air and marijuana too.

"The long hallway ended at the mouth of a large living room with at least six overstuffed sofas—also red— and quilted floor pillows.

"There were about twenty people in the room. Some were sipping champagne, while others helped themselves to the silver trays of petit fours.

"When we entered the room, people acknowledged us with a nod, a soft hello, or a quiet smile.

"The whole scene was very cozy. Very inviting.

"Neville took a seat near the windows, which were blacked out. Soft music came from somewhere—I think it was Middle Eastern, lots of bells and cymbals. It was nice.

"'How long have you known Cookie?' I asked Neville after she'd brought over two flutes of champagne.

"'Not long,' he said as he scanned the room.

"'This is a little weird, but nice,' I said. 'Is this my surprise?'

"'The beginning of it.'

"Before long, I began to feel funny. I mean, a little queasy, but more horny than anything. I had another glass of champagne, and then Cookie brought over two tall bottles of sparkling water.

"'Make sure she drinks all of it and then some,' I heard Cookie whisper to Neville.

"'Why is that?' I said, barely able to keep my hands off him by then. I was already in his lap, not even knowing how I got there. I was nibbling on his neck and my fingers were stroking his cheek. I wanted to touch him down there, but I controlled myself because we were in this public space, you know, Noah?"

"Uh-huh, go on, Ms. Crystal."

"Okay, well, he said, 'Drink this, baby,' as he poured me a tall glass of water. And I did, with no objections.

"The music seemed to swell, and all I wanted to do was to take my clothes off. I was hot from the inside out.

"'Damn, does she have AC?' I inquired when I finally pulled my lips off his neck.

"'Why? Are you hot, baby?'

"'I'm baking!'

"'Well, go on and take your clothes off.'

"I just looked at him. I thought he'd lost his mind. I mean, as much as I wanted to do just that, I wouldn't, because we were surrounded by a room full of strangers. But when I turned around, everybody was naked!

"'Ohmigosh!' I screamed, and threw my hands over my mouth. Not only were they naked, but they were all engaged in one sexual act or another.

"'What the hell is going on here!' I screamed, turning to Neville.

"'Whatever you want to go on here.'

"As absurd as his answer was, something inside me urged me not to fight it.

"I turned to look at the couples once again, and found myself getting hot just watching them. I mean, it was like watching a live porn show!

"'You get undressed first,' I whispered as I slid off his lap. And just like that, Neville stood up and disrobed. His cock reached out for me, and while I'm not a fan of fellatio, it was so beautiful, sleek, and shiny black that I suddenly had to have it in my mouth!

"So there I was, on my knees on the settee, blowing Neville Gill!

"When I was done, wiping his juice from my chin, I looked around to see if anybody had been looking, but Noah, all those people were in their own Kama Sutra world!

"After that, I stripped down to nothing. I felt so powerful at that moment that I didn't care who was watching, and all I wanted to do was ride Neville until the sun came up!

"And Noah, as weird as this story already is, it gets weirder!

"Neville was already seated when I tried to mount him, but he gently pushed me aside. 'Drink some more water,' he urged, and I was like, 'What is this with the water?'

"'Just drink it, trust me,' he said, and when I lifted the glass to my lips, he got up and strolled across the room and stood alongside a couple who were doing it doggy-style.

"He tapped the man on the shoulder just as nonchalantly as if he were interrupting him on the dance floor. I winced, because I expected that big black man to turn around and slap the shit out of Neville, but he didn't. He just pulled his dick out of that woman, smiled at Neville, then stepped away. Neville didn't miss a beat, he rolled a condom onto his penis and slipped right into that woman!

"For some reason, as shocking as the scene was to me, all I could think of was, Where in the hell did he get that condom from?

"I was sitting there with my mouth open, trying to rationalize what I was seeing, when I saw that the very same man that Neville had interrupted was staring dead at me.

"My mouth was still open by the time he was standing in front of me, and I realized that his short black dick was level with my open mouth, so I promptly snapped it shut.

"'You want me to eat you?' he asked.

"Noah, I tell you, I couldn't even speak at that point, I was in such shock!

"'Well, what do you want to do?' He grinned as he grabbed hold of his dick and shook it at me.

"Noah, I'm going to share this with you, and you better never repeat it to another living soul because I will hunt you down and kill you, but all I did was lean back and spread my legs.

"I didn't even know this man's name, and there I was, my legs cocked open, ready to receive him!

"He ate me first. Was down there chomping for a good long time before he finally reached into one of the crystal candy dishes—well, what I thought was a candy dish—and plucked out a condom.

"He put it on and rode me until I hollered for help!

"And Noah, he was the first of three strangers I would fuck that night.

"Noah? Noah?"

"I'm—I'm sorry, Miss Thing. I'm just in a bit of a daze is all."

"Me too."

"I mean, this is something that I would expect Geneva to do, not you."

"I know. I know."

"I mean, even Miss Drama."

"Well, there would have been money involved."

"Yeah, you're right about that."

"I feel so cheap."

"And you should!"

"Thanks a lot, Noah."

"I'm—I'm sorry. You know Neville gave you ecstasy, right?"

"What?"

"Ecstasy, girl. That's why you got so horny so quickly, and that's why he wanted you to continue drinking as much water as possible."

"He drugged me? I thought it was the champagne."

"Well, you thought wrong. Anyway, where is he now?"

"I don't know. He dropped me off and went out."

"Hmm, probably went to get some more pussy, the ho!"

Geneva

I'd been sneaking calls from the stockroom, trying my best to get hold of Crystal. But her secretary said she'd taken the day off. All I was getting at her apartment was her answering machine, and her cell phone kept going to voice mail.

I really needed to talk to her about this whole situation with Deeka. It was killing me, keeping it from her, and I just couldn't spare the ten dollars I'd have to spend for a phone card to call Noah.

So I was going to tell Crystal and get some decent advice for a change. I was about to pick up the phone and dial her number for the eighth time when Darlene's head popped around the door, and she exclaimed, "Lover boy is outside!"

"Shit. Did you tell him I was here?"

"Yes, I did," she said gaily before disappearing.

Panicked, I remained where I stood and was just about to dash out the back door when I heard Darlene's voice shrilly stating, "Hey, you can't go back there!"

"Geneva!"

I turned slowly around to face him.

"Why are you doing this to me, 'Neva?" he asked.

His face seemed drawn, his eyes red. Had I done this to him?

"Deeka, it's not right; it's just not right."

"What's not, 'Neva? That I love you? When did loving someone become wrong?"

"But you're so—"

"So what, Geneva? So young? Age is just a number; it has nothing to do with what a person feels in his heart."

"Look at me," I said, my eyes welling up with tears. I spread my arms out at my sides. "Is this what you really want?"

"Yes."

Deeka rushed to me then and embraced me. I fought weakly for a moment, and then I melted into him.

"I love you, Geneva. You've got to believe me," Deeka whispered into my neck.

"But—" I started, but he hushed my objections with a long, lingering kiss.

"But . . ." I began again when we finally came up for air, "but what if it doesn't work?"

"If it doesn't work, at least we can't say we didn't try."

We kissed again, and somewhere off in the distance I heard Darlene blubbering like a two-year-old.

Chevy

Surprisingly, I wasn't required to wear the usual ANJA's BITCH T-shirt to Babalu's. Anja sent around an email advising all the assistants that, while they would not be wearing the T-shirts, she expected all of them to be dressed smartly.

I was thrilled to read that, and while I had a dozen or so magnificent ensembles, I would splurge and buy myself something new.

The something new ended up being a psychedelic halter top that showed off my perfectly perky C-sized breasts and a pair of white denim jeans that hugged my pear-shaped behind. The final touch were the orange and silver slingbacks that cost six hundred dollars and added six inches onto my five-foot-five frame.

I went over to Everything Hair on Fulton Street and purchased me a ponytail, stopped to check out the wares of one of those African brothers who sell silver jewelry on the street, displayed on a strip of velveteen fabric on the sidewalk—you know the ones—and picked me up a pair of diamond-cut silver hoops. A quick stop at Duane Reade for some press-on eyelashes and my retro-chic look was complete.

I packed all of that into my Gucci overnight bag. I wasn't about to wear my outfit into work and then out that evening. Besides, I didn't want one of those ambitious bitches to run out on her lunch break and buy the same getup!

I had a lot to do that day. Anja shot me emails from her Blackberry like bullets. Last I'd heard, she was in Cape May, something about a luncheon with a sorority at the famed Akwaaba by the Sea, but she would be back in NYC in time to kick off the summer with her annual Memorial Day soiree.

I remember reading about the one she'd had last year at Vinshu. *People* magazine and *Upscale* had covered it. Everybody who was anybody was there. It was the summer party to attend—if you could get invited. Anja was very selective about her guest list. I'd been receiving emails for two weeks from society people and celebrities alike, all wanting to know what it was they had to do for *me* to get an invite to the party.

It was in my contract not to accept gifts, but who was I to turn down six pairs of Juicy Couture jeans? I told that publicist girl that I wore a size six and that she should send the jeans to my attention at 330 Stuyvesant Avenue in Brooklyn, and that not to worry, she would be placed on the list!

In the past week I had racked up so much designer shit, it was insane. I wouldn't have to shop for at least four months—but of course I would! The secretary to the chairman of Air Jamaica sent me a case of rum and a first-class round-trip ticket to anywhere the airline flew! You know I put sister-girl down on that list quick, fast, and in a hurry!

I wouldn't take lunch in the dining room that day. Besides the fact that it was eating into my salary, I needed to clear up the last-minute details for the Look-See next week.

Me and three assistants, including a photographer, Anja's makeup girl, and her stylist would be taking a morning flight out of JFK to Puerto Rico. From there we would take a puddle jumper into the island of Tortola, where the Little Dix Bay private yacht would collect us.

Anja wasn't flying commercially; she had hired a private plane to take her directly from Philadelphia to the private airstrip in Virgin Gorda.

I was so looking forward to this trip. But I had to get through the party first. Dante was still really heated.

* * *

Instead of the usual group transfer to the venue, I was assigned my very own sedan. Fine by me. That just meant I didn't have to make phony conversation with my co-workers and that there would be no chance of Dante and me ending up together.

When my sedan pulled up in front of Babalu's there was a line of wannabe guests stretched down the block and around the corner. There was also a crowd of people who'd come just to celebrity-spot.

The NYPD was working double time. They had uniformed officers on the roofs of the surrounding buildings, undercovers blending in with the screaming crowd, and uniformed officers patrolling the barricades with hefty German shepherds.

It was like a scene from the red carpet of the Oscars!

When I stepped out of the sedan, the paparazzi went crazy—well, at first sight they thought I was Anja; it had happened twice before. Personally, I thought I was much better-looking than Anja, and besides, Anja was an Amazon-sized woman! Nevertheless, I smiled and gave them my best Queen Elizabeth wave as I made my way toward the front entrance.

I loved being the center of attention!

It was just eight thirty, and already the club seemed packed to capacity. Beautiful men dressed in nothing but white loincloths walked around with trays heavy with flutes of champagne, while beautiful women dressed in tiny turquoise skirts and bikini tops served chocolate-covered strawberries off golden trays.

DJ Mike served up a nice blend of R&B, hip-hop, and rap music, and the sea of people moved in unison to the rhythm.

I looked across the room and spotted Snoop Dogg, Bianca Jagger, Tyra Banks, and Bill Clinton huddled together near the bar. I wondered what would come out of that meeting of the minds!

Me, I was looking for Loose Change. I had a serious wet spot for him and was dead set on getting his digits or at least giving him mine.

I flipped open my compact, applied a bit more lipstick, gave my ponytail a healthy shake, and went a-huntin'!

* * *

"Where the hell is your headset?" I heard a familiar shrill voice from behind me ask.

I'd been there two hours and had had a lively conversation with Chris Rock and Salma Hayek. Still on the lookout for Loose Change, I felt my head spin from the three glasses of champagne I'd consumed as I turned around to face Dante.

"What?" I said, throwing my hip out and rolling my head b-girl style on my neck.

"I said where is your headset?"

Poor little Dante, in his dark jeans that would have been nice except that the legs were too long and the cuffs dragged the floor even though he was wearing three-inch-heeled espadrilles.

He wore a white blouse that flared at the cuffs and had large shell-shaped pearl buttons down the front.

He'd bleached his short curly hair a golden blond that did nothing for his red complexion, and he had installed a gold loop in his left nostril.

In short, he looked a hot mess!

"Go away, little man," I said, and wiggled my fingers at him. "You're not the boss of me."

Dante grabbed his chest and stumbled backward before letting out a loud dramatic gasp. It was then that I noticed he was wearing nail polish. I knew the color well, Cotton Candy.

"Oh, no, you didn't, Miss Thing!" he bellowed.

I smirked and turned to walk away when my head was suddenly jerked back on my neck.

That queen had grabbed hold of my ponytail!

My hands went up and my champagne flute went sailing through the air.

"You ugly, backstabbing bitch!" Dante screamed as he tugged with all his might. I tried to pull away, but as small as Dante was, he was stronger than he looked because in no time I was on the floor, being dragged through the crowd.

Finally, the ponytail fell off and Dante fell forward. I lay there in a daze, looking up into the astonished faces of the guests.

I couldn't believe that this was happening to me, but before I could get myself together, Dante was on me, bitch-smacking me and screaming, "I hate you! I hate you!"

I tried the best I could to get him off me, but to no avail. Finally, a brawny security guy appeared, snatched Dante up by the collar, and dangled him in the air above me while he kicked and screamed like a banshee. When I was finally on my feet, my face stinging and my outfit soiled and ruined, I tapped the security guard on his shoulder. The security guard turned around and Dante turned with him.

"One thing," I said calmly, then balled up my fist and cold-cocked Dante right on the jaw.

No one bitch-slaps Chevanese Cambridge and gets away with it!

Dante went hurling to the floor, and before I knew it, Security had me too, so Dante and I were both thrown out onto the street.

Dante hurled a few curse words at me before scurrying away. I flipped him the bird, limped over to the curb, and hailed a cab.

* * *

By the time I got back to Brooklyn it was almost midnight. I was sore and pissed off. I'd fucked up again.

There was no way Anja was going to let me keep my job after this fiasco.

Usually I didn't really care about shit like that. But for the first time in a really long time, I felt ashamed of and disappointed in myself.

Could it be true? Was I really that much of a fuckup? I was getting too old to be acting like a twentysomething corporate newbie, jumping from job to job like I had a trust fund somewhere. Shit, I was just twentysomething years away from retirement age, and I didn't have not one dime saved. And if Bush had his way, there weren't going to be any Social Security benefits for me to live on either.

Walking into the dark house, I was feeling almost palpable despair, and for one weird moment, I didn't know what the hell was on my cheeks, because it had been so long since I'd cried.

Crystal

By the time the fog cleared, days had passed, and I woke up one morning to find myself in the midst of a moral crisis. "What the fuck did I do?"

Neville had spent the night out and I was still lying in bed, feeling ashamed and confused when he came bounding in the next afternoon all cheery and shit.

"Hey," he said as he strolled into my bedroom and took a seat on the edge of the bed. "Taking a vacation day?"

I just glared at him.

"What's wrong with you?"

Sitting up, I looked at the clock that sat on the nightstand. It took everything I had in me not to pick it up and knock him in the head with it.

"What's wrong with me?" I said sarcastically. "What the hell is wrong with you?"

Neville's jaw dropped. "Don't tell me you're angry because I didn't come home last night."

"This is not your fucking home!" I screamed, and slung a pillow at him.

"Whoa! Whoa!" Neville said, jumping up from the

bed and barely blocking the pillow. "Where is all this anger coming from?"

Could he be that fucking ignorant?

"You take me to some, some swingers' club, feed me ecstasy, let me fuck strangers, and you ask me where the anger is coming from?"

"I did not feed you ecstasy, Crystal. I wouldn't do something like that to you," he said defensively. "You had two glasses of champagne and, well, the incense that was burning was an erotic stimulant called Cupid, a perfectly natural narcotic. Like weed."

I blinked.

"That still doesn't change the fact that you took me to a place like that and that I did the things I did."

"No, it doesn't, but you made a choice to fuck those men. Nobody put a gun to your head, and besides, why are you so bent out of shape over it? You're a grown woman, a grown woman with a generous sexual appetite. I just thought for a change you'd enjoy being treated to a buffet instead of your usual nightly entrée." He said the last part with a wicked smile. "Besides, since I've been doing you, you've been happier and less stressed. If more people fucked, I mean really fucked, there would probably be no wars."

This man had lost his mind!

"Did you know," Neville said, looking down thoughtfully at his hands before looking back at me, "that the bonobos have sex not for the sole purpose of reproduction, but to ease tension, or to comfort? In short, they substitute sex for aggression."

Yes, yes, he was stone-cold crazy. Here I was grieving over the most immoral behavior I had ever involved myself in, and he was talking about some goddamn monkeys!

"What the hell are you saying?"

"I'm saying, Crystal," he said, reaching for my hands, "that the bonobos are our closest cousins, and they believe in making love, not war, and they're better for it. We should follow their example."

Now I'd heard everything! "You are crazy, aren't you?"

"Far from it," he said as he stood to leave. "Ask your mother, she'll tell you."

"My mother? What does my mother have to do with this?" I threw at his back.

"Just ask her," he said.

Geneva

After all of the attention at work, I just couldn't find it in me to remain there for the rest of my shift. The boss was out and Darlene, a sucker for a good romance novel, was still wiping her eyes when she told me to go on, that she would handle the rest of the shift alone.

Deeka drove me home, and I promised that I would meet him at his place later on that evening so that we could discuss telling Eric and everybody else about our relationship.

Charlie was with my mother, Doris B, and I called Mom and told her that I would need her to keep Charlie until about ten p.m. Mom acted as if it were a chore, but I knew she really enjoyed having Charlie around. They fussed with each other like two old women.

I sat on the couch, staring at my feet, wondering just how I would tell my son that I was in love with one of his friends. I set up what I would say scene by scene in my head, and each time it seemed to end badly. Shaking my head in despair, I reached for my cigarettes and lit one.

There was something else to consider too. I was going to meet Deeka at his place. Surely that meant there was going to be sex. I really wanted to be with him but wondered, once he saw me in the nude, if he'd still want me.

"Ahhhhhh!" I screamed out to the walls as I reached for the remote control and turned the television on. Flicking through the channels, I stopped when I came to BET. A Loose Change video was on, and for a moment I was enchanted. He was one good-looking man. I laughed to myself as I thought how Chevy salivated over him. I wondered briefly how her night at Babalu's was going and made a mental note to give her crazy ass a call in the morning.

Immediately following the Loose Change video was a Jill Scott video. Now there is a big, beautiful black woman, I thought. And wasn't she married? I thought she might be. I propped my feet up on the coffee table and watched.

An Angie Stone video followed. Hey, another big, beautiful black woman, and wasn't she and that fine-ass D'Angelo an item for a while? They even had a child together!

I shot straight up. It was like I had an epiphany. It was as if the spirits of all of the big, beautiful black women were talking to me all at once! What was wrong with being big?

"Not a goddamn thing!" I screamed victoriously.

In no time I was up from the couch and in my bedroom, rummaging through my underwear drawers. "I know I own at least one pair of thongs," I muttered to myself, tossing grandma panty after grandma panty onto the floor until I found the one and only thong I'd ever owned huddling in the corner of the drawer.

It was red silk with brown suede insets on the side and a lacy bow at the back. The tag was still attached to it, and I wondered why I'd never worn it.

Quickly slipping out of my uniform, bra, and panties, I hurriedly slipped it on and immediately knew why it had never been worn.

My bulging stomach sagged over the waistband, and when I turned around to see what the rear view looked like, the bow wasn't even visible—lost somewhere in the crack of my ass!

Yesterday, that view would have left me defeated, but on that day, I looked at myself and said, "Beautiful!"

* * *

After a long hot shower, I creamed my skin with Charlie's baby lotion—I just loved the smell of it—and then doused myself in Jean Naté. Slicking my hair back with some gel, I rummaged through my old makeup bag and found a tube of mascara that was damn near dust when I opened it. It must have been sitting in that bag for five years. I scraped out what I could and applied it onto my lashes.

I'd done some shopping since I'd been seeing Deeka. Not much, nothing like what Chevy and Crystal do. But I'd hit Lane Bryant on a few occasions and had managed to pick up some decent stuff from the sale rack.

Because, for the first time in a long time, I was feeling my femininity, I decided on the sunny white and yellow sundress that I'd purchased for under twenty dollars a week earlier. I didn't have any shoes to match it, so I just slipped on a pair of flip-flops that I'd bought to wear out to Coney Island Beach last year. They were yellow, so it worked for me.

I applied some raspberry-colored lip gloss to my lips, grabbed my pocketbook, and headed out the door. Chaka Khan's "I'm Every Woman" was buzzing in my head as I took the slow-moving elevator down to the lobby and headed out of the building.

"Hello, Ms. Geneva!" some of Charlie's little friends yelled at me when I walked by.

"Hey, kids!" I yelled back.

"Oooh, you look nice, Ms. Geneva!" they sang.

You're damn right I do!

"Thank you kindly!"

I looked nice and I felt good. I was on a natural high. Here I was, the mother of a grown son and young daughter, working as a waitress and living in the projects, on my way to see my twentysomething gorgeous band-manager boyfriend.

What wasn't there to feel good about?

* * *

When Deeka opened the door to his Columbus Circle apartment, he was dressed in a pair of blue sweatpants and a red tank top. His muscles rippled as he took a step back to let me in. In one hand he held a steaming pan of shrimp.

"Hey, baby," he said after he leaned in and kissed me quickly on the lips. "You look wonderful."

I glowed.

"Have a seat, make yourself comfortable."

The apartment was small but cozy. The walls were painted a warm brown and accented by creamy white moldings. There were family pictures on a small glass table beneath the window that looked out on the court-yard, and large framed prints of musical instruments hung on every wall. In addition to that, there were in-struments propped up against the walls. Some I'd never even seen before.

A scented candle sat flickering on the glass table in front of the sofa, alongside a stack of magazines. The floors were glistening hardwood, and I didn't see a speck of dust in sight. He's a better housekeeper than I am, I thought.

I sat down on the leather sofa.

"Can I help you with anything?" I yelled to Deeka, who was in the kitchen.

"No, no, just relax."

Teddy Pendergrass was playing on a stereo I couldn't see, and I just leaned back and allowed myself to let go.

Deeka came in with two glasses of white wine.

"What kind is this?" I asked.

"Chardonnay."

"Hmm." We clinked glasses.

"I'm glad you're here, 'Neva," he said after we'd sipped the wine.

"Me too."

* * *

Dinner was wonderful: shrimp scampi, spinach salad, and wild rice. We ate and laughed and talked and drank, until I looked up at the clock and realized it was practically midnight and we hadn't even touched on how we were going to tell Eric.

"Oh, damn," I said in a panic.

"What's wrong?"

"It's almost twelve o'clock. I didn't expect to be out this late," I said, jumping up from the table. "I have to call Doris B. I know she's having a fit."

Deeka just sat there looking at me.

"Where's the phone?" I said, spinning in circles.

"You're leaving?" he said quietly as he got up and picked the cordless phone up from its base on a wooden stand nearby.

I didn't even answer him. I snatched the phone from him and punched in Doris B's number. It rang three times before Doris B's sleepy voice answered. I began rambling my apologies, but all Doris B said was "Don't you have any upbringing, girl? Don't be calling me at this hour unless someone's dead."

And with that she hung up the phone. That was Doris B for you, but I was more than sure tomorrow I would be getting an earful.

"So?" Deeka said.

"So," I replied as I stared sheepishly at him, "I guess I'm staying."

* * *

All of a sudden I was nervous, standing there clasping and unclasping my hands as I watched Deeka dim the lights, then take a seat on the sofa, tapping the empty space beside him and indicating with a jerk of his head that he wanted me there.

I lumbered over and sat down, practically hugging the arm of the chair while I tried to remember the words to Chaka's song.

"Do you think I'm going to bite you?" Deeka laughed seductively.

I shook my head and gave him a small smile.

"I will, you know, if you want me to," he said, and winked.

I giggled like a schoolgirl as I moved closer to him. We kissed. Small pecks at first, then more urgent probings, and I felt my insides open up and my heart must have dropped down between my legs because there was some steady thumping going on there.

"I want you so bad," I murmured as he covered my face in kisses.

His only response was one hand pushing beneath my dress and massaging my vagina through the silky material of the thong, while the other worked at pulling my breast out from the confines of the sundress.

His mouth was on fire by the time it reached my nipple. I could hardly catch my breath, and then all the air went out of me when his hand, the one under my dress, suddenly found its way up inside of me.

"Damn, you're so wet, so fucking wet," he mumbled.

He moved his finger in and out of me, and I ain't going to lie, it felt good, but I needed something bigger!

"I want you, I want you," I breathed over and over again.

And suddenly I was in the air. That man had swooped my two-hundred-plus pounds up like I was as light as a feather.

In his bedroom, he placed me gently down onto his king-sized bed and began to slowly undress me. When I was just down to my thong, he looked at me and said, "You are one sexy woman, Geneva Holliday."

My excitement spilled over, and I flung my legs wide open while I watched him slip out of his clothes. There it was: the biggest, blackest, prettiest dick I had ever seen. "Oh, shit," I said, and then fear took hold of me. Would I be able to handle it all?

He moved closer and it seemed to swell.

Slowly, my legs began to close, but Deeka didn't seem to notice. He pulled the drawer to the nightstand open, pulled out a condom, and, ripping the package open with his teeth, he expertly rolled it onto his throbbing cock.

Something in me told me that I was in store for one hell of a ride! Climbing on top of me, he began to cover me in kisses again, as he tugged my thong off. It took a moment, seeing that the decorative bow at the back was lodged in the crack of my ass, but it finally came free.

As Deeka positioned the tip of his dick at my hole's entrance, I held my breath and squeezed my eyes shut while he slowly eased himself in. Damn, it felt good to have a real dick up inside of me and not a stiff plastic dildo!

He slid the tip of his penis in and out, in and out, until we could both feel my muscles relax and give way so that he could slip another inch in, and then another, and then another, until my legs were wrapped tightly around him.

"Are you okay?" he breathed into my ear.

I was just fine!

He smiled at me, kissed me beneath my eyes, and on the tip of my nose before sliding his hands beneath my bottom and raising it up off the bed. My breath caught in my throat.

"Breathe," he whispered as he sank deeper into me. "Breathe, baby, breathe." And I did, and that man's dick touched something up inside of me that had never been touched before.

"Oh, shit," I moaned as pleasure tore through me. I grabbed hold of his shoulders, bit down onto his shoulder blade, and churned my hips against his. I was in ecstasy. "Baby, baby, baby!" is all I could mumble over and over again. I had never had sex like that. Not ever!

We moved with each other, him up inside of me, our tongues dancing, our hands pressing and kneading; I swear it went on like that for hours. Whenever he asked, "Do you want me to stop?" my only answer was to pull him deeper inside.

When finally neither one of us could take any more, he wrangled my legs up and over his shoulders. I didn't know if I could take all that dick slamming into me at one hundred miles an hour, but it was apparent that he was ready to spew his load, so I squeezed my eyes shut and braced myself.

In and out, in and out—his rhythm quickly gaining speed until he was pounding into me—and still he managed to touch that spot up inside of me and I forgot that my head was banging against the headboard, and dug my fingers into his waist and helped him bring it on home!

We came together; me screaming my head off and him babbling in a language I'd never heard before.

Noah

I didn't want to look appealing, and I certainly didn't want Zhan to look appealing, but didn't he take a shower, lotion his body, and pull on the red raw-silk boxers I'd given him for his birthday? The ones that he looked totally scrumptious in! I always thought they were for my eyes only. I guessed I'd thought wrong.

"Is that what you're wearing?" Zhan laughed when he turned around to see me standing in the dingiest, holeyest pair of drawers I could find. In fact, I'd pulled them from the bag of rags we kept for dusting the furniture.

"Yes, I am," I said defiantly. Zhan just muttered something and reached for his Levi's.

"I don't want to do this, Zhan. I don't!" I whined, crossing my arms across my chest and stomping my feet into the green and gold area rug on the bedroom floor.

Zhan turned toward me, his eyes filled with disappointment. "But you said you would. You promised."

That I had.

"Well, I've changed my mind." I couldn't look at that pained expression on his face any longer, so I turned my attention to the window. "I won't do it."

Zhan stayed quiet for a moment. "Okay," he murmured as he pulled his T-shirt over his head. "I don't want you to do anything you don't want to do," he said in a defeatist tone. "But I think you should be the one to tell them."

I didn't want to be the one to break it to them. I didn't want to look like a chicken, a wimp, a scaredy-cat!

"Fine."

* * *

Ray-Ray greeted us at the door. He was dressed in vibrant green silk lounging pajamas. I could immediately tell that he didn't have any briefs on because his manhood was swinging freely beneath the material. For a brief second I regretted my decision. Averting my eyes, I brought them back up to Ray-Ray's face and smiled brightly. "Hey."

"Well, good evening," Ray-Ray responded, and kissed me lightly on the cheek, then did the same to Zhan. "Come in, come in."

The lights were dimmed, and there was soft jazz playing in the background. Incense was burning on Buddha stands in all four corners of the apartment. "Sit down. Aldo is still getting dressed. We figured we'd unwind with some wine and cheese here before heading over to the hotel."

Zhan looked at me and nodded his head for me to begin. I opened my mouth just as Aldo walked into the room. I knew Aldo had a nice physique, but I didn't know how nice. He hadn't bothered to dress and was standing in the doorway wrapped in just a blue and white terrycloth towel. He'd fashioned his silver hair into the style

Elvis Presley had made famous. His lips looked remarkably pink, and his chest appeared to be chiseled out of granite. My heart quickened.

Ray-Ray approached him and placed a long, smoldering kiss on his lips. As he did so, Aldo reached around and caught a good bit of Ray-Ray's behind in his hands and squeezed.

Zhan and I watched, shifting uncomfortably in our seats as they carried on as if we weren't even in the room. I felt my dick begin to stiffen. I looked at Zhan and saw his Adam's apple bobbing up and down in his throat. Something that happened whenever he was turned on.

I loudly cleared my throat just as Ray-Ray reached for the knot on Aldo's towel.

"Oh, dear me," Ray-Ray said, turning around and looking at us. "Please forgive me." His face had a crimson sheen to it. I didn't know if it was from the heavy foreplay I'd just interrupted or the fact that he was embarrassed.

"Yes, please excuse our display," Aldo added, and then he said, "Wine?"

"It's that damn Cupid is what it is," Ray-Ray said as he walked toward us. His dick was as stiff as a corpse and seemed to be pointed right at me. Zhan's mouth opened and then closed, and then he stood up abruptly and mumbled something about helping Aldo with the wine. I was left alone with Ray-Ray and his dick.

"Cupid?" I asked, looking down at the floor. He certainly wasn't making it easy for me. Already I felt my conviction crumbling. I pressed my knees tightly together and tried to think of something that would kill the heat growing in my groin area.

"Yes, Cupid. Haven't you heard about it? It's the newest thing in sexual stimulants."

"Oh, what is it—some type of pill?" Why was he just standing there in front of me like that? In a minute I was going to rip those fucking silk pants off and suck him off like a Tootsie Pop! And what was up with the heat? I was burning up. Or at least I thought I was. Could horny feel this hot?

"No, it comes as an incense stick," he said, and pointed at the burning incense sticks around the room. "My brother, Jo-Jo, and a cousin of mine developed it. It's all the rage."

"Oh, wow," I muttered and wiped at the perspiration on my face. "May I have some water?"

"Of course you can, but I'd rather you wait until we're ready to"—he paused, then smiled wickedly before grabbing his dick and shaking it at me—"hit the sheets, because the water really intensifies the mood. Aldo and I have had three glasses already, hence our erotic display."

Oh, great!

Crystal

I didn't speak to Neville for the rest of the day, or the evening for that matter. It didn't take much for Neville to get the hint because he'd prepared a tasty dinner, and when I didn't emerge from my bedroom, he left.

I lay in my bed like a stubborn child, even though my stomach was growling like there was no tomorrow. But when I heard that front door close, I was up and in that kitchen, digging into the pots like I'd just come off a hunger strike.

Don't get me wrong, I remained angry the whole time I was gobbling down the stew, peas, white rice, and fried plantains. Angry still when I drank the two glasses of freshly prepared sorrel he'd made. And just as angry when I picked up the phone and called my mother, who I hadn't called since she'd been in Vegas.

"Hey, Neville," she said when she answered the phone on the fourth ring. My breath caught in my throat. "You and Crystal still getting it on?" She snickered wickedly.

"Ma!" I screamed into the phone.

"Oh! Oh!" Peyton was flustered, and Peyton Atkins

never got flustered. "Hello, darling, how are you?" she said meekly.

"Don't 'Hello, darling' me. What the hell is going on?"

"What are you talking about, dear?" she said, trying to sound as innocent as possible.

"I'm talking about you and Neville!"

"Neville? Oh, is he still staying with you?"

"Stop it, Mother. You answered the phone fully expecting it to be him. Why?"

Peyton was quiet for a minute. "Well, sweetheart—"

"Cut the sweetheart shit—"

"Don't you dare speak to me that way, Crystal Atkins. You ain't too grown for an ass-whipping!"

"Just tell me what this is all about."

"Well, baby, you see, it's just that since Kendrick left and you stopped getting it on a regular basis . . . I mean, you've been so grouchy and miserable, and sex is such a natural thing, I just thought that you should be with someone you were already comfortable with, so Neville just seemed the logical choice because he's an expert and all—"

"What?" I said, astonished.

"He's an expert—"

"He's a male prostitute?"

"Well, he likes to be called a coastline executive, honey—"

"You got me a rent-a-dread, Mother!"

"Well, he doesn't like that title either, baby. You see—"

"I can't believe you turned your own daughter into a trick!"

"Oh, stop being so dramatic, Crystal!"

"Dramatic! As if what you've done isn't?"

"Look, from what I've heard, he has done his job and done his job well, because the reports I've been getting tell me that you've never been happier!"

"Reports? Reports from Neville?"

"Not from Neville, from Noah."

Geneva

I turned over and fully expected to open my eyes and see the chipped paint on my bedroom ceiling, but what I saw was the spinning wooden blades of Deeka's ceiling fan. I grinned; it really hadn't all been a dream.

He had spooned himself into me. His naked body felt so good pressed up against mine. It felt right.

"Morning," he whispered in my ear, and then kissed my neck.

"Morning," I whispered back, and then pushed my backside into him.

He snickered. "Well, you're a morning girl too, huh?" he said, his penis already growing hard against me.

We'd made love all night long, and I should have been exhausted, but I wasn't.

"I'm an anytime-of-the-day kind of girl," I said as I positioned myself for entry.

* * *

I wanted to cook him breakfast. I mean, he'd cooked me such a wonderful dinner, and made such sweet love to me, it was the least I could do. And so I'd put eggs and bacon to fry in this big black pan his grandmother had given to him. Somehow, I don't know, we ended up back in the bedroom, the eggs and bacon forgotten, my legs up over his shoulders, and then the alarm went off!

The apartment was filled with smoke, and we laughed as we, naked as the day we were born, ran around opening windows.

"Go put on a T-shirt, 'Neva," he said as he walked toward the front door. "I'm going to open the door and let some of the smoke out."

"Yeah, your neighbors are going to really love that," I said as I sashayed away. I slipped into the bedroom, pushed the door just far enough on its hinges so that I couldn't be seen, but I could see them.

When Deeka opened the door, Eric was standing in the hallway.

"Hey, man, I was just about to ring the bell," he started, then looked down at Deeka's dick. "Yo, sorry, man, I didn't mean to interrupt," he said, giving Deeka a wink and then turning his head away. "I just came to get my sticks. Remember, I left them in your truck the other night?"

Eric had taken Deeka totally off guard, and he stood there for a minute in shocked silence before finally muttering, "Yeah, yeah, man. Just wait here and I'll get them."

Removing the crochet throw from the back of the sofa and wrapping it around his waist, he scurried around looking for the sticks, all the while praying that I wouldn't come out of the bedroom.

Eric spotted his sticks on a small wooden table across the room near the kitchen. Deeka's back was turned when Eric said, "Oh, I see 'em, man," and started across the room. By that time he heard Eric laugh and say, "Damn, man, you certainly ain't no cook. These eggs and bacon burnt to a crisp. My mama do the same thing all the time."

He was peering down into the black pan, and I was skipping out of the bedroom dressed in one of Deeka's blue and white football jerseys that didn't even hit my waist.

Noah

"Baby, stop crying. I can't understand what you're saying?"

"He—he, and I—I, and then Eric and—"

"Take a deep breath, honey, a deep breath."

"O-okay . . . when, when I walked out, Eric was standing there and I—I was damn near naked, I mean I had the shirt on, but, but it wasn't long enough and everything was showing, you know?"

"Uh-huh."

"And at first I could tell that Eric wasn't even sure it was me, and then his face just changed and his mouth dropped open, and he looked at Deeka and then at me and started screaming, 'You're fucking my mother!' over and over again."

"Oh, God."

"And D-Deeka was trying to explain that it wasn't like that; he was trying to explain that we were in love, and I was trying to hide myself, and then Eric looked at me and called me a slut!"

"No, he didn't!"

"Yes, and Deeka went to him, and Eric shoved Deeka so hard that Deeka fell over the couch."

"What!"

"I was screaming, and Eric was screaming that he hated me, and then he just walked out."

"Oh, my God! Oh, my God!"

"Yes, and by the time Deeka drove me back home, Eric was gone."

"And that was two days ago?"

"Yes. I—I don't know where my baby is, Noah! I've called everybody, and nobody's seen him!"

"Maybe they're just saying they haven't, Geneva."

"I really fucked up, Noah. I really fucked up!"

"Geneva, let me tell you something. You are a grown woman and you've earned the right to fuck and love whoever you want to, do you hear me? That boy of yours ain't nothing but a spoiled brat!"

"But, Noah—"

"But, Noah, nothing. I gotta mind to get my ass on the plane right now and beat the black off of that boy of yours!"

"Noah, but—"

"How dare he call you those names? How dare he, Geneva!"

"I know, but—"

"I don't care if he walked in on you fucking forty of his friends, he had no right, none at all!"

"I—I—"

"You tell him to call me when you see him. You tell him to call me collect!"

I slammed the phone down and turned over roughly in the bed. I'd relegated Zhan's ass to the couch and didn't know when, if ever, he'd be allowed back into our bed.

He'd cheated on me. Yes, he did. So what, it was just a kiss; that's how it fucking starts!

When Ray-Ray went to get the water for me, I heard him squeal with laughter and then say, "Okay, boys, you can't do it right here on my clean kitchen floor!"

I don't even remember jumping up off the couch; I just remember being in the doorway, staring at my man and Aldo in a lovers' embrace up against the refrigerator and, oh, yeah, I remember lifting the rolling pin off the counter and clocking Zhan right in the head with it! After that, I left in a rage, Zhan following behind me with his pathetic apologies.

He tried to explain to me that he didn't know what came over him. He was talking wine with Aldo and had opted for a glass of water because of the heat, and then next thing he knew, he and Aldo were tonguing each other down!

Ray-Ray and Aldo had called a number of times. Of course they didn't understand why I had reacted the way I had; they didn't know that I'd changed my mind. I explained to them the reason for my behavior and they, of course, defended Zhan by saying that his reaction had more to do with the incense than anything else.

I didn't want to hear that shit! Hadn't I controlled myself when Ray-Ray's big dick was just inches from my face?

Crystal

"I won't be in today," I told my secretary.

"Under the weather?"

"Something like that," I said listlessly.

"Oh, okay. Tomorrow then?"

"Maybe," I said, and hung the phone up.

I'd ordered Neville out of my house, and I could hear him in the next room, gathering up his stuff. I was lying in bed, staring at the ceiling, feeling cheap and used.

We'd had a long conversation about the whole situation. I'd ranted and raved about how dishonest he and my mother had been. Neville didn't say much; he just nodded his head in the appropriate places and stared down at his hands.

"I can't believe you make a living being a whore," I'd said to him as I paced the floor.

"It's the oldest profession in the world, Crystal," he'd responded quietly. "And really, if anything, I'd rather you use the term *gigolo*. Because as you now know from your own personal experience, I didn't just fuck you, now did I?"

"Wh-what?"

"I romanced you, Crystal. Made you feel like a woman is supposed to feel. Special, honored, respected."

He wasn't lying.

"That's not the point!"

"Then what is?"

"I was deceived!"

"Yes, yes, your mother and I did deceive you, but for your own benefit. Not like it was with your experiences in the past."

"What are you talking about?"

"Men deceive women for their own gain all of the time, and I know you've experienced that yourself. Your mother tells me there was a man that you were in love with, but he was an addict and—"

"My mother talks too damn much!" I screamed.

Neville raised his hands in surrender. "Okay, I won't even go there, but the point is, what did you get out of that experience? Nothing, right?"

I didn't respond.

"Okay, fine. But this—this was all for you. All for your enjoyment and benefit," he said in a voice that was begging me to see things his way. But I was too angry.

"It's not like you didn't bust a nut, you know!"

"Of course I did." He grinned. "I enjoy my work."

That was it. My anger boiled over, and I walked over and slapped him dead across his face. His head jerked left, and when I raised my hand to do it again, he caught my wrist and said, "You get only one of those."

I snatched my arm from his grasp and backed away from him.

"How much? How much did my mother pay you to fuck me?" I said, my eyes filling with tears. "How much, you filthy bastard? How much?"

Chevy

I'd spent the entire holiday weekend in bed, feeling sorry for myself. All I could do was think about my life and the wrong turns I'd made. And worse still was the fact that nobody seemed to be thinking about me. The phone didn't ring not one time. Even the bill collectors had forgotten I existed.

Tuesday morning came, and I stood by the window watching the employed people hustle down the street toward their jobs. Me, I was dressed in my red teddy, with nowhere to go.

It was just past nine, and I was about to curl up on the couch and watch one of those tired talk shows when the phone rang. I almost jumped out of my skin when it did and was so frazzled that I snatched it off the base and didn't even bother to check the caller ID.

"H-hello?"

"Chevy?"

"Y-yes, who's this?"

"Anja is on her way to Virgin Gorda and has heard from the makeup artist that you are not at the airport. Anja wants to know why."

I pulled the phone from my ear and stared stupidly

down at the buttons. "'Scuse me?" I said when I pressed it back to my head.

Anja let out a long sigh. "Your plane leaves in an hour, and Anja expects you to be on it."

Click.

Geneva

I was sitting on the couch, crying my eyes out on Deeka's shoulder. He'd just come back to my apartment after having been out all night and most of the morning combing the neighborhood in search of Eric.

"I—I have to call his father," I blubbered as I reached for the phone. "He's a policeman. I think I'm going to need to file a missing person report." Just saying those words got me to crying again.

"Shhh, shhhh, 'Neva. He's all right. I'm telling you, he's just crashing somewhere, cooling off. He'll show up; believe me, he will."

I dialed Eric's father's cell phone number. Just when I was being transferred to voice mail, the lock on the front door turned and the door opened.

Eric stepped inside.

"Ohhh, Eric. Oh, my baby!" I wailed, jumping off the couch and nearly running over Deeka to get to my child. I threw myself on him and hugged him as tight as I could. "I'm so sorry, baby. I'm so sorry," I cried.

Eric stood as stiff as a board. He was so empty of emotion, I felt like I was hugging a tree. I stepped back and looked at him. "Eric?"

My son didn't even look back at me. "I came to get the rest of my things," he threw over his shoulder as he stepped around me.

"Yo, Eric, I need to talk to you, man—" Deeka began as he stood up, but Eric just put his hand up and said, "Don't say a fucking word to me, man."

I was about to go after him, but Deeka caught me by the arm. "Leave him, 'Neva. He needs more time."

Ten minutes later, I watched as my son walked out of the apartment and seemingly out of my life.

Chevy

After I'd recovered from the shock, I hurried into my bedroom and packed. I didn't know if I would make it to the airport in time, but I did know there was more than one flight leaving out of Kennedy that could get me to Virgin Gorda before midnight.

As expected, I missed the flight, but the agent was kind enough to reroute me through Miami. From there, I would take a flight to Puerto Rico and then connect from there into Tortola where I would catch the private yacht over to Virgin Gorda and Little Dix Bay.

As hectic as the connections had been and as many hours as I had spent on three different flights and in three different airports, I was reeling with excitement when I stepped onto that yacht. An elderly gentleman with skin as black as coal, a snow-white beard, and a bald head helped me on and then presented me with a cool glass of fruit punch. He introduced himself as Coyote.

"Any rum in here?" I whispered.

Coyote's eyes were glued to my breasts. I was wearing a floral halter top. The material was so thin, it was almost see-through.

"Of course," he said, and winked at me.

The sail over was wonderful. As hot as it had been on land, the cool breeze that sailed off the sea made me forget that the temperature dawdled near ninety-five degrees.

The island itself was small, and grew smaller the closer we came. It wasn't a lush island; in fact, some of the low-lying hills were dotted with cactus. Little Dix Bay itself sat on a half moon—shaped beach. Blue market-sized umbrellas dotted the beach, shading the guests who relaxed on the chaise lounges. I'd done all of my checking in on the yacht, so when we pulled up to the pier I was shown to my room.

My room was actually a cottage. One large room with plenty of windows, a king-sized bed, and generous sitting area complete with sofa. The desk and the bathroom rivaled the ones I had in my office back in New York.

It was fabulous!

"Is everything to your liking, Miss Cambridge?" the young man who'd escorted me asked.

"Oh, yes." I beamed as I threw myself down onto the bed.

"Well, then, if you need anything just dial zero on your phone."

"Okay, I will," I said.

The man turned to leave.

"Excuse me. Haven't you forgotten something?"

"Sorry?"

"My key," I said.

"Oh, no, Miss Cambridge. There are no keys here at Little Dix Bay."

Geneva

"The band has a gig tonight at the Zimba Lounge, and I can't imagine that Eric won't show."

I was gripping the phone to my ear, hearing but not hearing what Deeka was saying.

"'Neva, are you listening to me?" he softly asked.

"Uh-huh."

"Stop worrying yourself about this. It'll blow over; believe me, it will."

I could feel the tears welling up in my eyes all over again when the beeping sound came, informing me of an incoming call.

"Okay, I'm going to pick up my sister, and then we'll head over to the spot. Do you want me to swing by and pick you up?"

"No, I'm going to wait here for my baby to come home," I barked, and abruptly brought our conversation to an end.

In light of the situation, I was having a lot of mixed feelings about my relationship with Deeka. If I'd followed my first mind and kept that boy at a distance, none of this would have happened and my baby would still be home with me.

The phone rang and I quickly pressed talk, hoping against hope that it was Eric.

"Hello?"

"Yeah, Geneva, you called me?" The voice of Eric's father, Big Eric, came through. "I hope we're not going to have yet another conversation about child support. I told you when you decided to keep that baby that I didn't want any more children and you knew that—"

"Our son has run away!" I screamed like a madwoman into the phone.

Noah

"You no-good motherfucker!" I shrieked, and flew at Zhan when he walked through the door that evening. I looked a mess; my process was standing up on my head. I'd been eating chocolate all day, so there was a brown ring around my mouth. I smelled to high heaven, because I hadn't bathed or bothered to roll some deodorant under my arms.

"What!" Zhan cried, and threw his hands up to block the slaps I was trying to levy across his face. He caught my arms and pushed me backward. His pale face was bright red, and the vein in his neck was plump and thumping. "Noah, what in the world is wrong with you?"

"You cheater, cheeeeeaaaater!" I screamed as I jumped up and down in place. I'd spent the whole day obsessing over what had gone down the other night, and now I was mad all over again. I'd tried to call Zhan at work to cuss him out, but his secretary said he'd left for the day. That was two o'clock, so where the hell had he gone? 'Cause he certainly wasn't here with me! He and Aldo probably hooked up at the Savoy.

"Cheater?" Zhan truly looked perplexed. He ran his hands through his slick black hair. Something he did when he was trying to think. "Are we back on that again, Noah?"

I folded my hands across my chest and began rapidly tapping my hippo slipper–covered foot on the floor. "Where were you today, huh? Huh? Where?"

Zhan jumped at the crazed pitch my voice had taken on. "I was at work, Noah. Why?"

"But," I said, and threw my index finger out at him, "you left early! Where did you go, Zhan? Where?"

Zhan's face went a deeper red, and he dropped his eyes down to the ground. That was a clear look of guilt. It was true!

I felt the tears begin to well up in my eyes. "Oh, my God. Oh, my God," I said as I brought my hands up to cover my face and began to blubber into my palms.

"But—" Zhan started.

"Don't say a fucking word to me you lying, conniving, cheating British bastard!" I screamed, storming to the bedroom and beginning to pack my clothes.

I was so filled with rage that I didn't see the small, brightly wrapped package that Zhan held out to me, and I barely heard him mumble, "I left work early to pick up this gift for you."

Gifts brought on by guilt, I did not want!

I would go back to America, back to my brownstone on Stuyvesant Avenue, back to my friends and family. Back to my life!

"Fuck you, Zhan, and fuck Mother England!" I screeched.

"What are you doing?" Zhan's voice was filled with panic. "Are you leaving me, Noah?"

I spun around, and through a waterfall of tears I said, "Yes!"

Crystal

I stood with my hands on my hips, waiting for Neville to answer me. "How much?" I screamed again.

Neville looked at me and tilted his head to the side and said, "Nothing. I never cashed the check."

I was stunned. "What? I don't understand," I said, completely confused now. "Isn't this what you do? I mean, you charge women to . . . to—"

"Yes. But not you, Crystal. You were one of my best friends growing up. You were the only one who made me feel like I was okay when I wasn't." He laughed a little then. "You never made fun of my jug head or big feet. I know I wasn't the most attractive child.

"And besides," he continued, "you're a beautiful, sexy woman. What man wouldn't want to make love to you? I know I would have paid *you*, if the roles were reversed."

I just stood there with my mouth open.

"Most of the women I, um, service are wealthy white women who come down for their slave poundings—"

"Slave poundings?"

Neville snickered. "Yeah, that's what we call it. White women who feel bad about slavery and the continued oppression of black people. They feel so bad that they want to help us 'help' *them*, if you know what I mean."

I was starting to.

"But it's different for us with our own women. We may fuck for money, but when it comes to black women, we make love to them—it's impossible to do it any other way—at least it is for me."

I didn't know if he'd just made a beautiful statement about black women or a degrading statement about black men.

"But you want me to leave and I will," he said, turning and walking away.

* * *

Now, I was lying alone in my bed, replaying the whole scene, I wondered if I'd made the right decision.

I had overreacted. I knew that I had. Didn't I have a good time? Hadn't I had the best sex of my life? What the fuck was I so upset about anyway? Okay, that whole scene at the swingers' club was certainly not something I would ever want to do again.

But it had been something, hadn't it?

I laughed out loud at the memory, and then slapped my hands over my mouth. Little Miss Goody Two-Shoes Crystal had fucked a strange man. A few strange men! No one would believe it! I rolled over onto my side. Well, I had gotten what I wished for, right? I mean I had been pining for a good piece of dick since Kendrick left, and I'd gotten just that, hadn't I?

So what was all the fuss about?

Well, Mama being involved still left a bad taste in my mouth, but I guess she really thought she was helping me out. And hadn't she done just that? Yeah, she had. I pulled myself out of bed. A mother's love is something else, I thought, as I started down the hallway toward Neville's room.

Chevy

Attached to the bottle of rum and basket of fruit that had been delivered to my room that afternoon was a note from Anja, instructing me to meet her in the main dining hall for dinner at six p.m.

It was just about four, and I'd been able to take a quick dip in the crystal blue ocean, which was so calm, it felt more like an enormous pool.

I was starving and devoured the mango, banana, and a large portion of the pineapple before I felt anywhere near full. After a shot of rum and a glass of sparkling water, all I wanted to do was sleep. But I knew if I closed my eyes now, I would sleep way past six, so I put myself in an ice-cold shower. That woke me right up.

I was dressed by five, choosing to wear an orange tube dress that sat right above my knee and fit my figure like a silk stocking. I let my weave cascade down over my shoulders and popped my green-tinted contacts in my eyes.

On my feet I wore a pair of Stuart Weitzman six-inch-heeled, open-toed mules that were practically the same color as the dress. A pair of gold bangles and hoop earrings, and I was ready to go. I still had a half hour before dinner, so I took a seat at the bar and ordered a glass of champagne.

The bar area, like the resort itself, was small and very intimate. There were couples all around me, so I focused my attention on the bartender. "Are you enjoying your stay?" he asked, flashing me a row of beautiful white teeth.

"So far, so good," I said as I saluted him with the champagne flute. "So what's there to do here on the island after dinner?"

"Well, not much, you know. There is a bar on the waterfront that closes at about midnight."

"Ugh, midnight!" I screeched with disgust. "No place to shake my booty? No nightclubs?"

"Well," the caramel-colored bartender said, leaning in, "we have very few, but you can still shake your booty, as you say, in other places." He grinned wickedly at me.

I returned the grin and took a moment to really take him in. He wasn't fine, but he had a pleasant look, and from what I could see, his body was tight. I hadn't had sex in ages and the little tingle happening down between my legs that was quickly becoming a very loud TWANG told me that it had been too long.

"And where might someone like me shake her booty after dinner tonight?"

"Hmm, maybe on a private beach, under a moonlit sky."

"Oh, really?" I purred seductively, and rested my elbows on the bar and folded my hands beneath my chin. "And what might one do for music?"

"Ahhh, yes, music. Well the lapping of the ocean against the shoreline is all the music you'll need," he said, and eyed me evenly as he licked his lips.

"You don't say."

"Yes, I do."

"And would I have to find this beach on my own?" I asked as I batted my eyelashes.

"Oh, of course not. I would be more than willing to take you there."

"I'm sure you would." Anja's voice sailed from behind me. My face froze and the bartender blinked, removing my empty glass and slowly making his way down to the other end of the bar.

I turned around on my stool. "Anja!" I said as cheerfully as I could.

"Come, Chevy, Anja does not like to be kept waiting," Anja said, and turned on her heel and strolled away. She was dressed in a sweeping white tunic dress. Her hair was tied up in a matching turban, and she wore large wooden earrings in her ears.

I followed her obediently to the dining area, where a stocky maître d' seated us. I looked around for some of the other staff I knew would be traveling with Anja, but saw no familiar faces. I felt like I should say something about the Friday night brawl with Dante but thought maybe she hadn't heard about it, since she didn't mention it. But then again, Anja knew about everything.

She sat across from me with the menu open, blocking her face. When she did finally decide on what she wanted, she closed the menu and laid it across her dinner plate. I dropped my eyes, but I could feel hers boring into my forehead.

"Look at Anja, Chevy."

And I did.

"Anja does not like scandal," she began as she rolled the tip of her index finger along the rim of her water glass. "Anja only likes scandal when Anja is reporting it. Do you understand?"

I nodded my head.

"Dante has been punished. Which means you must be punished as well," she said in a goddesslike tone. "How do you think Anja should punish you, Chevy?"

Who was I? I couldn't believe I was sitting across from her like some cowardly little girl. The Chevy I knew and loved would never have put up with this bullshit!

Anja smiled, and I realized that this was the first time I'd been less than twenty feet from her since she'd hired me. At this close range, I could see that Anja had a serious stubble problem.

"Chevy?"

"Yes?" I said, dragging my eyes from her chin.

"How do you think Anja should punish you?"

And up close, even in candlelight, she really wasn't that pretty. I mean she was attractive, but something . . .

"Anja will not repeat herself!" Anja hissed.

"I don't know, Anja. Really, I don't," I said, reaching for my napkin and placing it on my lap.

Anja eyed me for a moment before doing the same.

"You admire Anja, don't you?" she said.

I nodded my head.

"Would love to be in Anja's shoes, wouldn't you?"

I nodded my head again.

Anja laughed. "What would you do to be in Anja's shoes?" she asked as she leaned in. I looked up and could have sworn she was leering.

Crystal

I walked up behind Neville, who was shoving something down into his duffle bag. "Neville," I called as I placed my hand gently on his shoulder, "I'm sorry. I behaved badly."

Neville turned around to face me.

I leaned in and pressed my lips against his, but he didn't respond at first. Then his tongue darted in between my lips and found my tongue. We kissed passionately for a moment.

"I don't want you to go," I whispered into his neck. "Not now, not like this," I said.

"But I will have to leave at some point, you know," he said, and I could tell without seeing that he was smiling.

"I know. When exactly will that be?"

"My ticket is dated for a week from now."

I stepped back and slipped my T-shirt over my head. "Wouldn't want you to incur any charges for making changes to your ticket," I said, tossing the shirt to the floor and reaching for the waistband of my sweatpants.

"They can charge up to twenty-five percent of the

ticket price," Neville said as he unbuckled his belt and unzipped his pants.

"That's a crying shame, a crying shame how much these airlines get away with!" I screamed as I threw my naked body against him, knocking him down onto the bed.

Geneva

I sat on the bench in front of my building, chain-smoking as I watched Charlie play with her friends. She'd asked me at least fifty times when Eric was coming home, and all I could say was "Soon."

I'd told Big Eric the whole sordid story and demanded that he haul out the troops to find my son, and all he could say was "I can't believe you're screwing a man half your age."

After I cussed him every which way, damned him to hell, and talked about his mama and ugly new wife, he knew I was serious and said that he would do what he could but that the bottom line was that "Little Eric" was a grown-ass man, and if he wanted to leave the nest, he had every right to do so.

I didn't want to hear that shit and told him so. After a few more choice words, I sent Eric scurrying out of the apartment with his tail between his legs. I told him the next time I saw him he'd better have my son or there was going to be hell to pay!

Deeka stopped by on his way to the club, just missing my ex-husband. He had his sister, Kendra, with him. She was all of seventeen years old. Kendra seemed nice enough, all happy to meet me, talking about how much she'd heard about me. I wasn't in the mood to make anyone's acquaintance, and to tell you the truth, Deeka should have known better, but true to his gender, he wasn't even thinking on that level.

I dropped Charlie off with my mother, lied and said I had some errands to run, and parked myself right outside on the front bench again.

I had my cigarettes and the cordless phone with me. While I chain-smoked, I tried calling Crystal, and when she didn't answer, I called Chevy. Now that was a sign of desperation.

* * *

The way it was told to me, Deeka arrived at the Zimba Lounge at around nine thirty, just as Eric and his band were getting ready to play. Deeka had tried to talk to Eric, but Eric wasn't having it and warned him to get away from him. They'd played four sets when Eric looked across the bar and saw some young fine thing all up in Deeka's face.

He would confide in me later that all he saw was red. This man who had claimed to love his mother flaunting some ho all up in his face like that. His words, not mine. Well, it was all he could do to keep his composure, and right in the middle of one of their songs, he threw his sticks down to the ground and made a beeline toward Deeka.

Deeka was taken completely off guard. I mean, he'd seen him coming on account of the ruckus Eric was causing. He knocked a waiter over and a couple who'd been dancing in the middle of the floor.

Deeka was in so much shock that at first he couldn't move. And then when he could move, he pushed the girl, who turned out to be his sister, out of harm's way. And just in time too, because before Deeka knew it, Eric was all over him like white on rice!

Tables went over and glasses shattered, while women screamed and some men tried in vain to pull Eric off. Deeka would tell me that he didn't want to hit him, but after Eric clocked him twice in the nose, he had no other choice but to defend himself.

They rolled and rolled until Deeka found himself pinned beneath Eric, a steak knife pressed against his throat. It could have gone really bad then. In one fell swoop I could have lost both the men I loved. One to the grave and the other to the penitentiary.

But God is good all of the time, and that low-account, deadbeat ex-husband of mine came upon the scene like Superman and snatched Eric off Deeka.

"What the hell do you think you're doing?" Eric had screamed at his oldest child.

He had ten cops with him, and they all had their guns drawn. When the call came over the radio that there was a fight at the Zimba Lounge, Eric Sr. had responded to it, not knowing that he was about to encounter our son and my lover!

It took a moment for Eric to realize who it was who was screaming at him, but when he did, reality must have come crashing down on him, because he looked at Deeka and then at the knife and then burst into tears.

I couldn't remember the last time Big Eric had held his son in his arms, but I knew he did that night.

Chevy

Anja had consumed over a dozen oysters and nearly a whole bottle of champagne. She'd stopped talking in the third person and to my surprise had even called for a cigar.

"They have the good shit here. Cubans!"

I'd smoked a cigar or two in my lifetime, but they were always very slim, very delicate, very ladylike. Not Anja, she was stomping with the big boys.

"So," she said, after taking a few puffs of her cigar, "how about if I make you an indecent proposal?"

"How about it?" I said loosely. Oh, did I forget to mention that I had also gone through a bottle of champagne and was now sipping on some very smooth cognac at the time? My head was light, the weather warm, and the bartender had made it his business to give me the eye as he cleared some glasses away from a nearby table.

I was feeling no pain.

Anja laughed naughtily before her eyes narrowed, then her face turned serious as she leaned in and said, "I want to fuck you, Chevanese Cambridge."

That wasn't something I was expecting. I felt my buzz begin to slip. "Wha-what did you say?"

Anja got up and pulled her chair around the table so that she was almost in my face. "I said I wanted to fuck you," she repeated, her hot smoky breath singeing my earlobe.

I made a face and looked at the empty bottles of champagne on the table. Surely she was drunk out of her skull.

"I'm straight," I said brightly, turning to face her.

"Yeah, well, so am I," she said, and winked. Her hand was slowly stroking my thigh. "I'm not looking for some free pussy; I'm willing to give you an opportunity to live like me for one week, if you let me . . ." She trailed off, and I could see that she was staring hungrily at my crotch.

Bells were going off in my head.

"What exactly do you mean, 'to live like you'?" I ventured.

Anja smiled. "Well, let's put it this way, you want to have your own television show, right?"

I nodded my head.

"I'll let you sit in as my replacement for one week."

I mulled over the idea. That really wasn't enough for me to spread my legs for a bitch and break umpteen years of heterosexual behavior, now was it?

"What else?" I pressed.

Anja sat back. "Oh, you know how to handle yourself. I like that in a woman," she purred, and then licked her lips. I shivered but kept my composure.

"How does five thousand dollars cash sound? Plus, you'll get to live in one of my homes and I'll give you access to my um . . . Nordstrom account."

My eyes popped.

"You're shitting me, right?"

"Not at all," Anja said, and her hand was suddenly on my shoulder, eagerly massaging it.

I twisted my mouth. The last time I'd agreed to use my body to make money, I almost landed in jail. I didn't know about this.

"Who's to say you'll do all of these things if I give myself to you?" I said, finishing the cognac and calling for another, my mind already made up.

"I have a contract and my notary public here," she said, leaning in and stealing a lick off of my shoulder. I saw a couple across the dining room point and giggle.

"Stop it," I hissed, moving my chair away from hers.

"Look-See," Anja began. "I gotta have you."

So this was really what a Look-See was all about, I thought as the waiter set a fresh snifter of cognac down before me.

"Okay, okay," I agreed when my buzz had returned and I realized I would probably never have this opportunity again.

Anja snapped her fingers, and out of nowhere appeared the geisha woman, contract in hand. "This is my mother," Anja said as she gently stroked the woman's face.

"Oh," I responded flatly.

Nothing after that would ever surprise me. If George W. Bush himself, sporting a pointed tail and dressed in a red cape, had suddenly walked across the floor and introduced himself as the devil, I wouldn't have even blinked an eye in disbelief.

"Sign here, initial there, and there, and sign here,"

Anja said, then her mother stamped the document and added her own signature before giving me a carbon copy and scampering off again.

"Well then, shall we?" Anja said.

"Um, yeah, but can I get that bottle of cognac to go?" I asked as I stood up.

* * *

We agreed that she would meet me in my cottage at midnight. I took a shower, shaved my legs, clipped the hair around my vagina, and then thought I must be mad, because I was preparing myself the way I would for a dude!

I was nervous as hell, even after all the cognac. At ten to midnight, I started to get dressed and go over to her suite to call the whole thing off, but just when I began to open the door, I saw through the crack that she was coming up the stairs!

I closed the door, and, hopping on the bed, I wiggled out of the skirt and blouse I'd thrown on and then lay there, stiff as a board, in nothing but a thong.

Like I said, I'd been preparing as if I were about to get some dick, so I had lit some candles and placed them strategically around my cottage.

"Hello, hello," Anja called when she stepped into the room.

"Hi," I said, my voice cracking.

Anja came to stand over me. "Why so uptight?" she said before she leaned down and pressed her lips against mine.

"I'm not uptight," I lied as I lay there, my arms by my sides, my legs crossed tightly.

"Don't worry, darling," she cooed. "You're really going to enjoy this."

I closed my eyes when she started rolling up the dress. I didn't want to look at her pussy and lose my dinner. She was humming. I didn't recognize the tune. But I thought it might be from a horror flick.

When I decided I would peek, she was standing there in nothing but a full-body girdle. I almost laughed out loud. Anja the Anaconda wore a girdle!

"Are you ready?" she said, her voice huskier than I'd ever heard it.

"Uh-hmm," I said.

Anja turned her back to me and slowly, seductively, began pulling one strap down and then the other. Her back was tight and her shoulders broad. She had the body of an athlete.

Anja tugged and tugged and then bent over and stepped out of the girdle. She had a rock-hard ass, and I wondered how I could get mine that way.

"Are you ready?" she purred.

I wasn't, so I said nothing and closed my eyes just as she was making a slow, dramatic turn toward me.

As I lay there waiting to feel her hands on me, I remembered a saying my grandmother was always fond of: "Y'all will know I've gone and lost my *whole* mind when you see me giving my money to a man or laying down with a woman!"

From the situation I'd found myself in, I assumed I'd lost at least *half* of my mind.

"Open your eyes, Chevy." Anja's voice filtered through my thoughts.

I took a deep breath, then slowly opened my eyes and found myself staring at at least ten inches of 100 percent prime FDA cock!

Anja wasn't an Anja at all!

Anja was a man!

Crystal

"Hello?" I said through a sex-induced sleepy haze.

"Crystal, I need you." Geneva's voice came back at me.

"What's wrong?" I asked as I sat up and gently pushed Neville's head off my stomach. My clock read 12:15 a.m. "Is Charlie okay?" My voice was slowly filling with panic.

"It's not Charlie, it's me, it's Eric, it's everything," Geneva's voice quaked, then she started to cry.

"I'll be right there."

I jumped out of bed and snatched up a pair of sweat-pants that were lying across the bench at the foot of my bed.

"What's happening?" Neville asked as he sat up and rubbed the sleep from his eyes.

"Geneva needs me," I said as I pulled my T-shirt over my head.

"I'll come too."

* * *

Geneva was sitting outside her apartment house on the bench when we arrived. Neville walked over to her and bent down and gave her a tight hug and a kiss.

"Hey," he mumbled, not knowing what else to say.

"What's going on, girl?" Sitting down beside her, I threw my arm around her shoulder and listened intently as Geneva unfolded the whole sordid tale. I struggled to keep my face sympathetic, but honestly, there were times when I really just wanted to slap her arm and scream, "Stop your lying, girl!"

I couldn't believe she'd been keeping all this from me. But then again, who was I to judge? Look at all that I'd been doing.

Neville and I exchanged uncomfortable glances.

Geneva fell into a fit of tears and I pulled her to me and cooed, "It's going to be okay, girl. You'll see, everything is going to be okay."

The sound of a car's motor caught my attention, and I looked up to see a dark blue Capri with tinted windows pulling up to the curb.

Chevy

"You have a dick!" I screamed, bolting upright and covering my bare breasts with my hand.

"Most men do, sweetie." Anja grinned at me.

"You're a man!"

"Well, isn't it obvious?" he said, pointing to his rock-hard penis.

"But, but—"

"But what?" he said, taking a step closer to the bed.

"I—what—why . . ."

"Okay," he began as he took a seat on the edge of the bed and crossed his legs, "I will give you the short version. I started out as a singer-slash-comedian-slash-gossip-whore in the nightclubs. I had a very David Bowie–like look: eyeliner, shadow, teased hair, the whole shebang, you know?"

I didn't, but I nodded my head anyway.

"It went over really well with the Wong Foo crowd and I started making a lot of money. That was when I was living in San Francisco." He added matter-of-factly, "By the way, I was married with two kids at the time. My ex-wife was the one who thought it would be fun to dress me up like it was Halloween all year long. I didn't mind, I'm very confident about my sexuality."

My eyes bulged.

"So one day this guy came up to me and offered me a gig with this underground radio station. I took it, and as my career developed, so did the Anja persona."

I just stared at him. Only shit like this happened to me.

"What's your real name?" I asked.

"Andre," he said, and then reached over and plucked a tissue from the box on the nightstand.

"Andre?"

"Yes," he said as he used the tissue to wipe the lipstick from his lips. "You know you can't repeat any of this. You did sign a confidentiality agreement, and we wouldn't want Anja to have you hunted down and killed." He gave me a little smirk, and for the first time he totally let go of his feminine voice. "So are we going to do this or what?" Andre said, cocking his head to one side and giving me a sly, sexy smile.

I gulped. "Why do you have to pay women to sleep with you?"

"I don't, sweetie. It's a tax write-off," he said as he leaned over and kissed me on the lips.

It was nice, I have to admit. And once his tongue pried through my clenched teeth, it was even better than nice.

He wasn't a bad-looking man at all, and he knew what to do with that big cock of his. I can't even remember the last time my toes curled during sex.

Well, at least I thought it was the sex. It might have just been the five thousand dollars and the Nordstrom account!

Geneva

We were all looking at the Capri Classic that was sitting at the curb, its motor humming loudly. I knew it was the cops. They always thought they were fooling somebody in those damn Capris, but everybody always knew it was the po-po.

Then the driver's-side door opened and my ex-husband, Eric, stepped out. "Isn't that Eric?" Crystal said, taking a step away from me.

"Yeah." My heart was thumping in my chest. This can't be good, I thought as I slowly rose from the bench.

Then the back door opened and Deeka stepped out. I just closed my eyes and shook my head. Something really bad had happened, but I willed my mind not to go there.

"There's Eric!" Crystal suddenly whooped. My eyes flew open, and there was my son, stepping out of the other side of the car. I wanted to run to him, but my feet refused to move.

All three men started toward us.

When Deeka and Eric passed beneath the streetlight I could see blood on their clothes. Deeka's eye was swollen and his lip was busted. Eric had a shiner under his eye as well, but otherwise he looked unharmed.

"Well, Geneva, I found your son beating the shit out of your lover," Big Eric said, a little too proudly for my taste.

Eric wrapped his arms around me. "I'm so sorry, Mama."

I pulled him to me. "No, I'm sorry, baby. I'm sorry."

"Look," Eric said, pulling away from me, "I don't know what came over me." He shook his head in embarrassment. "I mean, seeing you like that with him, I just went crazy, you know? You're my mother and—"

"I know, baby. You don't have to say anything else—"

"Ah, Geneva, let the man talk," Big Eric boomed.

"I just want to say that I'm cool with it now." Eric levied a friendly slap on Deeka's arm. "Me and my man here had a long talk, and I know that he really loves you."

I looked at Deeka.

"Who am I to stand in between two people who love each other?" Eric said, and stepped aside.

Deeka stepped forward and took my hand in his.

"Oh God, this is soooo romantic!" Crystal cried, and threw herself into Neville's arms.

Noah

"I'm sorry, Crystal," I apologized again in a low voice after Crystal repeated for the umpteenth time that she did not appreciate my working in conjunction with her mother to get her laid.

I was sorry. And not only was I sorry, but I was feeling sorry for myself. My relationship was coming to an end, and I was heartbroken. I wanted to share that with Crystal, but when I called to do so, she'd immediately ripped into me.

"Well, you need to be," she said, and then she released a long sigh and said, "Thank you."

"What?"

"I said, 'thank you,' Noah. Only a true friend would go to the lengths you did. Don't get me wrong—I'm pissed about the whole situation—but more grateful than anything."

I didn't say a word. I wanted to hear this.

"I really needed Neville here. I mean, I needed the sex, don't get me wrong—Lord knows I needed the sex!" Her voice went up a notch, and I found myself smiling for the first time in days. "But I also needed to be reminded that I am a beautiful, sexual being, and Neville did that for me."

"I'm glad to hear that, sweetie."

"It's funny how we know what our friends need, even when they don't express it, don't you think?"

"Yes."

"So I feel like you need a hug right now. You sound so sad. I wish I was there to give you one."

My eyes filled with tears and my lips began to quiver.

"Do you want to talk about it?" Crystal asked. Then the dam broke, and all of what I'd been going through came rushing out.

Crystal never interrupted me. She just listened the way a good friend was supposed to. After I was finished, she softly reminded me of something that I had seemed to have forgotten in my anger.

"Noah, remember the summer you had your little problem?" she began. My little problem was the fact that I had started sleeping with women. It was a dark, dark period in my life. "When you told Zhan, he was totally understanding and even went to a few of your Homosexuals with Heterosexual Tendencies meetings, right?"

"Yes," I whispered.

"He didn't get angry and walk away from you. He stuck by you, he forgave you, and continued to love you, didn't he?"

"Y-yes."

"He gave you another chance, so why can't you do the same for him?"

I hadn't even looked at it that way. Here I was putting the man I loved through the wringer for something as simple as a kiss. And not once did Zhan throw my indiscretions in my face.

"You're right, baby," I said through a fresh stream of tears. I let my jealousy hide the fact that this man loved me so much that he would let me walk out of his life, if that's what would make me happy.

"Of course I am," Crystal said, and I could tell she was smiling. I was smiling now too.

"Wow, is this what a hug feels like long-distance?" I teased.

"I guess so, baby. It feels pretty damn good, doesn't it?"

Geneva

How the summer had slipped away from us so quickly, I didn't know. It seemed the older we got, the quicker summer passed us by. It also seemed the older we got, the more bizarre our summers became!

If someone had told me back in January that during the summer a fine man nearly half my age would fall in love with me, that Crystal would break her celibacy with a gigolo, that Noah would turn down sex with gorgeous strangers, and Chevy would find and keep a job more than two weeks, I would have slapped that person into next year!

But it happened. Life is wild.

Neville left just yesterday and promised to come back to visit real soon. But it doesn't seem that *soon* is quick enough for Crystal because she's already planning on taking a trip down to Antigua before the year is out.

I asked her if it was a love thing, and she laughed and said no, it wasn't a love thing but it was certainly a lust thing. I suppose that's okay; I'd been involved in plenty of "lust only" relationships myself.

Me and Deeka are going strong. He is everything I ever thought I wanted, and then some. We definitely have a love thing, peppered with a healthy amount of lust! He's still managing Eric's band and recently got them signed to this small record label. They've started working on their first CD. I'm so proud!

I had to finally come to terms with the fact that my baby is growing up, becoming a man in his own right. We agreed that he wouldn't mess around in my romantic affairs and I wouldn't mess around in his. To further cement the deal, I had Juuuuuuuuuuuulie—I mean, Julie— over for dinner. She's a nice enough girl, seems to have a good head on her shoulders. Smart, quick, and from what I see, she adores Eric.

I'm trying real hard not to imagine them up in my apartment doing the nasty while I'm on this trip—even though I know they are!

Charlie is growing in leaps and bounds, and Deeka seems to love her as much as I do.

Noah is still in England. He patched it all up with Zhan, and he says that their relationship is as strong as ever. He says that he will reconsider the "key swapping" thing, but not with the neighbors; it's just a little too close to home for him. Both he and Zhan are going to try to come to New York for Christmas. I hope they do; I miss Noah something horrible!

Chevy, well, we didn't even know that she had been out of the country until we all met at Crystal's for a bon voyage party for Neville and saw that she had a tan that was out of this world! She didn't have much to say about the trip, which was unusual for Chevy because she usually uses every opportunity to dangle her jet-set lifestyle in our faces. But not this time. She just said she'd had a good time and that she'd worked hard. But I noticed that the whole time she was speaking she was also grinning like a Cheshire cat.

She even paid Noah the back rent she owed him, and we all got one-hundred-dollar Nordstrom gift certificates with little note cards that said, "Just because."

Maybe Chevy is finally growing up. It's about time too, because she is damn near forty years old.

She even invited me, Deeka, Charlie, and Crystal up to Martha's Vineyard for the Labor Day weekend. Apparently Anja has given Chevy her home in Oaks Bluff for the whole month of September. Chevy claims that it's one of the perks of working at La Fleur Industries. If that's the case, I told her, bring me home an application!

Anja's house is supposed to be a magnificent eight-bedroom mansion overlooking the ocean!

We're on the ferry now. I'm so excited, all I can do is grin. The only place I've ever been outside of New York is New Jersey, and that was just to Newark Airport.

I feel like I'm at the beginning of a great change, and that feels damn good. Looking over at my man, my friend, and my daughter, I suddenly understand the saying *Today is the first day of the rest of your life.*

I hope the rest of my life feels as good as this day does.

Someone named Dante is supposed to meet us when we dock. Chevy said he'll be easy enough to spot. Just look for the short little man with the nose ring and bad dye job who's wearing a T-shirt that says CHEVY'S BITCH.

Acknowledgments

I'm grateful to everyone who had any part in the life of this book and to those who dug deep into their pockets to purchase it!

You all know who you are!

Good things,
Geneva

About the Author

Bernice L. McFadden is an associate professor of English at Tulane University and the author most recently of the memoir *Firstborn Girls*, and of several critically acclaimed novels, including *Sugar*, *The Warmest December*, *Loving Donovan*, *Nowhere Is a Place*, *Glorious*, *Gathering of Waters* (a *New York Times* Editors' Choice and one of the 100 Notable Books of 2012), *The Book of Harlan* (winner of a 2017 American Book Award and the NAACP Image Award for Outstanding Literary Work, Fiction), and *Praise Song for the Butterflies* (longlisted for the 2019 Women's Prize for Fiction). She is a five-time Hurston/Wright Legacy Award finalist, as well as the recipient of three awards from the Black Caucus of the American Library Association.